THE FATHER-DAUGHTER CLUB

❖

ALISON RAGSDALE

This book is a work of fiction. Names, characters, places and incidents either are products of the author's imagination or are used fictitiously. Any resemblance to actual events or locales or persons, living or dead, is entirely coincidental.

THE FATHER-DAUGHTER CLUB
Copyright © 2014 by Alison Ragsdale

ISBN-10:0990747832
ISBN-13:978-0-9907478-3-3

Also by this author:

TUESDAY'S SOCKS

THE FATHER-DAUGHTER CLUB

CHAPTER 1

---◆---

The room at the Grande Bretagne hotel overlooked Syntagma, Athens's Constitution Square. Elizabeth Fredericks stood at the window. An oversized toweling bathrobe wrapped around her, she looked down at the scene below.

"What's going on down there?" her husband David called from the shower.

"It's a hive of activity," she shouted back.

At the base of the adjacent parliament building, two Greek ceremonial Evzone guards goose-stepped away from each other. The short white skirts, in tight concertina pleats, swirled around sturdy white-clad legs as the two soldiers stopped and swiveled back to face each other. Their red shoes with black pompoms looked comical and somewhat incongruous in the overall grand seriousness of their uniforms.

Yellow taxis and a steady trickle of cars circulated the square. In the center were clusters of tables under large umbrellas.

A handful of tourists wandered around and photographed each other while teams of waiters emerged like ants from within the cafés and restaurants that lined the edges of the square. The servers wove expertly between the tables, huge trays balanced precariously over their shoulders. Looking down on all the activity, it was hard to believe that this was a country deep in crisis. Kate would love to see this.

The thought of her daughter brought with it the customary wave of sadness, and Elizabeth wondered what Kate was up to today. She would be at the university in Edinburgh, either lecturing or in the library. Whatever she was doing, Elizabeth was sure that Kate would not be thinking about her mother.

In the bathroom, David turned his face up and let the warm water run over it. The restorative power of water never failed to amaze him. They'd had a less-than-smooth arrival in Athens the previous day, as a result of it being Easter. Their bags had taken two hours to show up, and they'd had to take a shabby, unlicensed taxi to the hotel. It had seemed a better option than waiting for a further two hours among a crowd of gesticulating travelers, all arguing over the few cabs that were still running on the national holiday.

It wasn't the best of beginnings for their European adventure, the trip they'd dreamed of and planned to mark David's retirement from the bank in Dundee. However, the hotel was pleasant and the bathroom spacious and clean, which he knew to be extremely important to Elizabeth.

He reached for the soap and lathered it over his head. His morning shower always set him to rights, preparing him for the workday ahead. At least it had for the past forty-plus years.

As the sudsy water trickled down his temples and filled his ears, it felt surreal to David that the workday routine he had followed for almost five decades was over. The faces he'd seen circulating his office would no longer be part of his days. Someone else would be sliding into the branch manager's parking space and sitting in the small, dark office overlooking the car park.

As he turned off the large brass tap, David felt a new rush of both excitement and fear at what lay ahead. Most of all, he was looking forward to the luxury of time to spend on traveling and on his passion for classical architecture. The newly unlimited time with Elizabeth, however, was what scared him.

They had been through a rough patch over the past three years. After thirty-seven years of marriage, he had made a colossal mistake and had an affair. Every time he remembered it, he cringed. Now, not having his work to hide behind, he'd have to face the reality of having changed the dynamic of his and Elizabeth's relationship forever.

David pushed open the glass door, reached for a towel, and stepped out onto the cold marble floor. He caught sight of his reflection as he rubbed himself dry. Despite all the past hurt and recriminations, it was a new day, and he was determined that this trip would provide the opportunity to heal the wounds that he'd inflicted upon their lives, once and for all.

The bathroom door was ajar, and he saw Elizabeth at the window. She was staring down at the square. As he looked at the familiar line of her neck, her hair wrapped up in a toweling turban, he wondered how they would get along spending the next month together, without the customary visits from Kate to dilute any tension.

Elizabeth twisted the latch on the window and tried to open it. It was stuck hard so, after several unfruitful attempts, she re-locked it, disappointed. Despite the heavy glass between her and the street below, she imagined she could smell the aromatic coffee, mixed with the ubiquitous cigarettes and car fumes, emanating from the square.

She took a deep breath and shoved her hands into the fluffy pockets of the robe. She had slept well but still felt fatigued. The month-long trip stretched before them, and she was hopeful that it would be everything they had dreamed of. They both needed this.

In contrast to the activity at her feet, the Acropolis and Parthenon stood in stoic silence far to her left. The harsh scaffolding, erected as part of a massive restoration project, did not detract from their ghostly beauty. She twisted her neck to take in the sight and marveled at the idea that all those people down in the square might not be paying sufficient homage to these ancient structures. From what she could see, they seemed more intent on their pastries and coffees than on the breathtaking temple that watched over them, asking nothing of them in return.

Hearing David moving around, Elizabeth turned.

"So what are we doing today, sensei?" With a towel wrapped around his waist, David placed his palms together in front of his chest and bowed.

Elizabeth stuck her tongue out at him and reached for her glasses on the bedside table.

"Nothing, if you don't watch out, grasshopper." She laughed and then looked down at the notebook where she had written the list of things that they had earmarked for their time in Athens.

They had agreed on various must-see landmarks – the Acropolis and Parthenon, of course, the Temple of Zeus and Hadrian's Arch, then Plaka, the ancient marketplace. David also wanted to visit the Odeon of Herodes Atticus. Some additional recommendations from the hotel concierge had increased their list to include the National Gardens and a climb to the top of Lykavittos Hill where they would be able to enjoy a bird's-eye view of the city.

"We could do Lykavittos today, if you feel like a climb?" Elizabeth watched David nodding as he leaned into the wardrobe and shuffled the hangers, searching for the tan cotton trousers she knew he wanted.

"They're underneath the blue shirt." She indicated with the notebook. "There weren't enough hangers." She shrugged. "Perhaps we can go to the Odeon of Herodes this afternoon?" Elizabeth's glasses slipped to the end of her nose as she looked down at the list.

David, now wearing the trousers, shook the small plastic kettle that was sitting on the dresser.

"Do you think this thing works?" He gave a mock grimace.

"Let's go down into the square for breakfast." She smiled.

"Good idea."

The sun was already hot, and David's nose shone with the sunblock that Elizabeth had insisted he use. She sipped on a sweet, gritty coffee and watched the activity around them.

"This coffee is pretty good, really." David tipped his head back, draining the tiny cup. "Oh, god." His face screwed up in distaste as a tiny trail of dark grounds trickled from the side of his mouth.

"I don't think you're supposed to drink it all the way to the bottom." Elizabeth couldn't help laughing.

"Well you might've said." David reached for a paper napkin and wiped at his mouth. "Ugh, that was nasty." He chuckled.

"As with all good things," Elizabeth said, "you should quit while you're ahead."

Having finished with their coffees and two warm *spanakopita*, they were ready for the day. Elizabeth watched her husband count out some euros and was overtaken by a wave of contentment.

"All set?" Elizabeth looked at David and tried to guess what he was thinking. She still enjoyed the fact that his face was an open book whose index she had memorized. This man, with whom she had spent the better part of her life, could still make her heart twitch with his simple candor and naivety. When he wasn't driving her crazy, of course.

"Let's go and climb that hill." David stood and reached out his hand to her.

"I hope it's not too hot for this." As she stood up, Elizabeth felt a trickle of sweat meander down between her breasts. She needed to get moving and hopefully, once they were out of the square, there would be a breeze.

CHAPTER 2

Kate Fredericks paced across the floor of her Edinburgh flat. Her backpack lay on the bed, a messy pile of clothes next to it. She wasn't sure what to take for such a short trip. She knew that Greece would be hot, so she had pulled out a pair of shorts, a summer dress, and a long floral skirt she could wear with a couple of different T-shirts. That should be enough for two days.

She glanced in the mirror. Her chin-length fair hair was a mess, and she had dark shadows under her pale blue eyes. She looked older than her thirty years today. A knot of anxiety in her middle had become her constant companion this past week, and tonight it had moved so high up it had made its way into her throat.

"What else should I take?" Kate walked into the bathroom.

Charlotte Macfie lay in the bath. She was surrounded by bubbles, with a glass of red wine balanced on the ledge behind her and a paperback propped up on her bent knees. Her long dark hair was tied up in a curly bundle, and her cheeks shone pink from the heat of the water.

"A swimsuit, maybe?" Charlotte looked up.

"You're getting that book wet." Kate tutted.

Charlotte slid her knees closer to her body, raising the book above the foam, as Kate opened the bathroom cabinet.

"I doubt we'll be lounging at the pool, somehow." She smiled at Charlotte. "It's not that kind of visit."

"I know that." Charlotte sat up abruptly, sending a surge of water over the edge of the bath. "Oh shit, sorry." She grabbed her towel from the floor and began dabbing at the puddle.

"I'll get it. You daft bugger." Kate laughed, took the towel from Charlotte's hand, and knelt to wipe up the spill.

"Are you sure you don't want me to come with you? I can stay out of the way. Hide in the hotel room or something." Charlotte put a hand on Kate's shoulder to stop her frantic dabbing. "Kate?"

"No. I think it's best if I go alone. I should have done this before they left, but having them gone has made the decision easier, somehow. Makes no sense, I know." She shrugged.

"No. I get it. It had to be the right time for you. I'm just worried about you being alone."

"I'm a grown-up, and they're my parents. What's the worst that can happen?" Kate stood up and threw the sodden towel into the laundry basket.

"I don't know. I just think you might need moral support." Charlotte reached for her glass and took a sip. "Want some?" She held the glass out to Kate.

Kate took a long swallow and handed it back.

"Dutch courage?" Charlotte smiled.

"Absolutely." Kate nodded, then leaned over and kissed her.

CHAPTER 3

———◆———

Charlotte tipped the large bag of coffee beans into the top of the grinder. The nutty scent made her nose twitch. She loved watching the glossy beans cascading into the metal chamber, like a waterfall of roasted ball bearings. The morning rush was about to start, and the present serenity inside The Bakery, the coffee shop she owned, would soon give way to the bustle of the breakfast crowd grabbing some of her homemade sustenance on their way to work. She had built up a good number of regular customers and always did her best to memorize their orders, making them feel valued – greeting them by name and having their "usual" ready for them. Her two helpers, Mungo and Chloe, would be arriving in half an hour, and then it would be all hands on deck for the next three hours.

She loved the time she spent alone in the kitchen each morning, baking and preparing the fresh morning fare. It was her time to think, reflect, and drift between the long metal counter-tops. Her headphones whispered Vaughn Williams, Ravel, and

Debussy to her as she filled the ovens with rolls of soft dough, rounds of biscuit batter, and trays of cut scones.

This morning, however, she was distracted. The silence she usually treasured felt heavy and awkward. Kate had left for Greece the previous evening, and as Charlotte scanned the café tables, making sure they were clean and had sugar containers and menus placed in the center, she mentally calculated what time it was in Athens. It would be a while before Kate would be able to call her, so she needed to try to focus on the day and get on with her work.

The commercial ovens in the kitchen were full of the last batch of crusty morning rolls, and the long glass display case in the shop was already filled with fresh doughnuts, parkin biscuits, flapjack squares, sausage rolls, and three kinds of scones.

Her daily routine started at 4:00 a.m., but she had had a head start this morning, going down to the bakery at 3:00. Unable to sleep, she had paced around the flat for over an hour, worrying about Kate, before deciding that she might as well use the time productively.

Charlotte knew this trip wasn't going to be easy on Kate. She had little idea how the much-feared confrontation with her parents would go, but she guessed that the Fredericks would not make it easy for their daughter to tell them what was going on in her life.

Kate was everything Charlotte had hoped to find in a partner. Apart from being gorgeous, with her tall willowy frame, softly freckled face, and captivating blue eyes, she had many qualities that Charlotte felt she lacked herself. Kate was both intelligent and erudite. She carried herself with confidence and yet was not arrogant or unapproachable. She was kind and loving, generous to a fault, and also had a great sense of humor. Her students at the university admired her, but they also liked her.

Charlotte smiled to herself as she adjusted the pile of newspapers on the Welsh dresser. She had hated most of her own professors at Glasgow University and had left after a year to travel to India with her cousin. She had promised her parents, Elsie and Duncan, that she would come back and finish her degree, but of course that had never happened. Instead Charlotte had trained as an assistant baker in a classy French patisserie in London. The lure of the regular salary and independence from her family proved stronger than her desire to finish her formal education. She knew that she'd disappointed her parents in this respect, but overall, they had always been proud of her and her achievements. They had been overjoyed when she'd told them four years ago that she was returning to Edinburgh and was making an offer on The Bakery in Rose Street.

Thinking about her parents brought a familiar twinge of pain as a picture of her mother floated into her mind. Elsie had been her best friend and confidante. When Charlotte had come out to her parents, they had been amazing. They had been concerned for her and the potential cruelty of others judging her, but had taken the news in their stride. Elsie had even offered to go to a Gay Pride event in London with her. They'd taken the train down to the city and stayed in a small hotel on the Tottenham Court Road. They'd laughed together and had a fun weekend, seeing *Chitty Chitty Bang Bang* in the West End and wandering around Covent Garden. Elsie had held her hand the entire time at the Pride meeting.

As she scanned the row of tables inside the bakery, Charlotte's vision blurred. It had been over a year since Elsie had passed away, and she still missed her mum. Charlotte knew that Kate and Elizabeth had never been close and she couldn't help but wonder if, when she learned of Charlotte's existence, Elizabeth Fredericks would be able to accept her as her daughter's partner. Despite Kate's trepidation, Charlotte remained optimistic that ultimately both Elizabeth and David would want their daughter to be happy, whatever that happiness looked like.

Turning her back on the two bay windows overlooking Rose Street, Charlotte walked towards the kitchen. The rolls smelled wonderful, and before she opened the oven to remove the perfect golden orbs, she turned up the volume on her iPod. The gentle strains of "Claire de Lune" lifted her spirits, and the thought of Kate coming home to her in just two days carried her on towards the rest of her morning.

CHAPTER 4

◈

The café at the top of Lykavittos hill was basic but busy. The ascent had proved more challenging than anticipated but now, sitting in the hot metal chair, Elizabeth looked down at the view and her fatigue faded. The Acropolis stood in the distance, silent and stoic amidst the mayhem of modern-day Athens. Behind the temple, she could see all the way to the Aegean, a tantalizing blue ribbon floating behind Piraeus, the town from which they'd soon be taking the hydrofoil to the island of Hydra.

Incongruous suburbs sprawled out to the left and right of Athens. To Elizabeth's mind, they diluted the magnificence of the historic structures at the city's heart. She sipped her icy lemonade and wiped at her throat with an already damp napkin. David was staring down at the view and nodding, as if agreeing with her silent assessment.

"It's an odd mixture, isn't it?" He nudged his sunglasses back up the bridge of his nose with a knuckle. "The old and the new, cheek by jowl."

"Yes. It's beautiful, and sad somehow." Elizabeth's voice was soft.

"A statement of the world we live in, eh?"

David turned to his wife and placed his hand over hers on the table. She was the yin to his yang, the cheese to his ham. He remembered making her laugh by telling her that on their honeymoon. His youthful attempt at romantic metaphor had gone somewhat awry, but had remained a classic "David-ism" – the label Elizabeth had given to his little verbal eccentricities. He was lucky. Lucky that she found them charming and not irritating or ridiculous. He loved her. How could he have risked all they had together when he had strayed three years ago?

Elizabeth had been depressed at the time, and her lack of interest in all the things she loved to do had alarmed him. She had withdrawn from most of her social activities, become distant, dismissive, shoving him off in the morning with a pat on the shoulder rather than the customary hug and kiss on the lips. He'd seen the signs of her sadness but had mishandled everything.

Connie was a colleague, a kind woman and a friend. David, feeling all but abandoned by Elizabeth, had confided in Connie about the situation at home and had felt important, valid, when she had listened to him and shown real interest in what he had to say. He had fallen headlong into the classic mistake of consoling himself in the comfort on offer before him.

All that said, there was no excuse for his behavior, and David felt the familiar surge of guilt as he looked at his wife. He thanked all the gods that she had stuck with him despite his lapse in judgment. He had been a fool.

"Cooling off yet?" Seeing her still-flushed cheeks and empty glass, he gestured for the waiter.

"Yes. The breeze is perfect." Elizabeth had left her hand beneath his and now turned to see his face. She knew he worried about her, but she was fine. He was here, and she was here, and all the old unpleasantness was in the past, she hoped.

"We can order some lunch if you like, then walk back? Should be easier going downhill." David reached for the menu and, extending his arms out across the table, cursed the elusive three or four extra inches he needed to see the small script.

"Give it to me." Elizabeth laughed. Taking the menu from his hand and slipping her glasses on, she began to read out the bill of fare.

Once full and rested, they made their way down the hill. David had been right, and the descent was relatively painless. The temperature had eased a little. The afternoon sun slid behind the hill, casting long shadows across the tree-lined steps that gradually dropped them back down into Kolonaki.

Back in their cool room, they were surprised to discover that it was already four. The idea of more adventures that afternoon had lost its shine. David had showered and was lying flat on his back on the bed in his underwear, his arms folded behind his head. Elizabeth sat at the small desk overlooking the square, writing a postcard to Kate.

Their daughter was a professor of civil engineering at

Edinburgh University. Since her immersion in the heady culture of academia, her communication skills had become less than optimal, as far as her mother was concerned.

Elizabeth sighed as she twisted the pen in her mouth. She wondered if Kate had even remembered that they were away. She resolved to make a greater effort to visit her daughter more often, once they got home. Smiling resignedly, she mumbled, "If the mountain won't come to Mohammed…"

"So, let's rest until dinner, then tackle the Odeon of Herodes tomorrow?" David circled his left ankle, which gave a loud crack. He winced and then shifted on the bed.

"Yes, perhaps we can do that in the morning?" Elizabeth finished writing and turned the postcard face up on the desk.

"What did you say to Kate?" Turning on his side, David propped himself up on one arm.

Elizabeth picked up the card and began to read.

"'Dear Kate, Arrived safely in Athens. Climbed Lykavittos today. Magnificent views. Tomorrow – National Gardens. Hotel is perfect. Love, Mum and Dad.' Want to add anything?" Elizabeth waved the card at David.

"Nope, sounds good to me." He rolled onto his back.

They had decided to walk into Plaka for dinner. Elizabeth was looking forward to seeing it, having read so much about that part of the city. The historic gathering place had been the true heart of ancient Athens. From her research, it seemed that the terraced streets that wound up the gentle hill overlooking Syntagma were lined with shops, tavernas, and bars.

Dressed in a light cotton dress and gladiator sandals she had bought for the trip, Elizabeth glanced at herself in the long mirror. She found her reflection satisfactory. Her face was sun-kissed, her eyes appearing a little bluer as a result. Tucking her shoulder-length fair hair behind her ears, she nodded. She had long ago given up the notion of being considered empirically pretty, but she would do, for a sixty-two year old.

David stood behind her, watching her in the mirror. She was a handsome woman; even after all these years, he thought her lovely. Her floral dress and Greek sandals made him feel dowdy by comparison. He looked down at his pale-blue polo shirt, safe beige trousers, and the new sandals that she had bought for him. Not something he'd have chosen himself, they were surprisingly comfortable.

"Ready, love?" He gestured towards the door.

As the elevator slid down to the ground floor, David caught his reflection in the polished brass panel of the door.

"Gosh, I caught the sun today."

Elizabeth glanced at the top of his head. The skin was an alarming shade of pink under the thinning grey hair.

"Yes, you did. Lucky you had the sunscreen on." Elizabeth smoothed a stray damp curl that had sprung up over the back of his collar.

"Yes, sensei, you were once again correct."

She tightened her hand around the base of his neck, squeezing his muscles.

"Careful, grasshopper. I have the credit cards, so if you want to eat tonight, you better watch your P's and Q's."

Elizabeth laughed, and as the doors opened onto the busy lobby, they walked out, hand in hand.

A tall, slim woman stood behind the concierge desk and nodded at them as they passed.

"Have a good evening," she said as David pushed on the revolving door, letting Elizabeth step into the wedge of space ahead of him.

"*Efharisto* – thanks, we will," David spoke over his shoulder, stepping in behind his wife and then guiding her out into the warm night air.

The famous stone steps of Plaka were lined with rows of crimson geraniums in terracotta pots. Fragrant lemongrass and lush ferns draped themselves over the stairs' time-softened edges. Lush vines crept up trellises and wove themselves over arbors as hundreds of gold lights twinkled from amidst the green leaves, warming the walkways beneath. Whitewashed buildings hugged the stairways on either side as David and Elizabeth climbed towards the central *agora*.

Looking ahead, they could see the Acropolis standing guard, and as they walked on, they passed numerous market vendors. Colorful clothing hung from the stalls. Marble figures of the gods sat amidst bolts of delicate cotton, and sparkling jewelry hung on rough nails that had been driven into warped wooden shutters. A variety of sweets and pastries, wrapped inside crinkled cellophane pyramids, lay on blankets on the ground, forcing Elizabeth and David to pick their way around them to make any progress at all.

Numerous tavernas had placed their tables out on the edges

of the wide steps, the gingham table covers and wooden chairs beckoning to passersby. As they walked underneath the lush green canopies, Elizabeth could smell the tantalizing scent of lamb roasting on rustic open grills.

The strains of bouzouki music followed them from one terraced level to the next and, as they turned another corner, Elizabeth stopped in her tracks and gasped. A small cluster of tables sat ahead, draped in white covers. Behind them lay an almost unobstructed view of the floodlit Acropolis. The tables each had a small pot of fresh rosemary at the center, a single flickering candle, and two round-backed chairs. The wooden sign read *Taverna Irini*, which, from studying her guidebook, Elizabeth knew to mean Tavern of Peace.

"Oh, David." Her words trailed away, and she looked at her husband.

"Right, let's get a table." David moved towards the small doorway buried deep in the thick stone wall just as a waiter walked out to greet him.

"Table for two please – em – *dio parakalo*?" David gestured toward Elizabeth, who was still standing on the step below, transfixed by the view.

"Sure. No problem." The waiter clapped his hands together, then led David to a table close to the edge of the widest step. A few of the other tables were occupied, most by couples leaning in close to each other. The music, while still Rebetika, was subtler than at some of the other restaurants they had passed.

As they settled themselves at the table, Elizabeth felt unexplained tears prickling her eyes. David, looking up from the menu, caught sight of the glimmer of moisture the candle highlighted and pressed his hand onto her thigh under the table.

"Everything OK?"

Elizabeth sniffed and shook her hair out of her eyes.

"More than OK," she replied, allowing the feeling she recognized as peace to encapsulate her. She hadn't given herself the luxury of relaxing into this feeling in a long time. Maybe now she could?

Dinner was a triumph consisting of tender, spit-roasted lamb with garlic and oregano, fluffy roast potatoes with lemon, and another fragrant Greek salad accompanied by a bottle of chilled retsina wine.

David had been chatty and full of praise for their first day. They talked about the next day and what they would like to do for the remainder of their time in Athens.

"I wonder if perhaps we're trying to cram too much into the days?" David spoke through a mouthful of lamb.

"Probably." Elizabeth picked an olive out of the salad bowl and popped it into her mouth.

"We should just take it easy and go with the flow, as Kate says. No need to have an agenda, I suppose. We are on holiday." David emptied the last drops of retsina into her glass.

"Yes – and if we don't see every single amphitheater in Greece, it won't be a disaster, right?" Elizabeth grinned at David's mock-horrified expression. "Seriously, Dave, we have about twelve of them on the list at the moment."

"No, of course, that's fine." David sensed her seriousness. He knew that she had suffered through his obsession with architecture over the years, and that he had pushed her over the edge at times with his need to visit as many historic structures as humanly possible, regardless of where they were.

To David, the true art in architecture was in the balance of the designs. He would soak up the symmetry and sense of order in beautifully designed historical buildings. The perfectly matched columns supporting a gate on an Hellenic structure, or the sweeping buttresses over the door of a Gothic church, held a certain magic for him. He could not abide modern architecture. Seeing the harsh angles, like huge bruises of steel and glass, on the faces of otherwise classical cities hurt his sensibilities.

He had wanted to be an architect ever since visiting the Eiffel Tower as a young child. However, when he was selecting courses for his university applications, his father had pressured him away from the career he longed for. Albert Fredericks's logic was that a banker would never be out of work and, if David wanted a solid career he could always count on, being an architect would not be the way to go.

In David's day, children listened to their parents and made their choices accordingly. So he had opted for business and finance courses at Edinburgh University and had had the "solid" career in banking that his father wanted for him. A part of David had always regretted his decision, but after a few years of being trapped inside a profession he had become well qualified for, and which provided a good living, he was loath to make changes that might upset the apple cart.

Once he and Elizabeth were married, there had been no question of him taking any risks, so he had stuck it out, pursuing his passion for design and architecture on his own time.

He watched Elizabeth drain her glass of wine. "Shall we have another bottle?"

Elizabeth wiped her mouth with a napkin.

"Not if you want me to walk back to the hotel under my own steam."

David was amazed that the market vendors were still at their stalls as they made their way back down the stepped hillside towards the square. It was 9:45, and life was still very much in motion in Plaka. Music wailed from the many cafés and restaurants they passed, and for every person climbing down the steps there was one climbing up, just beginning his or her evening.

Realizing Elizabeth wasn't next to him anymore, David looked around. Spotting the familiar shape of her, he saw that she had stopped a little way back. She was at a stall with piles of large, petal-shaped sheets of leather in a rainbow of colors stacked against the makeshift walls. She was thumbing through some samples on a narrow glass counter and appeared to be talking to the tall man standing behind it. As David approached, he heard the man speaking in competent English.

"All best-quality leather, hand-cured and crafted." The man's voice was low and melodic. Elizabeth was obviously enraptured.

"Dave, look at this. This gentleman is a cobbler. Look at these shoes." She pointed behind the man to the rows of shiny leather shoes lined up along the walls. David saw brogues, with the customary holed pattern across the toes, smooth casual loafers, moccasins with tassels, ladies' high-heels, and flip-flops in every color. It was mesmerizing. Perhaps it was the wine, but these were some of the most beautiful things he had ever seen.

"I measure you now and make for you – whatever you like – ready in two days." The man was courting Elizabeth's attention.

She raised her gaze to David and nodded. She didn't need his permission, but she silently asked for it anyway.

"Go ahead." He smiled. "As long as I get to pick the color."

Elizabeth turned back towards the man.

"I'd like a pair of those." To David's surprise, rather than the flat, comfortable-looking flip-flops, she pointed to the high-heels.

"Of course – and what color you like, madam?" the vendor asked, turning to pick up a thick pencil and a piece of brown paper.

"Blue." She and David spoke in unison and then laughed at each other. They both knew why they'd chosen blue, but weren't willing to share that information with the cobbler, who waited while their private joke rolled over them.

It had been their first official date. In her first term of studying English and Scottish literature at Edinburgh University, Elizabeth had agreed to meet David at the dance being held in the Student Union. She was nervous about her dress for the evening. Her best friend, Freya, had suggested Elizabeth liven it up by borrowing her new pale-blue high heels. The shoes were the most beautiful things Elizabeth had ever seen and, terrified that she might ruin them, she'd tried to resist Freya's urging. Despite her concerns, the shoes had seduced her, complementing the soft floral tones of her dress. So Elizabeth had relented, slipping her feet into the gentle embrace of the leather.

Walking into the union that night, she and Freya were arm in arm. As she stepped down the rough metal staircase, she spotted David at the bar and raised her hand to wave. Just at that moment, the group behind them surged forward and Elizabeth felt an inexplicable tug at her right foot. As her weight shifted forward, she grabbed for the banister, and her hand tightened on the railing as Freya went down in a cloud of pink and white cotton.

Elizabeth recalled the slow-motion scene unfolding before her. Her friend was lying in an inelegant pile at the bottom of the stairs, laughing as her boyfriend, Sandy, tried to help her to her feet. Elizabeth stood rooted to the spot, still gripping the banister, while her right foot remained trapped behind her, the long heel of the shoe buried deep in a hungry, metal-toothed hole in the stair.

Searching frantically for David's face, she saw him come towards her. He walked up the stair, reached down, and slid his hands around her ankle, slipping her foot out of the trapped shoe. She remembered the thrill of his touch as she self-consciously moved to the lower stair, allowing him the room he needed to maneuver the shoe out of its metal prison. Eventually, having freed it, David stood and held it out to her.

"Ready for a drink now, Cinderella?" He had smiled at her, and for Elizabeth, the rest had been history.

Selecting a pale, sky-blue sample of leather, Elizabeth edged her way inside the small shop. The leather pieces were stacked like hundreds of miniature Persian carpets, layers of color and texture that she couldn't help but touch.

"Come, madam – come, please." The man beckoned her towards a small wooden platform at the back of the shop.

"You take off your shoes and stand here, please." He placed a sheet of brown paper on top of the platform and stood back to let Elizabeth remove her sandals.

Offering her his elegant hand, the craftsman helped her stand up on the platform, then settled himself down onto folded knees on the ground.

"I measure now – OK?" He bent, hands poised over her foot, awaiting her permission to make physical contact.

"OK," she replied, watching David, who in turn was staring at the cobbler.

Placing one long-fingered hand over her instep, the crafts-man gently pressed her foot onto the paper and drew around its contours. When she eventually lifted it, the thick pencil had left what looked like a rudimentary and childlike outline on the paper. She wondered how he could make a decent shoe from it.

He indicated her other foot. Elizabeth placed it forward on the opposing edge of the paper so he could repeat the exercise.

Once the outlines were done, he measured around the width of each foot, across the arch, from the tip of her big toe to her ankle, then from underneath the heel along to the big toe.

"You want this style?" He showed her a red leather court shoe – the heel around three inches high. It was cut low at the front, with a gently pointed toe.

"Yes, they're beautiful."

Her smile said it all, and David felt the familiar tug at his heart that happened when she indulged herself this way, which was rarely. He wished she would do it more, but he could not often persuade her that she deserved these little luxuries.

Having left the required deposit and the name of their hotel, the two shook hands with the tall cobbler and left. For the re-mainder of the walk they remained silent, savoring the smells, sounds, and sights of the *agora* and the gentle, cooling lick of the night air on their skin.

CHAPTER 5

The warm water lapped over Elizabeth's thighs, and she lay her head back in the bath. As she submerged herself, her ears filled up with soothing fluid, and the noises of the air conditioning, the hum of the TV from the bedroom, and the rumble of cars and activity from the street below all became subdued. It had been a great day, and she was now enjoying the special kind of relaxation that having no agenda, no specific demands on her time or attention, afforded.

David was dosing, watching BBC World News. She, on the other hand, had no desire to know what was going on in the world. She had left that behind for a while and unless there was some global disaster of epic proportions, she was staying focused on the here and now.

As she rocked her hips from side to side, moving the warm water around herself, Elizabeth tried to remember the last time they had had a proper holiday, at least one that didn't involve going to a theme park, seaside resort, or similar place that Kate had insisted upon. At the thought of her daughter, Elizabeth felt a familiar jolt to her stomach. She missed Kate.

While they both adored their clever, accomplished girl, when she'd been growing up, David had indulged her beyond what Elizabeth had felt was reasonable. Memories of feeling isolated, left on the outside of their father-daughter club, flooded her mind, and while she knew that it was childish to feel left out, she still did sometimes. David and Kate had a deep bond, a way of communicating without including her, that hurt. She hoped it was unintentional, and over the years had come to terms with it as being endemic of their special relationship, as opposed to them just being thoughtless about her feelings.

She remembered Kate's eighth birthday party. The house had been filled with little girls running around the garden and spilling through the French doors into the living room. Their frills and ankle socks had sparkled white, and squeals of delight had floated in the air. She couldn't find David or Kate anywhere until she walked into the dining room. They sat at the far end of the table amidst a wave of little girls playing noisy chase around them. Kate was on her dad's knee, and she had opened her gift from them both. The baby doll lay on top of a mound of tissue paper, and Kate's arms were clasped around David's neck, her head buried in his shoulder.

As she floated in the bath, Elizabeth relived the pain that she had felt at that moment, when she realized that they hadn't waited for her. Kate had looked up at her and David had said "Oh, look, darling, it's Mummy. The doll's from mummy too."

Elizabeth had felt then, and many times since, that her

presence was unwelcome, and David's gesture of inclusion an ill-timed afterthought.

When David had had the affair three years ago, Kate had all but accused Elizabeth of driving him to it with her detachedness. Elizabeth had recoiled, burned by the venom spewing from her angry daughter, and it had taken weeks for them to reconnect in a true sense.

Elizabeth knew that the vitriol sprang from fear, but it had taken time for her to see Kate again after the awful confrontation. Kate had eventually shown up one day with a bunch of stargazer lilies and apologized for defending her father's obvious wrongdoing. Once Elizabeth had assured Kate that she had no intention of leaving David, the two women had formed a tacit agreement to repair their relationship.

Sliding back up in the bath, Elizabeth felt a stab under her ribs. Her hurt at David's betrayal had been compounded by her anger at the ridiculous cliché of him choosing Connie – a blowsy, middle-aged teller who worked at the bank. She had thought that he might at least have been a little more discerning in choosing the woman who had the potential to bring about the demise of his marriage. A young, blonde, brainy trainee would have made more sense – but then a young, blonde, brainy trainee wouldn't have been interested in balding, safe, skimmed-milk-in-his-de-caffeinated-coffee David.

As she reached for the olive-colored soap on the edge of the bath and began lathering her arms, Elizabeth remembered how hard she'd tried to reason things out when it had happened. Her lack of attention to him had seemed to be the catalyst that had driven David to take the leap towards another woman. She imagined Connie finding every word that he uttered fascinating and erudite as she tittered and fawned over him at the coffee machine, or in the cafeteria. Elizabeth supposed that could have been seductive, and been enough to make David feel valued when he wasn't feeling so at home.

The one thing she would concede to in that whole mess was that she, Elizabeth, *had* been less than interested in him at the time. However, that did not excuse his shocking decision. She had been severely depressed, retreating into the house and to the comfort of food, becoming a tearful, sleepless, angry, and over-weight reflection of her former self. She knew that she had shut down for a while, in so many areas, but had been powerless to stop the momentum.

David had not known how to cope with being left on the outside of any part of her life. She had been aware of his confusion but had still been unable to alter her behavior. After his transgression had been discovered, she had let him marinate in his guilt for many months. A pink sticky note with details of a rendezvous, and a small childlike heart drawn around the words, had not been a very dignified way to find out that her husband was being unfaithful. David never did check his trouser pockets before throwing them in the wash basket.

As she lay in the now cooling water, Elizabeth felt a stirring of the old feelings of betrayal. No, it was enough. They had moved on.

As she twirled the olive-colored soap in her hands, it felt marvelous, creating creamy bubbles that slid through her fingers. She made a mental note to sneak a bar of it into their case when they left for Hydra in a few days.

CHAPTER 6

The flight had been smooth, and Kate now watched the changing scenery as the taxi wove through the city. Old and new buildings stood cheek by jowl and were growing exponentially taller as they passed. She wondered if they were nearing the center of town.

"How much farther?" She leaned towards the driver, hoping to be heard over the thumping radio. The music was local, heavy on the bass, with dueling bouzoukia playing a fugue that was beginning to put her teeth on edge.

Mercifully, the driver reached out and turned the volume down.

"Five minutes. Hotel Grand Bretagne, yes?" His brown eyes sought hers in the rearview mirror, and Kate nodded.

"Yes. Thanks." She sat back in the seat and pulled her bag closer to her hip. As she watched the light rising behind the buildings to her left, she tasted salty dread. What was she doing here? This was insane. It was only 5:45 a.m., far too early to wake her parents, but she'd flown all the way to Greece to hijack their trip and break the news that had been burning a hole in her heart for years. There would be no more hiding, no more avoidance, just honesty, raw and present. How would they take it?

A picture of the scene came to her: her father silent and pale, supporting her mother's arm as Elizabeth stood red-faced, her voice stolen by disappointment. Kate swallowed. It was too late now. It was time she faced the music, and time that her parents learned to accept her for who she was. Charlotte Macfie, the amazing woman that she had been seeing for months, was the love of her life and hiding that was an injustice, not only to herself and Charlotte, but also to her parents.

The taxi slowed down as it approached a large square. There was a steady flow of traffic, surprising for the early hour, and Kate watched as a motorcycle with an oversized trailer full of vegetables squeezed past them on the right. The taxi driver shouted something out of the open passenger-side window, and the motorcyclist responded with a gesture that Kate had never seen before. She presumed it was the Greek equivalent of the middle finger, and despite the nerves that bubbled under her ribs, or perhaps as result of them, she giggled to herself.

The square opened up in front of the car, and on the left, a long building with a pinkish hue and centralized columns stood at the top of a set of marble steps. The Greek flag flew from the center of the front portico. She presumed that this must the parliament building she'd read about, which meant that they were in Constitution Square. Kate looked to her right. Behind a group of closed umbrellas with tables underneath them, she saw a tall building. She counted seven floors, and as her eyes swept up to the top, the name Hotel Grand Bretagne glowed against the blue-pink dawn.

The taxi pulled up to the entrance, and within moments, a doorman was helping her out of the car.

"Welcome to Hotel Grande Bretagne. You are checking in, madam?" The tall man bowed slightly as he spoke, his English impeccable.

She knew her room wouldn't be ready this early, and rather than sitting in the lobby until it was a decent time to wake her parents, Kate decided she'd go in search of coffee.

"Um, no. Not yet. I…" Kate stumbled over her words and felt her face flush. "I'd like to leave my bags and go for a walk first. Can I do that?" She ran a hand through her hair and stepped to the side of the taxi, handing the driver a handful of euros. The driver took the notes and pulled away, leaving her looking up at the building, her bag in the hands of the doorman.

"Of course, madam. Please follow me." The man pushed through the revolving door and Kate followed in his wake. "You can leave the bag with the concierge." He spoke over his shoulder as he guided her across the wide, bright lobby.

Having left her name and passport with the concierge, Kate slung her handbag over her shoulder and headed out into the square. It was 6:10, and already some of the cafés that sat around the edges of the square were opening. Spotting one that looked promising, with yellow umbrellas shading several small wrought-iron tables, Kate wandered over.

It was warm, the morning sun causing her to squint as she searched her bag for her sunglasses. Charlotte had reminded her to take them, and as her hand found the familiar shape, Kate smiled.

The coffee she ordered was bitter and sweet and quite marvelous. She ordered another and a pastry in the shape of a horseshoe, filled with apricots and scattered with toasted almonds. As she bit into the flaky round, she wondered how Charlotte would rate it compared to one of her own. Perhaps it was the contrast to the strong coffee, but Kate thought it one of the most delicious things that she had ever eaten.

Having finished her breakfast, she checked her watch again: 7:16 a.m. was early, but it wasn't totally uncivilized. Besides, if Kate knew her parents, they'd have been awake for an hour at least.

Her waiter had disappeared, so she walked inside the small café to pay the bill. The woman behind the counter smiled and thanked her. Kate left a tip and wove between the tables then crossed the square towards the hotel.

As she swung out of the revolving door into the reception area, her heart began to clatter under her ribs. This was it. It was time.

CHAPTER 7

The telephone rang shrilly and, wrenched from a deep sleep, David's heart flip-flopped in his chest. Diving from the bed to grab the phone, he knocked his glasses onto the floor. He glanced at his watch and, squinting at it, saw that it was 7:35 a.m. He lifted the receiver to his ear.

"Yes, hello?" His voice was rough.

"Mr. Fredericks, good morning. This is Giorgos, the concierge. Sorry to disturb you, but you have a guest in the lobby."

The words settled on David's morning-dull brain. As he looked over at Elizabeth, he saw that she'd already slid her glasses on and propped herself up on one elbow. She was mouthing, "Who is it?"

David shrugged in response.

"Sorry? A visitor – for us?" He raised his eyebrows and looked at Elizabeth as he spoke.

"Yes sir, your daughter. She is here. Shall I put her on the line?"

David felt another lurch in his chest. Kate? Here? What had happened? He instantly thought through the series of catastrophes that must have occurred at home. Their house had burned down. She had crashed her car. She was seriously ill. She'd been fired from the university. None of the scenarios he imagined, however, could account for her presence here in Greece.

Elizabeth was now looking very worried. She tapped David's shoulder, shaking her head in question. David nodded at her as he answered the concierge.

"Yes, put her on."

"Dad?"

"Kate, what's going on? You're here?"

At this, Elizabeth sat bolt upright, and both hands flew to cover her mouth. David knew she was running through the same worrying scenarios in her head that he himself had imagined. To reassure her he squeezed her leg and shook his head. "S'OK," he mouthed.

"Yeah. Surprise! Can I come up?" Kate sounded young.

"Well, yes, of course, but what are you doing here?" David shrugged as Elizabeth bounded from the bed and headed to the bathroom to retrieve her robe.

"I'll explain when I get up there. Everything is fine, Dad, honest."

"OK, well, we're in room 306." David tossed the covers off with his free hand and placed his feet on the cool marble floor. "See you in a few, then." With that, Kate was gone.

Elizabeth trotted back into the bedroom. Wrapped in the robe, she dragged a brush through her hair.

"What's wrong?" she asked, her eyes wide.

"She says nothing is." David scratched his head, rose from the bed, picked up his glasses from the floor, and passed Elizabeth to get into the bathroom.

"Well, what the hell's she doing here, then?" Elizabeth heard the edge in her own voice. Fear angered her, and Kate's turning up out of the blue while they were on their dream holiday could only mean that something was badly wrong.

Scanning the room, Elizabeth ascertained that all was in order to receive Kate. Their clothes were hung away, and the small sitting area at the far end had been tidied. Their Fodor's guidebooks and camera sat on the low coffee table, and her sun hat lay on the arm of the chair.

Walking to the mirror, she examined herself. Tying the robe a little tighter around her middle, she looked at her reflection. Did she look a mess? Was she disheveled? Then, a wave of irritation at her own concern overtook her. Why was she worrying, anyway? This was their holiday, and even if Kate had turned up unannounced and found them sitting stark naked, reading the paper amidst toenail clippings and half-full cups of cold tea – so what? She'd just have to live with it.

The notion that she couldn't completely be herself with Kate struck her as both odd and sad, as it had for many years. She remembered feeling judged by her daughter all through Kate's teen years. Kate would make sarcastic remarks about Elizabeth's clothes, her preference for traditional furnishings and colors, and the food she cooked. That behavior had gone on for years, even after Kate was well into her twenties.

When they had redecorated the living room a few years ago, Kate had dug the dagger in once more.

"Gosh, Mum, what happened? The sofa looks like it's from

this century. Was there no sale on at chintzy-furniture.com?"

Elizabeth had laughed it off at the time, but Kate's mockery hurt her. She knew that some of her friends' children had treated them the same way. Kate's my-mother-is-an-idiot phase hadn't ended with the teen years, however.

Elizabeth stared at her reflection and felt the familiar emptiness that being unable to figure out her only child always left her with. Why did Kate resent her so?

A sharp knock on the door snapped her out of her thoughts. David was there in a flash, and then Kate was in his arms.

"Dad." Kate buried her face in his shoulder and he patted her back as he had done since she was a baby.

"Hi, baby girl." David rocked her, not releasing her from the circle of his arms.

Kate opened her eyes and met Elizabeth's across the room.

"Hi, Mum." She released herself from David's grip and walked towards her mother.

"Hi, love." Elizabeth opened her arms. Kate wrapped her arms around her mother's waist, taking the breath out of her with the uncharacteristic intensity of the hug.

Alarmed, Elizabeth gently pushed Kate far enough away to look in her eyes.

"What's going on, sweetheart?" Elizabeth scanned her daughter's face. The smattering of freckles across the bridge of her nose was still just as it had been when she was twelve years old. The blue eyes, David's eyes, were clear and unblinking, and her short sandy hair with its deep natural waves was tucked behind each ear. Her face totally lacked makeup, as was Kate's style. All looked normal. But there had been some seismic shift. As a mother, Elizabeth knew it, could sense it, and no one could tell her otherwise.

Leaving her mother's grasp, Kate tucked an imaginary stray hair behind her ear and shrugged her heavy backpack onto the floor.

"Nice room." She looked around and smiled at her mum; then, receiving no response, she turned to find her dad.

David had picked up the small kettle and was in the bathroom filling it with water.

"Shall we have some tea?" he called into the bedroom.

"Yes, please." Kate walked over to the large window and looked down onto Syntagma Square below.

"Great view."

Elizabeth felt irritation again and inhaled, trying to get a hold of herself before she asked again about what was going on.

"Kate – darling – while we're glad to see you, I'm pretty sure you didn't take time off work, fly all the way to Athens, and wake us up to admire the view."

"Can we just have some tea first, Mum?" Kate fired back abruptly. Sliding her jacket off, she sank into one of the small armchairs.

Elizabeth bit down on her lower lip and turned to watch David tearing open two tea bags and placing them into both available cups. Leaving him to this small domestic task, she walked over and sat down on the sofa, tucking the robe around her legs.

"I'll have a cup when you two are done," David said, turning back to face the women in his life. The tension was palpable, and he coughed, clearing his throat.

"So, Kate, what's this all about?" He placed a steaming cup in front of them both and settled himself on the sofa, opposite his daughter.

"I just wanted to see you, I mean, see you in person." Kate picked up her cup and blew on the hot liquid.

"Kate, we're not idiots. What has happened?" Elizabeth could take it no longer.

"OK. I wanted to tell you something, and I didn't want to do it in a letter, or on the phone. It's too important." Kate's voice faded as she took another sip of tea.

"We're listening." There was an unusual edge to David's voice now.

"Well, I wanted to let you know that I'd met someone, some-one special."

Elizabeth felt the flood of relief. Thank god – Kate wasn't terminally ill, or moving to Australia, or something equally as devastating.

"For goodness' sake, why didn't you say so right away? We've been dying here." Elizabeth leaned forward and lifted her own cup.

"That's great news. But why the dramatic entrance, love?" David draped his arm behind Elizabeth's shoulder as she settled back against the cushion to sip her tea.

"It's not quite that simple." Kate shifted on the chair and placed her cup back on the table.

"Go on." Elizabeth's newly relaxed stomach re-clenched and she waited for the hit.

"Well, I've wanted to tell you this for a long time. There's just never been a good time, a right time." To Elizabeth's alarm, Kate's eyes filled up as she spoke.

"Darling, whatever it is, it can't be that bad. Just tell us." Elizabeth leaned forward, put her cup down, and placed her hand on the table as she spoke, reaching out across the void to her daughter.

Kate met her mother's eyes, blinked, then spoke.

"She's amazing and we've been together for almost six months now. Her name is Charlotte."

Silence wrapped itself around the three of them, and Elizabeth drew a long, slow breath. Were her ears deceiving her? Did Kate say 'she'?

David sat, silent and pillar-like, his arm heavy and stationary around his wife. The only muscle moving was one twitching in his jaw as he clenched his teeth.

Kate looked at her parents, her eyes flitting between their faces, searching for some sign of life from either of them.

"Say something." Her voice, beseeching, gave way to her emotions, and tears began to flow, leaving a tiny trail of salty footprints on the front of her pale-blue T-shirt.

The sight of those sad little marks jolted Elizabeth out of her state of suspended reality.

"OK, let me get this straight. You are seeing a woman, a woman named Charlotte?"

Kate nodded. Patting her jeans pocket, she rose – then dug in her backpack searching for something.

On autopilot, Elizabeth stood up and walked to the bathroom, picked up the tissue box from the counter, and returned to the room.

"Here you are," she said, placing the box on the table as Kate returned to her chair.

"Thanks." Kate pulled two tissues out and blew her nose loudly. It was something that had always annoyed Elizabeth. Did she have to make a sound like Horatio Hornblower? It was so unladylike. As the random thought filtered into her mind, Elizabeth felt a second shock of realization. A woman. Kate was seeing a woman.

The thirty years of her daughter's life began to swim before her eyes. Scene by scene, it opened up to her and told the story of an unhappy girl. The arguments they'd had when Kate was only four over her refusal to wear a dress to a family party. The letter Elizabeth had written to the school principal when Kate was twelve, asking if she could play on the boy's football team as there was no facility for girls to play football at the time. Kate's decision to have blue hair in secondary school and the lack of boyfriends all through her teen years. Rose, the one close friend Kate had ever had, had abandoned her after their joint sixteenth birthday party. Elizabeth had never gotten to the bottom of that. The harsh, boyish haircuts, the refusal to use makeup of any kind, did it all add up to this? How could she not have seen it? She was Kate's mother.

"Mum?" Kate was looking at her, and Elizabeth didn't know how long she'd been standing still.

"Yes, sorry. Just getting my thoughts together."

"You've no idea how hard this is. I've wanted to tell you so many times." Kate continued to dab at her eyes and look at their faces, searching for a reaction.

David remained still, his mouth tightly closed and his eyes unblinking.

"Dad. For god's sake, say something," Kate whined as she

twisted the tissue in her hand into a thin twine.

"What do you want me to say?" David finally spoke. His eyes were hard, and he didn't sound like himself.

At his words, Kate sat up, straightening her spine, and Elizabeth thought she could see a glimmer of familiar defiance flash in her daughter's eyes. She willed her to keep a lid on that particular reaction for the moment. Widening her own eyes at Kate, she hoped that she'd get the message. *Just stay calm. Don't start any fires you can't put out.*

"Well, I'd like to know what you think." Kate's voice had a distinct sting to it.

"Are you sure about that?"

Kate nodded, meeting his eyes.

David removed his arm from around Elizabeth's shoulder and ran both hands through his thinning hair. Head down, he examined the carpet before looking up.

"If this is not some kind of cruel joke, I'm not sure what to say, Kate. Whatever I say will make no difference to the situation, so I may as well keep my thoughts to myself." He shrugged then rose heavily from the sofa and, turning his back on them, walked to the window.

"This isn't about you, you know?" Kate was angry now. "This isn't something I am doing to you, like a teenage prank." Her tears gone, Kate stood and gestured to her mum, asking what she should do.

Elizabeth was at a loss. She stared at David's back and knew that this was something he would need time to absorb. His perfect little girl had thrown him a curve ball, leaving him struggling as to what to do next. Seeing the stoop of his back, Elizabeth felt sorry for him. It struck her as bizarre that she was more concerned with what was going through his mind than her own.

What did she think? This was not news she was expecting and yet, now that Kate had told them the truth, she was not rocked by the information. She was not shocked or afraid. No, much to her surprise, she was actually relieved. Whatever the barriers had been to her and Kate understanding each other, perhaps this would bring them down, once and for all?

"Mum?"

"Sweetheart, I think we just need some time to absorb this." She patted the air, indicating that Kate should sit. David still stared out the window, seemingly unable to look at them.

"I understand." Kate's voice was now small. "I'm sorry to spring this on you. It's just that I couldn't wait until you got home to tell you. Charlotte and I are moving in together, and I needed everything out in the open before we take that next step."

Elizabeth untied and retied the belt of her robe and, picking up the cooling tea, took a long swallow.

"How could you do this?" David turned, his face scarlet, his voice low and hard. "After everything... all the years, all the... everything we've..." His voice faded, and he shook his head slowly from side to side as he spoke, unable to look at Kate.

"After what, Dad?" Kate was up and moving towards him. "Everything you've done for me? All the wonderful opportunities you gave me? How could I let you down by not liking men?"

Elizabeth's nerves were jangling. This was escalating into an awful scene that they might all live to regret. Without a doubt, this could be a defining moment in all of their futures, and she knew she could not let things get totally out of hand.

She scanned David's face, desperate to get a read on what was going through his mind. For some reason, his locked subconscious was not yielding to her customary keys. He looked eerily absent from his body, obviously shaken but still too controlled somehow. She wanted to grab his arms, bring him back into the room, and remind him that this was Kate, his beloved daughter.

"I just can't…"

"Can't what, Dad? Believe that your daughter is a lesbian?"

Kate now stood in front of her father, her hands shoved deep into her pockets. Her thin shoulders rose up towards her ears as she spoke, her collarbones forming perfect cups out of the translucent skin that stretched across them. The stance reminded Elizabeth of a much younger Kate, the teenage version who crashed the car into the back of the garage but had still argued that someone else had left the car in gear, so it wasn't her fault.

This particular runaway car, however, had no one at the wheel but Kate, and the damage threatened to be far more substantial.

"I was going to say, I just can't take it in." David's eyes repopulated themselves, and he engaged Elizabeth's, seeking help.

"Well, I'm sorry, but you'll have to try." Kate was newly defiant.

"Kate, just back down a little. I mean it." Elizabeth's voice was firm, her eyes never leaving her husband's. "Take a moment to consider our position, and calm down." She released David's stare and turned to warn Kate with her eyes that she needed to stop for the moment.

Kate read her mother's face and, stepping backwards as if physically struck, returned to the armchair.

"Do you want me to apologize for my sexuality, is that it?"

In a wavering voice, she asked the question of them both, all the time looking at Elizabeth.

"If nothing else, you need to apologize for bursting in our holiday and, like a spoiled child, announcing this thing without a moment's consideration of what the news might do to us." David was now trembling. The color had drained from his face, and he extended a hand to steady himself on the chest of drawers.

"'This *thing*.'" Kate was livid.

"David, sit down." Elizabeth walked towards him and placed her hand under his forearm. Leading him to the sofa, she pushed him gently down onto the seat. "Sit there for a few minutes. I'm going to make some more tea."

Elizabeth beckoned to Kate, picked up the small kettle, and walked into the bathroom. She turned to her daughter.

"Just slow down. Do you hear me? You have to give him time, give *us* time."

"I know. I'm sorry, Mum, I've just been living with this secret for so long – trying to come to terms with things myself, doing everything I could to protect you both from the truth of who I am." Kate once again melted into tears. "Why do you think I stayed away from home so much, spent school holidays and summers at the university, didn't join you for more weekends, missed all those trips and Christmas dinners?"

Elizabeth looked at her daughter and, for the second time since Kate had dropped this ill-timed bombshell on their lives, felt a sudden flood of relief. As a million small scenarios ran through her mind – Kate's habit of distancing herself, the increasing lack of communication that had grown customary over the past few years, the obvious excuses for her inability to participate in family events and holidays – it all began to make sense.

As she tried to fill the kettle with water from the tap, Elizabeth could no longer see clearly. Her eyes filled up with years worth of unshed tears, tears of hurt, of frustration, and most of all of fear, that she was losing her daughter to something she could not fathom all began to slide down her face.

"How come you seem to be taking this better than Dad? To be honest, I'd have put money on you being the one to freak out." Kate wiped her eyes with the mangled tissue, placed a hand on her mother's shoulder, and searched her face in the mirror.

"Because it's so much better than what I was thinking." Elizabeth placed the full kettle down on the small shelf over the sink and looked in the mirror at Kate standing behind her.

"What were you imagining?" Kate sounded puzzled.

"That you hated me." Elizabeth turned to face her daughter. "I just thought that if I were gone, if your dad and I had divorced after his affair and you could've just spent time with him, that you'd have been home a lot more."

"Oh, Mum." Kate put her arms around her mother and pulled her in. Elizabeth put her chin on her daughter's shoulder and let the tears flow. For now, this was all she needed, to have Kate hold her and tell her that, despite all her fears, she wasn't the world's worst mother after all.

After a few minutes in Kate's embrace, Elizabeth gathered herself and, seeing her tearstained reflection in the mirror, splashed some cold water on her face, then patted it dry with a small white towel.

"OK, we need to deal with your father." She turned and walked into the bedroom, placed the kettle back into its cradle and, pressing the small button down, she addressed David.

"Are you all right?" She sat next to him and took his hand in hers. "David?"

CHAPTER 8

———◆———

Kate had gone to her own room to shower, rest, and give them all some time to themselves. Elizabeth now sat opposite David and picked at the salad that she had ordered from room service. His beef burger sat untouched, a small pool of grease congealing underneath the French fries and the lettuce that was wilting on the plate. Three small empty bottles of Metaxa brandy from the mini-bar sat on the coffee table. David lay back, balancing a half-full glass on his stomach, his feet up on the table next to the tray of wasted food.

"What are you thinking?" Elizabeth asked into the silence, spearing a small piece of cucumber.

"I don't know what to think," David replied, raising the glass to his lips and sipping some of the caustic liquid. He knew that he should be getting his thoughts together at this point, forming an opinion, dealing with the shock of it all, but he seemed unable to get a grip on the situation. "I mean, how did we not know?"

He looked at his wife, his eyes wounded and questioning. "Were we so blind, so ridiculously naïve, that we missed some glaring signs?" He paused mid-thought. "What does it mean for the future, is what I want to know?" David crossed one leg over the other, then, looking uncomfortable, lowered both to the ground, sitting up straight and adjusting the cushion behind his back.

Elizabeth chewed and waited for him to continue, not wanting to stem his newly accessed stream of consciousness.

"What about her career? Could it have a negative effect on that? What does this mean for her in terms of everyday life? How will she cope with the possible prejudice she could face? Will we have to meet this Charlotte person? I suppose we can kiss any grandchildren goodbye." He raised his glass, as if in a mournful toast to a beloved notion gone by.

Elizabeth turned towards him abruptly.

"What century are you living in, Dave? Are you serious? She's not dying. She's not emigrating. She hasn't committed some hideous crime that will see her rotting in jail for the next thirty years. She's simply…"

"Simply what?" he shot back. "Simply gay? That in itself is an oxymoron, my love." David let out a harsh laugh, and Elizabeth winced at the jarring sound.

"I was going to say that she's simply fallen in love. It doesn't change who she is, or who we are, for that matter."

Elizabeth pushed her plate away and, taking her half-full wineglass in her hand, sat back and folded her legs up underneath herself.

"Who we are?" David looked at his wife.

"Yes, as in, her parents. It changes nothing." Elizabeth

nodded as she spoke, as if by saying it out loud she was accepting the concept, the words giving the thought life, momentum, and credence. "It changes nothing, in that we need to be here for her now more than ever, David. If her own parents aren't in her corner, then who will be?"

"I just can't believe how calm you are." David stared at her and then sipped some more brandy.

"I'm not exactly calm, I just think that so much of her behavior over the years makes sense now." As soon as she'd said it, Elizabeth wished she'd restructured the sentence.

"I beg your pardon?" David was now leaning forward, the glass dangling between his knees, amber liquid sloshing dangerously close to the rim as he moved.

"I mean, some of the questions I had about her refusal to communicate, her aggression towards me, staying away on holidays, and canceling visits – this kind of answers them."

"Well, it would have been good of you to share your thoughts and concerns with me." David's voice had an edge to it now that she was unaccustomed to hearing.

"What do you mean by that?"

"If you suspected something of this nature was going on, why the hell didn't you talk to me about it?" David's voice rose to a shout.

"Hey, just calm down. Why are you shouting at me?" Elizabeth held her hand up, protecting her chest from the verbal onslaught.

"Just tell me, Elizabeth. Did you know?" David slammed the glass down on the table, sending a shower of tiny droplets into the atmosphere.

"No, I didn't know, for god's sake. But let's just say that I'm not totally surprised."

David shook his head in disbelief. She was sitting there, so smug, so in control. In all the years they'd been together, he'd never once considered hitting her, but now, in this moment, he wanted to slap her face.

"You're not surprised?" he managed to growl.

"No. Not entirely."

CHAPTER 9

———◆———

David had never for one moment considered that Kate might be anything other, or less, than he imagined. As he had watched her grow up, his pride in her and his adoration had grown exponentially. When she'd reached her teens, he had recognized a deep resilience in her. It was not hardness, but more of an inner resolve which he felt that she would be able to count on in the future, should she face tough times. She had generally chosen the less traveled path, and at times he had wondered why she seemed bent on making her own life what he considered to be more difficult in some respects.

As he listened to the water pattering in the shower, he imagined Elizabeth washing the news they'd received off of her body, soaping it away with each sweep of her hands. He visualized Kate's words dropping into the shower tray, spent and invalid as they swirled around the drain and then disappeared into the darkness of Athens's sewers. If only he could wipe them as easily from his mind.

He wasn't a narrow-minded man. At least, he didn't think he was. He had always prided himself, in fact, on being tolerant, and perhaps even a liberal to Elizabeth's opposing conservative. In this situation, however, it was Elizabeth who seemed to be coping with Kate's news with more grace and acceptance than he was. Did she not worry about the same things his mind was now plagued with? Did it not scare her that their daughter was taking this path?

Early afternoon or not, he opened the door of the mini-bar and scanned the remaining contents. The brandy he had already drunk lay heavy in his stomach, and he hadn't been able to eat his lunch, so he knew this was not a good idea. Regardless, he reached in and grabbed a cold beer, the frigid can feeling good against his palm.

He switched the TV on and sat back on the sofa, taking up his previous spot. The images of BBC World News flickered as he sipped the beer and felt his stomach contract at the chill.

Glancing at his watch, he saw that it had been three hours since Kate had left their room. He hoped she was asleep. In fact, he hoped she slept for the rest of the day. He didn't think he could face another encounter – not yet, anyway. The idea that he didn't want to see his beloved daughter brought a hard lump to his throat. What was happening to him? How could this be?

Elizabeth padded out from the bathroom encased in a large towel. Her hair was wrapped in a smaller one, and she looked like a figure from one of Russell Flint's famous bathhouse water-colors. Massaging cream into her hands, she walked past him and perched on the edge of the chair opposite.

"You OK?" she asked, eyeing the beer can in his hand.

"Yep," he replied without taking his eyes from the TV screen.

"David, we need to figure this out. She is here, this is happening, and we have to deal with it."

David sighed and, placing the half empty can on the coffee table, turned his attention to his wife.

"I need some time to process this." He ran his hands down his thighs as he spoke.

"I know you do, but you can't just ignore her in the meantime."

"I'm not up to another confrontation. Not today." He looked at Elizabeth, his face illustrating the truth of the statement.

"Look, why don't you go and see the Odeon of Herodes this afternoon? I'll stay here in case she wakes up and looks for us. Then, once you've had a few hours to yourself, we'll regroup, have dinner together this evening, and talk more then. Besides, I've already seen enough amphitheaters to last me a lifetime." She attempted a small joke, instantly questioning her judgment when David didn't respond.

"Would you mind?" he asked, relief flooding his face. She had given him a get-out-of-jail card, at least for this afternoon, and he clearly intended to take it.

"No – that's why I suggested it." She smiled. "Go on. Get cleaned up and go. You've got plenty of time to enjoy it, and we'll figure out what to do for dinner when you get back. Maybe we can walk up to Plaka, take Kate to that wonderful taverna?"

David rose from the sofa and walked over to her. Taking her hand in his, he lifted it to his lips and kissed it softly.

"You are a queen amongst women," he said, looking into her eyes.

Elizabeth felt her heart contract. He looked exhausted again. The refreshed David whom she had begun to see emerge over the past couple of days had disappeared, and the grey-skinned, distant version was back in his place.

She patted his hand and pushed him gently towards the bathroom. Watching his heavily burdened back as he walked away from her, she felt a tiny bubble of frustration towards Kate. Not at the momentous news which she had flown here to deliver, but at her timing. They'd been planning this holiday for so long, and they had their own issues to deal with, but now, typically, Kate had taken center stage. Elizabeth knew that was part of the job description of a parent. She had accepted it willingly, all those years ago, when the six-pound, five-ounce bundle was placed in her arms. Occasionally, however, she still resented the fact that they always put Kate first, without question.

Dragging the wet towel from her hair Elizabeth picked up her brush and began pulling it through the tangled fronds. She would dry her hair, get dressed then, once David had gone, pop over to Kate's room and see if she was awake. They needed to talk, and she wanted some time with her daughter before David got back.

CHAPTER 10

Kate lay on top of the bedcovers. Although the room was air-conditioned, her skin felt hot after her shower. The cool air moved across her body in waves, and she felt the film of fresh perspiration evaporate, leaving tiny goose pimples on her arms and legs. Enjoying the sensation, she let her mind wander to Charlotte. She wondered what she was doing. What time was it at home?

Glancing at the clock on the bedside table, Kate calculated that it was 10:10 a.m. in Edinburgh. Charlotte would have opened her small bakery in Rose Street, and the early morning rush of workers coming in for their coffee, sandwiches, and pastries would have passed. She longed to hear the mellow voice and tinkling laugh of the woman she loved.

Kate rolled off the bed, pulled her backpack onto her knee, and felt around for her mobile. She felt a slight flutter of nerves as she dialed the familiar number knowing that Charlotte would be waiting to hear that she had arrived safely.

As she listened to the ringing on her end of the line, Kate pictured the old-fashioned phone in The Bakery. It sat on the shelf behind the counter, surrounded by glass-domed cake stands housing the elaborate gateaux, Danish pastries, and crumbly fruit pies that customers raved about.

"Hello? The Bakery." Charlotte's voice was there at last.

"Hi, love, its me." Kate was desperate to connect with Charlotte's calm energy – suck it through the wires and have it wrap itself around her twitching heart.

"Kate, oh good, you're there. How was the flight, sweetheart?" In the background, Kate could hear the clinking of china dishes and Vaughn Williams's *The Lark Ascending* underlying the voices and general hum of activity. The small bakery was where she loved to spend her Saturday mornings.

"Fine, fine. It was good."

"How are your parents?" Charlotte's voice sounded a little less confident.

"They're OK. I told them." Kate blurted the words. Hearing the flatness in her tone and being anxious not to transfer her sense of doom at the way the meeting had gone, she mustered some positivity and continued.

"Mum was amazing. She's being so, I don't know, un-Mum like." Kate laughed and waited for a response.

"So, is she OK with everything?"

"Well, let's just say I think she *will* be. They'll both need some time, love. It's a big pill to swallow and …"

"So what about your dad?" Charlotte interrupted Kate and dove characteristically, if gently, towards the heart of the unsaid.

"He's not taking it so well. I think he's just shocked – he doesn't know what he's supposed to do. There's no manual for this, no procedure to follow. He's a bit lost, Lottie."

"Well, we can't expect anything else. We talked about this, right? It's a different generation and a tough concept for them to deal with. Patience, my love."

As always, Charlotte placed herself in the other person's shoes. One of the many things Kate loved about her was her empathy – her ability to give others the benefit of the doubt and her gentle acceptance of and patience with their struggles. Kate, on the other hand, tended towards the intolerant.

As she thought about Elizabeth crying in the hotel bathroom earlier that day, she was washed with a fresh film of guilt. She wondered – if she'd only told her mum years ago what she'd known to be true, could they have been friends all this time instead of adversaries - rivals for David's attention and affections? She knew that a large part of the tensions between the two of them were of her own making. She had given Elizabeth a hard time over the years, but she had not realized that her mum believed that she didn't love her. The notion made her feel nauseous. That her sharp tongue and occasional thoughtlessness could have made her mother so unhappy turned her stomach.

"Kate? You still there?"

"Yeah, sorry. Lost in thought."

"Are you all right? Do you need me to come out there?" Charlotte's voice was soft.

"No, not at all. It's my situation to deal with, and it's fine. Don't worry."

"I miss you, sweetheart." Charlotte's words caused Kate's

throat to clamp tight with emotion.

"Me too. I love you, Lottie." She felt the prickle of tears behind her eyes.

"Well, be strong but be compassionate, OK?"

Kate laughed. "I will, I promise."

Just as she hung up, there was a tap at the door. Kate slid off the end of the bed, walked over, and opened it.

"Hi, sweetheart." Her mum stood in a floral cotton dress Kate had not seen before, a hopeful smile on her face and a book in her hand. Kate smiled at the coincidence that her mother and Charlotte were the only two people to ever call her 'sweetheart.'

"Come in. What's the book?"

"The Fodor's guide. I thought maybe we could go out for a walk or something. Get out of the hotel." Elizabeth waved the dog-eared book as she spoke.

Kate was suddenly desperate to get outside, feeling the room beginning to close in on her.

"Good idea. Where's Dad?"

"He's gone out for a bit." Elizabeth walked past Kate and stood at the window. This view was not directly of the square, but if she craned her neck to the left, she could almost see the steps leading up to Plaka.

"Oh. Where did he go?" Kate was unable to hide her disappointment.

"Just to see yet another amphitheater." Elizabeth turned and winked at Kate. "I thought I'd save you from it."

"Right. Well, I suppose some ancient ruins are more up his street than facing a sullied daughter who's shattered his illusions."

Kate's voice was hard.

"Stop it, Kate. He's doing the best he can."

"He's running away from me." Kate's eyes were full of tears. "I never thought I'd see that. Not from him."

Elizabeth put her arms around Kate's shoulders and hugged her tightly. To her surprise, Kate yielded to the pressure and sank into her mother's arms.

"I've missed you, Mum." Kate spoke into Elizabeth's shoulder.

Elizabeth let out a low gasp, then swallowed the raw emotion Kate's simple words had evoked. Her daughter had summed up the pain of the past few years in a sentence. She had missed Kate too, and yet had been unable to put her finger on why. Kate had been there but had still been absent. Today, in this moment, she felt her daughter's presence, whole, true, and in her arms, just where she should have been all along.

Elizabeth and Kate walked along Panepistimiou Street. The strawberry *granitas*, pulverized ice with fresh crushed fruit and syrup, melted with the heat of the afternoon inside the thin paper cups the women held. They had walked and talked for almost three hours. Spent from their conversation and the exposure to both their situation and the hot sun, they headed back towards the sanctuary of the hotel.

"Do you think he'll be OK?" Kate stepped nimbly to the side to allow a young woman pushing a little boy in a stroller to pass between them. She smiled at the dark-eyed child, who raised a chubby fist in greeting as his mother pushed him on.

Kate turned to look after the woman as she walked away, and Elizabeth saw it. If she was not mistaken, she'd witnessed the first hint of that familiar dreaminess, just the merest sense of Kate feeling the undeniable tidal pull of maternal longing. Elizabeth remembered it well. She and David had been married seven years before she became pregnant, and by that time, she was cooing at babies and peering inside prams everywhere she went. She would find herself welling up when passing the children's section of a department store. An indescribable pain high up under her ribs would take hold, and she would have to move on quickly to avoid making a complete fool of herself in a public place.

"Dad will be fine. It might take a while, but he'll get there. He's just afraid for you."

"What do you think he's most afraid of? Is it the fact that your friends will know about me? Is he embarrassed? Is it about how this will affect him, or is he genuinely afraid for me?" Kate licked at the dribble of sticky fluid that ran from the squishy cup onto her clenched fist and looked around her for a garbage bin.

"I think he's just afraid of everything. You know how he is with the unknown? It was so unexpected, he'll just need to proc-ess it the way your father processes any life-affecting situation." Elizabeth gestured towards a large green canister, and the two women walked over and, shoulder to shoulder, deposited their sticky cups inside. Ever the mother, Elizabeth rifled through her large handbag and pulled out some wet wipes. Offering the open packet to Kate, she nodded towards a low wooden bench close to the base of a large building, which offered some much-needed shade.

"I think the part that he is struggling the most with is the future. He's always wanted to think of you married, settled, with a family around you. This just makes it …" Elizabeth's voice faded.

"What? More awkward? Less orthodox? Less acceptable? God

forbid we buck the norms. Lesbians do have families, you know, Mum."

"I know, sweetheart. It's just not the way he'd – we'd imagined it."

Before Kate could jump in, Elizabeth cut her off. Her hand, placed on her daughter's arm, was eloquent as she continued.

"You know that all we want, that we've ever wanted, is for you to be safe, fulfilled, and happy?"

Kate opened her mouth to speak again, but Elizabeth closed her down with her eyes. She wasn't finished, and her question had not required Kate to speak, just to acknowledge the truth of what her mother was saying. Kate nodded obediently.

"So when we imagined your future, we saw you with a husband, children, a fulfilling career, social life, etcetera."

Kate nodded again.

"The idea of you being in love with a woman… It wasn't on our radar. It's not that we are necessarily opposed to it, we just never imagined one day meeting your wife or life partner or… what are we calling it now?" Elizabeth looked at her daughter.

"Life partner, wife-to-be, whatever you want to call her. She is the love of my life, Mum."

"I understand that." Elizabeth smiled at her daughter. In a million years, she could never have imagined this conversation taking place. Life certainly did have some odd tricks up its sleeve, for them all.

Kate watched her mother's face. Was this the woman who could be relied upon to question, criticize, and give the unwelcome advice that she had come to expect over the years? Was she really having this balanced conversation with her mum? The unexpected nature of the situation was not lost on Kate. She wondered what Elizabeth was afraid of, as their conversation had focused on David for most of the day. As if to answer her question, Elizabeth spoke.

"What about children, Kate? Have you two talked about that?"

Kate's eyes snapped up to her mother's.

"Yes, in fact, we have. We both want a family. Lottie is an only child too, so we want at least two." Kate smiled for the first time since she had arrived, as she thought of Charlotte and their life together. She hoped that the honesty of her expression was obvious to Elizabeth.

"Well, sweetheart, I think we need to go and find Dad and have a chat. He needs to know everything that you've told me today about your work, your moving in together, your plans for the future. I think it will put his mind at ease somehow to know you've thought all these things through."

Kate watched a dark yellow bus pull up in front of the bench, and a group of tired-looking locals disembarked. They carried a mixture of briefcases, backpacks, and open baskets of brightly colored groceries – a perfect cross-section of Athenian life. She wondered if any among them were, like her, going home to a same-sex partner. Odds were that somewhere amongst the weary little throng were some kindred spirits.

They walked the last stretch back to the hotel in companionable silence, navigating around commuters, shoppers, and tourists. Another ten minutes and they'd be able to cool off in their rooms, take showers, and rest before dinner. Kate wanted to call Lottie again. She missed her so much.

Elizabeth wondered whether David was back yet. She hoped that he had been able to calm himself while surrounded by the ruins of the amphitheater, and perhaps even find a little perspective on this whole thing. Again, as she glanced over at her daughter, Elizabeth felt a tiny lilt of happiness at the day that had passed. She couldn't remember the last time she and Kate had spent this much time alone. Despite the circumstances, this day had meant a great deal to her.

Kate looked over at her mum and marveled at her sense of calm. She also wondered about her dad and hoped he was ready to hear what she had to say. If he couldn't come to terms with her news, she was afraid this trip would end up being totally counter-productive. Had she misread him so badly when she had thought she should tell him about Lottie before they moved in together? For the first time that she could remember, she was at a loss as to how to deal with her father.

CHAPTER 11

———◈———

David stood in the center of the amphitheater's stage. The sun shot an arrow of light through the sparse clouds and speared the checkered stone at his feet. Sweat ran in a rivulet down his back, and the burn on the top of his head was a pleasant discomfort. As he imagined his skin bubbling and curling up under the intense heat, he heard Elizabeth's voice in his ear. *Sunscreen, David – sunscreen.* An ironic smile twitched the corner of his mouth. There was no sunscreen on earth that could have protected him from the scald of Kate's announcement, and no matter how hard he tried, he couldn't shake the sense of confusion she had inflicted on him.

Watching a small group of tourists crawling amongst the elegant stone benches stacked up towards the sky, David felt his stomach tighten. Had she really no idea how this would affect them all? The idea of explaining his daughter's sexual inclinations to their neighbors at their annual summer garden party sent a shiver down his spine. How on earth would he explain this away? What if she turned up with this Charlotte? What if they were openly affectionate in public? How would he handle the questions, the stares he was concerned he might catch sight of if his daughter held hands with this woman or, even worse, kissed her?

David felt anxiety rising again in his chest. He knew he needed to get this under control. He tried to remember what Elizabeth had said, that it could be so much worse. And yet he couldn't, at this particular moment, imagine what could possibly have trumped this situation in terms of general awfulness. As far as he was concerned, it was a nine on a scale of one to ten, and there seemed to be nothing he could do to stop the startling new momentum in all their lives.

The sun at his back now, he reached for the camera and looked through the lens, focusing on the towering stone walls that stood behind the stage. The arched windows were vacant, showing only the afternoon sky and the tips of the cedar trees that lined the distant hillside. As he concentrated on the composition of the shot, beads of sweat ran into his eyes, the sting causing him to wince.

"Damn." He wiped at his face with the bottom of his damp T-shirt, the motion revealing his winter-white stomach. Lifting the camera once again, he tried to focus on the shot he wanted. A sudden breeze raised the hairs on his arms and ruffled his hair as he clicked the shutter, uncertain whether the photo was going to come out right.

Giving up, he stored the camera in its bag and walked through one of the lower arches, seeking some of the shade the walls would provide on the other side. As he emerged at the back of the theater, a young woman was sitting on the ground, leaning against the wall and packing a sophisticated camera away. Spotting his camera bag, she raised her eyes to David's and nodded in acknowledgement of a fellow photographer.

"Get any good shots?" she asked while he searched in his pocket for his handkerchief.

"Not sure. I hope so," he said, wiping his forehead.

The woman looked to be around Kate's age. She was slim, fair, and dressed in faded blue shorts and a yellow T-shirt, with a pair of dark sunglasses pushed up into her hair. Her skin was lightly tanned, just enough to highlight a dusting of freckles, and her smile was engaging.

"The sun's going down now, so…" David's voice faded.

"Yes. I get my best shots in the last ten minutes of daylight," she said zipping up her camera case.

"So are you done? There's another twenty minutes or so before sunset." David was curious.

"Yes – but my husband will leave me if I'm not back at the hotel in time for dinner tonight." She winked as she spoke, stood up from the dusty ground, and swiped at her bottom to remove the thin film of dirt clinging to her shorts.

"Ah." David felt his heart sink. She had a husband, of course. Just as it should be, but, it would seem, never would be for Kate.

"Well, have a nice evening," he said as she walked away.

"You too," she called back over her shoulder.

Feeling deflated, David left the theater. He needed a cold drink and something to eat. As his stomach growled, he remembered that he had eaten nothing that day.

As he approached the street at the base of the Acropolis, he spotted a small bakery. The smell of the fresh pastries inside assaulted him. The window displayed all manner of things he could not describe, but there were also what looked like *spanakopita* stacked in a tantalizing row. Gesturing to the man behind the counter, David spoke.

"*Spanakopita?*" He pointed and smiled.

"*Oxi, tyropithakia,*" the man replied, no hint of a smile.

"*Um, spanakopita parakalo.*" David tried again.

"*Oxi kale. Afta einai tyropita. No spanakopita, is cheeeese.*" The man used his hands to illustrate the word cheese, stretching his fingers out to show the elasticity of the substance.

"Oh, OK, that's fine. One of those please." David nodded, relieved that the man spoke some English, and pulled his wallet out of his pocket.

With his cheese pie wrapped in some thin paper napkins, and holding an ice-cold bottle of water, David walked towards the parliament building in search of a bench. Settling himself on a seat in a small section of shade, he felt its stored warmth permeate his shorts. He was too tired to move on, so he rocked from side to side and waited for his skin to adjust to the heat. He sank his teeth into the pie. It was delicious. The pastry was thin and flaky and the cheese piping hot, salty, and fragrant with oregano.

Syntagma Square pulsed with gentle activity. The end of the day was causing some of the crowds to dissipate, and with rush hour coming to an end, even the traffic circulated more sedately. David watched clumps of people walk past him as he ate and wondered, for the first time since leaving the hotel, what the women were doing. He imagined that they had gone out too, perhaps gone to Plaka or somewhere else where Kate could shop, as was usually her wont.

His stomach thanked him for the food, and as the pie did its work, he felt his nerves settle slightly. He knew that he would not be able to avoid seeing Kate that night, so he glanced at his watch. It was 6:48 p.m., and he needed to get back to the hotel.

Within a few minutes, he was crossing the cool lobby. As the elevator rose towards his floor, David's stomach re-knotted itself. What if Kate was already in their room? What would his heart do? How would he be with her? For the first time since he was a young man, David felt completely at the mercy of his emotions, and the feeling was disconcerting, to say the least.

As he looked at his reflection in the polished brass wall of the lift, he was shocked to see an old man staring back at him. He ran a hand over his disheveled hair and spoke to his reflection.

"She is still your daughter."

As a tiny ping indicated that he had arrived on the third floor, David took a deep breath, stepped out into the corridor, and headed towards the room.

CHAPTER 12

The three of them walked up the wide stone steps towards Plaka. As it happened, Kate and Elizabeth had not gone there during the day, as David had thought they might, so they had decided to take Kate to the little taverna from two nights ago to have a late supper. None of them was particularly hungry, but the action of getting outside, walking and observing their surroundings, seemed to ease the tension that crackled between them.

David walked a few paces behind Elizabeth and Kate, noticing how their heads were close together as they talked. Observing the surrounding streets, Elizabeth pointed at things as they passed. The same streets that he had been so enchanted by just two days ago now seemed mundane, predictable, and touristy. Was it so easy for the shine to wear off of life?

Feeling irritated with his irrationality and tendency towards self-pity, David pushed his shoulders back. He shook his head as if to banish the current thought and increased his pace, trying to catch up to his family.

"Hang on, ladies," he said, trotting the last few steps that separated them.

Kate turned to look at him as he reached her side. She smiled at him, and David felt his heart tear just a tiny bit as he found he could not reach out and wrap her hand in his arm as he might have done a week ago. He gave her a weak smile and stepped to the other side of Elizabeth, taking his wife's hand in his.

Elizabeth squeezed his fingers. Encouragement was what he needed now, and she knew this tiny gesture, his coming to them, was progress that she would acknowledge even in the face of Kate's obvious disappointment.

The taverna was quiet, with just two other tables occupied. The waiter, smiling, led them to their seats and left menus for them to look at.

"The squid we had here was fabulous." Elizabeth spoke to Kate as David cleaned his glasses on a napkin. The magical setting seemed lost on him as he studied the menu in silence.

They ordered a selection of small plates, a mezze of three local favorites to match their limited appetites, and a bottle of chilled retsina. The food arrived, and they moved the plates around the table, tasting each one. Kate asked Elizabeth about the rest of their trip, and David listened to their interaction, contributing only when one of them addressed him directly.

As Kate swirled the last of her wine around the glass, the Acropolis sat behind her like a floodlit postcard. She drained the glass and flashed an angry glance at her mother. Before Elizabeth could warn her off, she spoke coldly to her father.

"So, Dad. Are you going to carry on with the ostrich act, or shall we talk about things?"

David's eyes swiveled to meet Kate's as Elizabeth pressed her foot against his ankle under the table. *Careful, David. Careful.*

"I know we need to talk, Kate. I am just not sure you'll want to hear what I have to say." He wiped at a small pool of water on the table with his fingers and shrugged his shoulders.

"I do. Go on, please." Kate's voice was all business.

David looked at Kate, then drew a long, slow breath.

"Do I approve of what you're doing? No. Do I understand why it's happening? Possibly. Am I afraid of what the future holds? Yes. Regardless of whatever else you expect of me, you need to give me time to assimilate."

Kate softened visibly at her father's speech, and Elizabeth watched her husband and daughter, who were at opposite ends of both the table and the conversation.

Her voice tight, controlled, Kate replied.

"I can give you time, Dad. Time is free. But it won't change the reality of who I am or what I want out of life. I've spent too long hiding, and I'm happy for the first time in years. What I'm asking is if there might be a time when you think you can be happy for me. If you tell me that I can at least hope for that, then I can give you all the time in the world."

A long silence followed. The night was suddenly dark around them and Elizabeth, afraid to move, watched the two people she loved most in the world circling each other like caged animals. She held her breath, willing David to say something positive, anything that might alleviate Kate's pain.

He raised his chin and stared at the star-spattered sky above them. Without looking down, David said, "There's always hope, Kate."

They walked back to the hotel in silence. The trio, while together, were not closely connected, with Kate up ahead and Elizabeth and David lagging behind by a few paces. A bright moon lit the night, and the shops and stalls along the way were active in the business of closing down. Kate paused at a shop with a selection of colorful scarves draped through large metal rings and big, soft-brimmed sun hats stacked in piles. The woman packing the merchandise away smiled and nodded at her, but did not make any visible effort to entice her inside.

Kate eventually moved on and they followed, leaving a small distance between them, as she meandered down the steps towards Syntagma Square. From behind, she looked like Kate, just as David had always known her, her shoulders square and boney, her back straight, and her fair hair brushing her collar. Her pale-colored T-shirt was loose over the top of a long, patterned skirt that swung around her ankles as she walked, and a tote bag slung across her body bobbed against her hip with each step she took away from him. As he watched her move, David was overwhelmed by the sense that he was losing her.

Grasping Elizabeth's hand, he whispered to her.

"What should I do?"

She leaned in towards him.

"Talk to her, love. Ask your questions. We're leaving in two days, and we won't see her for weeks. Do it now."

Elizabeth gently pushed David ahead, then hesitated for the

few moments necessary for him to catch up to Kate. She watched as he walked up beside their daughter and nodded approvingly as Kate slid her hand through David's arm. He did not pull away, and as Kate leaned in towards her dad, she could sense her daughter relaxing a little.

CHAPTER 13

Kate sat at the small desk in her room, her mobile at her ear. Listening to the rings, she tried to picture Charlotte in her flat above the bakery, moving across the old wooden floorboards towards the phone.

"Hello?" Charlotte sounded tired.

"Hi, love, did I wake you?" Kate's anxiety bled into her voice.

Charlotte laughed.

"I'm not that much of a lightweight. It's only nine o'clock here."

"Oh, god, of course. I got it round the wrong way. I thought you were two hours ahead of me. I'm so tired, sorry." Kate rolled her eyes at her own confusion.

"Is everything OK?" Now Charlotte sounded anxious.

"Yes. No. I don't know." Kate shrugged in the empty room.

"What did you do today?"

"Walked a lot with Mum. We talked for hours. It was really …" Kate hesitated.

"What?"

"Really good, actually. She is being amazing. Dad, on the other hand, is taking it so personally. Like I am choosing to be gay to spite him, hurt him. We went to dinner, but it was painful, Lottie. He hardly said a word." Kate's voice faded.

"Just give him time, sweetheart."

Kate closed her eyes and pictured Charlotte looking out the window at the dark Edinburgh street below. Rose Street, which was home to her business and her flat, ran parallel to Princes Street, which flanked the beautiful gardens at the base of the castle walls.

"I know. I will. I'm just so disappointed in him." Kate squeezed the water bottle she held, and the sides caved inwards under the pressure, letting out a cracking sound that made her wince.

"Well, at least you have that in common, then." Charlotte held her breath. The joke, such as it was, could either work or not. She needed to see Kate's eyes to know her true state of mind, so this was a shot in the dark.

The wide swathe of cobblestones beneath Charlotte's window shone silver from a thin layer of rain and the reflection of the moon. As she looked down, she could see a man playing the harmonica. A hat lay on the ground at his feet, and groups of passersby stopped and dropped coins in it as he blew into his cupped hands, shoulders hunched and foot tapping. The wine bar across the way glowed golden as shadows moved around inside, arms and coated backs brushing up against the wide frosted windows.

Finally, Kate let out a laugh, and Charlotte released her breath, relieved.

"Good point. You are so good for me Lottie."

"I know." Charlotte was laughing now, too. "You need to sleep. I can hear it in your voice."

"You're right. I do."

"Call me in the morning?" Charlotte tucked the phone under her chin and reached up to pull the heavy curtains across her living room window.

"Of course. Sleep tight."

"Sweet dreams, sweetheart."

Charlotte turned off her phone and padded to the sofa. Her hot chocolate was getting cold, and her bed awaited.

CHAPTER 14

Elizabeth sat on the bed while David soaked in the bath, which was unusual for him. He was a shower man, and this odd development concerned her. She knew he was tired and had drunk more than he had eaten that day, so she insisted he leave the door open in case he slid under the water.

"Have you gone down the drain?" she called into the bathroom.

A sloshing sound assuring her that he was indeed alive, David replied, "Not yet."

"Can I come in?" Elizabeth moved towards the open door.

"Sure."

She stepped over his abandoned clothes and sat on the edge of the bath. Without speaking she held her hand out and David, understanding, passed her the dripping washcloth over his shoulder. She dipped it into the tepid water and wiped it across his back.

"So, what's going on?" she asked. His wet hair, spiking out over his ears, looked comical from the back. She reached over and smoothed it down.

"I'm just ruminating," he said, leaning into her hand as she continued to wash his back, seeming to enjoy the ritual and the pressure of the rough cloth against his skin.

"Reach any conclusions?" Elizabeth wet the cloth again and resumed her task.

"Nothing significant." David handed her the soap.

As she rubbed the soap across the cloth, Elizabeth gathered her thoughts.

"So what did you two talk about on the way back tonight? It looked as if you were talking," she coaxed.

"Yes. We did, a bit." David took the cloth out of her hand and slid back against the end of the bath, submerging himself more deeply into the cloudy water.

"So?" Elizabeth waited.

"She said that she'd thought this through. Knows what it means for her, and us, and her future. She says she's not afraid – of anything."

"Right."

"She seems resolved. I mean, there's no question of this being a phase of some kind, or a fit of pique over something we did." He closed his eyes.

"Dave, what on earth are you talking about?" Elizabeth stood up abruptly and leaned back against the sink.

Obviously taken aback by her tone, David opened his eyes immediately.

"Do you know how ridiculous that sounded?" Her anger was

evident. "Of all the things I may have had cause to call you over the years, narcissistic was not among them."

"Whoa, what do you mean?" He sounded hurt.

"Just listen to yourself. That you would even consider that Kate could do this out of spite, or in protest at something we did or didn't do to her, is ridiculous."

"I was just ..."

"Well don't, *just*." Elizabeth walked quickly back into the bedroom. She heard the splashes as David rose from the water. A few moments later, wrapped in a towel, he walked across the room to her and took her shoulders in his hands.

"Look, I may not be dealing with this as well as you are, but I think as her father, it's somehow harder for me to take in that our daughter is... well, not..." David searched her face as if trying to get a read on whether he should continue.

"Not what?" Her eyes blazed. "Not normal? Is that what you were going to say?"

David dropped his hands to his sides and turned his back on her.

"Yes. OK. I want her to have a normal life." His voice was hard. "I want her to get married, have babies, be around more, be happy, be part of this family. Is that so bad?"

Feeling chilled, Elizabeth pulled on a cardigan.

"She can have all that, David. Being gay and being happy are not mutually exclusive."

She turned to face him and caught him wincing at the harshness of her words, or perhaps it was just the reality of hearing them out loud.

"You have to look outwards. Stop seeing this as something

she is doing to *you*. This is her life we are talking about here, and if we want to be part of that, we need to learn to accept this." Elizabeth sank onto the bed. "I will not watch you destroy your relationship with her over this, David. I'm telling you."

David looked at his wife. How quickly things had flipped. Here he was on the outside, looking in on her and Kate, unexpected allies in an arena that was foreign and uncomfortable to him. He had always been the one Kate came to, the one she could confide in. He had prided himself on their closeness and had to admit that he knew that they excluded Elizabeth from things at times. They had even made fun of her habits and tastes, laughing quietly behind their hands and pretending that they didn't know she was being hurt by their actions. But didn't all fathers and daughters do that, to some extent?

"So what did you say to her when she told you all that?" Elizabeth tried again.

"I said it was wonderful that she was so comfortable with her decision but that we would need a little more time and consideration before we'd dance at a wedding that has two brides." His eyes flashed as he spoke. "Where's the balance in that picture?"

"Don't you dare speak for me in this. Don't you include me in your sad inability to see our daughter for who she really is, and with the potential to be happy." Elizabeth felt tears slide down her face and trembled with the force of her own words.

David's face softened. He hated to see her cry. It hadn't happened often in their lives, but it undid him every time.

"Look, love. I'm just working through this the only way I

know how. Don't cry, please, Liz. I can't bear it when you cry." He put his arms around her, and Elizabeth melted into his chest.

"We'll figure it out, love, we will." He patted her back as he rocked her to and fro.

Elizabeth raised her head and looked him in the eyes.

"Yes, we will, because I won't lose her over this, David. It's not an option. What you choose to do is up to you, but I will not let this come between her and me."

David saw her distraught and yet determined expression, one he recognized from three years ago, when he had confessed to his affair with Connie. That was one of the other times he had made her cry, and it twisted his insides to see her tears again.

"OK. We'll figure it out."

CHAPTER 15

The following day had been an uncomfortable stretch of time, with the three of them moving politely around each other as if on tiptoe, assessing facial expressions, avoiding eye contact and any further, overt confrontation.

David had lagged behind the two women as they walked through the National Gardens. They seemed to be talking easily while he remained ill at ease in Kate's company. They had visited the library, the parliament buildings and then had walked the length of Panepistimiou Street as Athens hummed around them, unaware of their strained interactions.

After a rest in their respective hotel rooms they had walked through Plaka, selecting a new taverna to eat dinner at. The night sky had been clear, stars sparkling above them as they talked in quiet voices, as if afraid to disturb the surface of the tentative film of peace they had let settle over them. On the walk back to the hotel David had once again lagged behind while Kate, her arm looped through Elizabeth's, had laughed softly at something he had been unable to hear his wife say. As he watched their backs moving away from him, David realized that he didn't want to know what was being said.

They exchanged awkward good nights in the hotel corridor and went to their rooms. Elizabeth had been quiet, answering him in monosyllables when he spoke to her. As she eventually slid into bed beside him David felt his heart tilt. Her silence was more disconcerting than her anger. He slept badly and then watched the dawn creep up the window, slowly lighting the room around them.

As agreed, they took Kate to the café in the square for breakfast. Her flight was at noon, so after another rather stilted conversation, over coffee and baklava, David and Elizabeth stood outside the hotel and watched as she loaded her bag into the back of a taxi.

"Safe flight, darling." Elizabeth hugged Kate close. "Call us when you get home, will you?"

"Sure, I will. Thanks, Mum. You've been great." Kate spoke into her mother's shoulder.

Elizabeth felt herself tearing up and nodded silently as Kate turned to David.

"Dad?"

David opened his arms, and Kate walked into his embrace. He patted her back briefly before pushing her away. "Fly safe." His voice was full, and he looked over at Elizabeth, seeking her eyes.

"See you when you get back. Enjoy Hydra and Italy, and take lots of good photos." Kate brushed her hair tightly behind each ear. "Bye, you two. I love you."

"We love you, too." Elizabeth spoke alone.

Kate smiled at her mum and then looked over at her dad. He stayed silent, nodding as she slid into the back of the taxi. Kate looked away, Elizabeth was sure, to hide her disappointment.

As the car pulled away, David put his arm around Elizabeth. He felt her lean away from him, and as the taxi disappeared into the square, she turned and walked into the hotel without a word.

David knew this meant trouble. Elizabeth rarely pulled away from him anymore, at least not since they had made their way back to more solid ground these past few months. He knew that Connie still crept in between them at times, and with every cold look or removal of her hand from his, he regretted anew his decisions back then.

He watched her back as she walked across the hotel lobby, analyzing her mood. Her head was held high and her shoulders were pulled down and back, indicating that she was holding a firm position. Her hands swung loosely at her sides, showing that she was comfortable and confident with that position. Her steps were wide and evenly spaced; she knew exactly where she was heading. She did not look back to see how far behind her he was or if he was following. She didn't care if he followed her or not; in fact, she'd probably prefer he didn't.

David sighed and shuffled after her. They had a lot of holiday ahead of them so he needed to fix this, and quickly.

When he got to the room, Elizabeth was already packing. Her clothes were piled on the bed and she folded them methodically, building thin layers into the case as she went. Her shoes were tucked neatly around the corners of the case, and last to go in would be her cosmetics, all wrapped inside plastic bags to prevent any spillages. As David watched her pack, he marveled at her system, thinking how much she lived her life by the same method. Everything was considered and balanced, spread across the available space. Awkward things were tucked away into corners and perishables kept near the surface, under a thin layer of protective coating.

She had not spoken to him since he had come back into the room, and the silence was heavy.

"Nearly done?" he asked, zipping his own case closed.

"Yep. Did you order a taxi at the desk?" she asked without turning around.

"Yes indeed. Arrives at twelve thirty. The concierge said it'd take about forty-five minutes to get to Piraeus, so that'll give us plenty time to get to the boat for two o'clock."

Today was their departure for the island of Hydra, which promised to be a place in direct contrast to the noise and bustle of Athens.

"Fine," she said, pulling her closed case off the bed with a thunk.

"I'll get that." David walked towards her.

"I'm fine." Her voice was thin, and she avoided his eyes.

"Liz, come on. Let's not allow all this to spoil things. We've got so much time ahead of us on this trip. We can't tiptoe around each other or…"

"I'm not tiptoeing around anyone," she barked back. "I'm just so angry that I can hardly look at you."

David felt her words like a fist to the throat. He knew he hadn't perhaps shone as father of the year these past two days, but all things considered, neither did he think he was the devil incarnate.

"Why are you so angry?" he asked, flopping down on the sofa.

"Because you couldn't see beyond the end of your own nose. Your daughter tells you something that will change all of our lives, most of all hers, and you make it about you." Her voice shook.

"Well, excuse me for feeling rocked by the announcement. It wasn't exactly what I expected on our dream holiday," he shot back.

"Me either, but neither did I want to make Kate feel as if she had declared herself a leper just by being brave enough to tell us the truth for once." Elizabeth stared at him, her face white. "You can still touch her, be compassionate, support her, David. She is not contagious."

David started at her words. Had his physical discomfort around Kate been that obvious? Apparently so.

Elizabeth rounded on him again.

"And what gives you the right to be so bloody sanctimonious anyway? You're judging her against what? Some twisted moral compass you have? Well, perhaps your compass is off – have you considered that? Weren't you the one to sleep with someone else? Glass houses, David, glass houses."

CHAPTER 16

K ate closed the warped paperback that she had stolen from Charlotte and shoved it into the seat pocket in front of her. She could never focus to read on planes.

The two days she had spent with her parents had been running through her mind, over and over. She had asked herself a thousand times if the choice to go to Athens had been a well-thought-out strategy or a knee-jerk reaction on her part that they'd all live to regret.

The last thing she wanted was to spoil her parents' long-awaited holiday, but there had never been a right time at home to talk to them about Charlotte. Numerous times she'd been on the point of it – standing in their kitchen as Elizabeth cooked or sitting on the arm of the chair while David read the paper. For one reason or another, she'd always thought better of it. Perhaps the underlying reason was that she was fundamentally a coward?

Suddenly, David's face swam before her eyes. His look of

bewilderment and the leaden silence after she'd told them were not what she had expected.

Had her mother had a fit of the vapors and stormed out of the room, that would have been more predictable. Having spent an entire day with Elizabeth, Kate now mentally corrected herself. No, her mum had been amazing – calm, supportive, and best of all, non-judgmental. Kate had to give her credit for the way that she had handled everything. She'd been extremely classy. The fact that Elizabeth had seemed relieved to hear that Kate was gay was a definite turn-up for the books.

David, on the other hand, would obviously take careful handling. She knew that her dad had pretty traditional views on life, but she had thought that he would be more accepting of this new version of herself. It had always been Kate and her dad in one corner and her mum in the other. For the first time in as long as she could remember, she wished her mum were here so they could talk again. She wanted to share more about Charlotte and their life together. David had not wanted to hear it, but Elizabeth had been interested, had asked questions about Charlotte, and had even said she'd like to meet her when they got home.

At this point, Kate had a hard time imagining Lottie and her parents existing in the same mind-space, never mind the same room. It would be so odd, having her two worlds collide after spending so long deliberately keeping them apart. Although she wanted the meeting to happen, she had no idea how she would manage it or how they would all cope with the inevitable tension and awkwardness.

Lottie was being calm and positive, but what felt odd was that Kate was usually the grounded, practical fixer in the relationship. She generally carried the bigger load when it came to their joint concerns. When Lottie's business had hit trouble, Kate had walked her through the small-business loan procedure, had helped her refinance the building and restructure her staffing in order to stay open. When Lottie's mother had passed away, Kate had taken over the funeral arrangements, as neither Lottie nor her father had been able to cope with the practicalities.

Kate had met both Lottie's parents, Elsie and Duncan Macfie, and was fond of them. They had accepted her as they would anyone their daughter loved, and consequently they had spent a few happy weekends with them the previous winter in their cottage on Loch Leven. They had huddled near the big fireplace, eating soup from mugs and playing endless rounds of charades.

Lottie had been devastated when Elsie died, but Kate had been there to pick up the pieces when Lottie wouldn't leave her flat for days. She had wrapped her in a big blanket and set her up on the sofa, fed her tea and toast, and refilled her hot water bottle numerous times a day. That had been a terrible time, but Lottie was gradually bouncing back, and the fact that the business was picking up again had given her a much-needed boost.

The captain announced that they were forty minutes from Edinburgh. She couldn't wait to get home and hold Charlotte close. Lottie was her home.

CHAPTER 17

Piraeus was every bit as hectic as expected. The taxi dropped them at the ferry terminal, and David went to locate their boat. Elizabeth stood guard with the bags, wishing for a cup of tea to take the edge off the noise and activity around her.

Boats were not her favorite mode of transport, but the trip was only an hour and a half, so she could grit her teeth and try to enjoy the scenery on the way over to the island of Hydra.

David came rushing back towards her.

"It's this way. Come on, love." He grabbed the larger two bags and jutted his chin towards the closest jetty.

The hydrofoil was a tall vessel with streams of passengers already walking up the ramps onto the lower decks. Elizabeth trundled after him, and they were swallowed up in the crowd moving on board.

They wasted no time in snatching one of the few available

tables in the cafeteria on the main deck, and David had stayed inside with the bags to let Elizabeth get some air.

The wind blew her hair off her face, and she leaned against the railing. She watched the white water curl around the odd ski-like blades as the hydrofoil rose up and then pulled through the waves. The mainland was behind them, and the small island of Aegina was already visible on the left. She had read that it was a big producer of pistachios, and looking at the small landmass, she wondered where on earth they all grew. Kate loved pistachios. She had spent an entire weekend when she was fourteen trying to make pistachio ice cream. Elizabeth laughed as she remembered the bags of shells and Kate complaining of sore fingers from opening the stubborn nuts one by one and dumping them into the blender. The ice cream had turned out to be a green, gritty mess that they'd been wary of tasting, but true to form, Kate had stubbornly eaten a bowl, only to throw it up later that night.

She wondered where Kate was now. Would she be home already? Elizabeth looked at her watch and calculated the time in the UK. Charlotte was probably meeting her at Edinburgh Airport. She wished she knew what Charlotte looked like. It would be easier to picture Kate with someone if she'd seen her face, shaken her hand, and looked her in the eye.

Elizabeth shook her head and moved some stray hairs that the wind had blown across her mouth. Whatever she looked like, Charlotte would be evaluated as any other potential partner would have been. It made no difference to Elizabeth what sex she was. As far as she was concerned, any person with whom her daughter intended on spending the rest of her life would undergo the same scrutiny.

From what Kate had told her, Charlotte seemed like a very levelheaded young woman. As a business owner, she was obviously hardworking and enterprising. Elizabeth was always impressed by women entrepreneurs, as she felt that they had more stacked against them than men wanting to set up similar ventures would. Despite how far society had come, there were still many deeply rooted prejudices in place.

As her mind went to the concept of prejudice, she took a deep breath. She wondered if Kate and Charlotte came across much of that in their daily life together. Did people still make a fuss about same-sex couples – tut their disapproval, stare at them if they held hands in the street? She couldn't imagine why they would, not anymore. And yet, there was an element of concern for her daughter that wouldn't leave her.

Elizabeth wondered whether, if Kate had been telling her that she had met some nice man she, Elizabeth, would have been any less concerned about that new relationship. She thought not.

The boat bounced abruptly, and Elizabeth felt a salty spray on her face, startling and refreshing. She licked her upper lip and ran her hand through her now-matted hair. This was so exhilarating. She'd never have thought she'd enjoy this part of the trip, being so wary of boats in general. She wondered if David was all right inside. Then, as she started to move away from the railing to go and check on him, she changed her mind. No. Let him sit and guard the bags, and when she was good and ready, she would go and relieve his watch. The idea that he was trapped, unable to abandon their belongings until she returned, gave her an odd sense of power. Putting her hand up to her mouth, she covered a tiny smile. Was she being wicked? So what if she was. He had not behaved in a stellar fashion, so why not let him stew in his own juice for a while? Maybe some time to consider might make him realize what an idiot he had been with Kate.

A small woman with a camera edged in next to Elizabeth at the railing. She leaned out over the side and took several pictures of the waters ahead.

"There's Hydra. See that dark line over there?" The woman nodded back at Elizabeth.

"Oh, yes. I see it." Elizabeth was surprised that the stranger had spoken to her.

"Comes up pretty quickly, once you get past Aegina. " The woman stared ahead and spoke without turning around. "Is it your first time?"

"On Hydra? Yes, it is." Elizabeth smiled.

"There are some great fish places in the harbor. Do you like fish?"

Elizabeth watched as the woman slid her camera into her pocket and turned to face her. Her face was tanned and smooth, her dark brown eyes somehow incongruous to the white-blonde hair. She wondered what the woman's story was. Was she here with someone, or a brave soul traveling alone?

"We do like fish. I mean, *I* do, yes," Elizabeth corrected herself. She always answered questions like that, on behalf of herself and David. "We like to play chess." "We think we'll take the blue one." "We're happy for you." We, we, we. She tried to remember the last time she'd said "I" in response to a question about how she felt or what she wanted. This conjoined state of mind had crept up on her gradually, along with the years of marriage and ever-increasing familiarity. Being half of a couple had become her identity.

She recalled when they'd taken a trip to Paris seven or eight years before. They had been in a brasserie on the boulevard Saint-Germain, and the waiter had asked if they would like sparkling water or still. Elizabeth had never liked sparkling water and was on the point of saying, as she had on numerous occasions in this situation, "still," when David piped up, "Oh, sparkling. We like sparkling." Much to her annoyance, she had swallowed her protest and drunk the gassy water. So many times like that she had capitulated, not wanting to rock the boat.

Now, however, when it came to Kate's new situation, she and David were on opposite sides of the fence. Staring out at the sparkling Aegean, she knew with calm certainty that this time there would be no "we" unless David jumped to *her* side.

Perhaps it was time, after all these years, for her to rediscover her "I," her "me," and her "mine"?

CHAPTER 18

Hydra was one of the few islands that remained pedestrianized, which made it a welcome change of pace from Athens. The crescent-shaped harbor was everything David had imagined. Fishing boats of all shapes and sizes, along with the occasional yacht, bobbed on their moorings against the glistening stone walls. A wide, paved walkway stretched out behind the boats, and a strand of restaurants, shops, and galleries stood closely behind it, beckoning in Hydriots and tourists alike to browse, eat, and drink.

Elizabeth had gone to the market, leaving him to read his book. He read the same paragraph four or five times before giving up and closing the paperback. There was too much going on to concentrate on reading. So much to absorb, to smell, and to taste on this tiny island.

The Hotel Sophia was in the perfect spot. It was right in Hydra town, and their balcony overlooked the port. David had watched several ships unloading cargo and was amused by the string of donkeys patiently waiting to be loaded so they could distribute merchandise across the island.

Steep stone steps led up and outwards from the harbor to cobbled streets that wound up the hillside. The town was densely constructed, with houses cheek by jowl, and it seemed that most of the local residences on the island were located here. Higher up the slope stood the great manor houses that he had read about. Stacked on the steeper hills, they'd been built in the eighteen hundreds, during Hydra's trading boom. While grand, they now appeared to loom ominously above the smaller whitewashed homes below.

The sun beat down on his face as he tried to count the various sounds floating around him. There were church bells, wind, laughter, the lapping of water against the harbor walls, a dog barking, some distant local rebetika music, and a woman calling to her child. The mixture of noises was oddly soothing, not at all jarring or invasive to his calm.

No sooner had he acknowledged the deep sense of calm than he was stabbed by a shard of guilt. He could see Kate's disappointed face as she sat in the back of the taxi. He hadn't been able to tell her he loved her. How ludicrous was that? She was his everything, his beloved girl. There was no doubt in his mind that he loved her, but for some reason, he'd chosen to hold that back. What was wrong with him? Was he punishing her? Had Elizabeth been right?

Made uncomfortable by the direction his thoughts had taken, David stood up and stretched out his back. When Elizabeth got back from the market, they planned on walking across the island to Mandraki Bay for a picnic. It was a long walk, but the afternoon sun would be less strong, and David was looking forward to the exercise.

A movement in the street below caught his eye. A small crowd of children trickled out of what looked like a schoolhouse. A large yellow dog sat on one of the steps outside. As David watched, a small, dark-haired girl emerged from the building and, as she approached, the dog's tail waved frantically back and forth across the stone step. The child leaned over and attached her book strap to the dog's collar, and then she patted its head and started up the steps. The dog padded happily behind her, the books dangling from its shoulder.

The beauty and simplicity of this scene touched him so deeply that David felt tears tingling in his eyes. He remembered how Kate had begged them for a dog. On her tenth birthday, she'd cried with disappointment as she unwrapped the stuffed collie they'd given her, as she'd hoped that this was the birthday when she'd get the real thing. He couldn't remember whether it had been he or Elizabeth who had decided that she was too young for the responsibility of a puppy – he just remembered Kate's face crumpling and the tears that tore into his heart.

As he swam around in the poignant memory, he saw Elizabeth a little farther down the stone staircase below. She was walking with a basket over her arm. It looked to have tomatoes and some tangerines inside. Her hair was tied back in a colorful scarf, and her long, gauzy skirt floated around her ankles. She looked up at the balcony and waved, and his heart caught in his chest. He loved this woman so much. For the millionth time, he asked himself how he could have strayed and hurt her so much.

Raising a hand, he returned the wave, then walked into the room to wait for her.

CHAPTER 19

❖

Elizabeth couldn't remember the last time that they had been to a beach. In many respects, she wasn't a big beach person, disliking all the sand and flies, lotion and mess. This, however, was nothing short of bliss. The wind in the little cove was high enough to blow the flies away and keep them comfortably cool. The sand was pristine and not so fine as to be blown around too much. The best part, however, was that there were only three other groups of people camped out at various spots along the shore, and all were far enough away to allow her and David to believe that they had this beautiful spot entirely to themselves.

Elizabeth unwrapped a hunk of feta and the crusty loaf she'd bought at the market. Sea air always made her hungry. David leaned over and filled two small plastic glasses with cold Robola, the fragrant Cephalonian wine they'd discovered the night before at a taverna in the harbor. With a small tub of olives and two huge tomatoes, which they each ate like an apple, their lunch was manna from heaven.

The waves advanced slowly towards them, leaving glistening trails of algae and fragments of bleached shells with each retreat. Elizabeth, full of their glorious repast, lay back on the blanket and watched a few scant clouds skirt across the clear sky. She was tired, as she hadn't slept well the past two nights, being preoccupied with thoughts of Kate. Perhaps she could nap here, with the waves, the wind, and the warmth of the sun on her skin?

David lay next to her, reading, the guidebook held above his head to block the sun. She looked at his familiar profile, noting the silver-grey temples, the pink skin around his neck where he always forgot to put sunscreen, and the way his lips moved ever so slightly with the content of the book. He was sweet and infuriating, kind and unkind, stubborn, accommodating, fair, selfish, caring, and careless. All these qualities made up the man she loved, and yet, at this moment, she wished for more. She wished for understanding to obliterate his conservatism where Kate was concerned.

They had not talked about her visit since arriving on Hydra and now, despite the pervasive peace of this perfect moment in time, she knew she needed to bring it up again.

"Kate wants us to meet Charlotte when we get back." Her words cut through the silence.

David nodded, not taking his eyes off the page. After a few moments, Elizabeth tried again.

"You realize that we'll be meeting her, don't you?"

David dropped the book onto the blanket and turned towards her, propping himself up on one elbow.

"I suppose so. Eventually." He lifted his glass from the blanket and took a long swallow of wine. "I was trying not to think about it."

Elizabeth swatted his arm. "David, I'm serious."

"So am I." He looked at her, no smile, no wink, nothing.

Elizabeth reached for the bottle and topped up both their glasses.

"Hiding from reality will change nothing."

"I know. But I don't have to go rushing towards it with open arms, either." David's bottom lip protruded as he spoke. If it hadn't been somewhat ludicrous to see a grown man pouting, it might have been endearing.

"We will face it, embrace Charlotte, and deal with everything Kate needs us to with good grace." Elizabeth looked at her husband as he eyed the horizon. She could swear his chin was trembling.

"David?"

"I heard you. I'm not a child. You can't issue edicts like that and expect me to just conform, tip my hat, and trot along behind you." His eyes flashed as he turned to her. "This is my daughter we're talking about."

Elizabeth felt the wind go out of her. "My daughter." His words summed up the way he thought of Kate, and perhaps had always thought of her, as his. She shifted her hips towards the edge of the blanket. The thought of physical contact with him right now was more than she could bear.

"She's my daughter, too." She felt her throat constrict. No – she wouldn't let emotion take over here. She was going to stay in control.

David stared out to sea, swirled the wine around his glass and then ran a hand over his thinning hair.

"Once we get home, we'll make a plan. There's no rush, is

there? What can we do from here, anyway?" He looked over his shoulder at her.

"We can talk, prepare, get our minds around it. We can be open to what's coming and see this as the beginning of a new future for all of us." Elizabeth met his glare.

"You accept it all so easily. Don't you struggle with any of it?"

"What's the point?" Elizabeth shrugged. "Kate is who she is. We need to accept and move on. If we want to be in her life, then *we* need to do the changing."

"You amaze me." David stared at her.

"Why?"

"You've always been the one... I mean you were always..." his voice faded.

"What, the rigid one? The demanding one, the disciplinarian, the bad guy, right?" Elizabeth heard the pitch of her voice rising. "Did you ever think that maybe that happened because you wouldn't take on any of those responsibilities?" She felt tears coming.

"What do you mean?" David looked blankly at her.

"Oh come on, Dave. You know exactly what I mean. You never wanted to be anything but the good guy where Kate was concerned. Good old Daddy. Soft-touch Daddy. When Mummy wouldn't give in, Daddy could be counted on to do just that. You were happy for me to take responsibility for all our unpopular parenting decisions."

David shook his head and stared back at the water.

"Did you think I didn't know all the times you and Kate laughed about me behind my back? You both made fun of me constantly, and you undermined me so often when you'd give way on something we'd agreed on, making sure you stayed the favorite." A sob escaped Elizabeth, and she swallowed a second one down in frustration.

Despite its bitter flavor, David knew that what he was hearing was the truth. There was no hiding from that.

Elizabeth continued.

"To me, this revelation explains so much. Kate has been struggling with her identity, her sexuality, for who knows how many years. Now that she's taken this leap of faith I will not disappoint her by judging or pretending to be concerned over tradition or conformity when I'm not. Maybe now she can stop trying to be who she thinks we expect her to be and just *be*?" Tears made their way down her cheeks, the breeze instantly drying their saltiness onto her skin.

David leaned towards her and placed his hand over hers on the blanket. Elizabeth pulled away and wiped at her taut face.

"Dave, if you are prepared to let this drive a wedge between you and Kate, you'll be on your own."

David was still disturbed by the notion that he and Kate were distant from each other, and now, far from feeling that he and Elizabeth were united in concern, he was feeling distanced from her, too.

He looked up at the hillside rising gently behind the beach and watched the silent arms of a windmill turn in the gentle breeze. The sun was dipping into the water, and a golden sheen rippled across the waves towards them.

"We should be getting back." He pushed the cork back into the wine bottle.

Elizabeth responded by gathering up the glasses, wrapping the remaining bread in a napkin, and shoving everything into the basket she'd brought along. As she stood up, David lifted the edges of the blanket, dragged it to the shoreline, and, with two violent snaps, shook the sand off it.

They were silent on the walk back to the hotel. Neither of them wanted to re-open Pandora's box that evening or to tap the other's emotions any further. They both focused on the sea wall that they were following and the amber lights of the fishing boats bobbing off the shore. By their mutual silence, they were in tacit agreement that the most eloquent conversation they could have now was one with no words.

CHAPTER 20

———◆———

Charlotte stood in the arrivals area at Edinburgh Airport. She watched the people around her surge towards the barrier as another planeload of passengers filtered through the doors, pushing children in strollers and trolleys laden with luggage. She yawned, a great, wide, jaw-breaking yawn, and then checked her watch. Her hair was loose around her shoulders, and her eyes swept the gathering crowd. Looking down at her jeans, she saw a floury hand print, and, suddenly self-conscious, she swatted her thigh to brush it off.

As people filtered around her, Charlotte saw Kate's familiar form appear through the sliding doors. She was taller than most of the other women on the concourse, and Charlotte's heart twinged when Kate, spotting her, raised a hand to wave. She looked tired and disheveled, and Charlotte guessed that she had not had much sleep over the three days that she had been away.

Pushing her way carefully through a group of football

supporters in front of her, Charlotte stepped into an opening in the crowd and then into Kate's arms.

"Hi, sweetheart." She spoke into Kate's shoulder.

"Hi, love." Kate's eyes were darkly shadowed, her hair was messy, scraped back into a band, and her backpack hung heavily from her shoulder.

"Let me take that." Charlotte lifted the pack onto her own shoulder, and the two women walked towards the exit, hand in hand.

Kate was quiet in the car while Charlotte, sensing that now was not the time to broach the subject of her parents, filled the silence by chatting about all the activity at the bakery since Kate had left. She talked about a new, local supplier for fresh fruit that was working out well and how the pipe in the kitchen that had been leaking had burst and that she had averted a disaster by figuring out how to turn off the water main until the plumber arrived.

Kate looked out the window at the winking eyes of the passing traffic and let Charlotte's talk drift over her. Her voice was soft and lilting, calming Kate's frayed nerves.

"You're staying at my place tonight, right?" Charlotte glanced at Kate over her shoulder.

"Yes, please."

"Good. I made a cracking quiche, and I've saved a bottle of that Montepulciano you love." Charlotte placed her hand on Kate's knee. "We'll talk it all out later, when you've had a nice bath and relaxed a bit, OK?"

Kate put her hand over Charlotte's and squeezed the slim

fingers. Charlotte always knew when to dive headlong into something and when to back off, and Kate felt a surge of love and gratitude for her intuition and selfless patience.

"I'm so glad to be home."

The flat above the bakery smelled of coffee, fragrant pastry, and pine floorboards. Kate loved this place. It was a sanctuary in so many ways, and she felt the tension slide off her shoulders as she walked into the lounge and flopped onto the sofa.

"Want some wine?" Charlotte dumped the backpack on the floor in the hallway and walked into the kitchen.

"I think a cuppa first, if you don't mind. One thing the Greeks don't do well is tea."

Sitting at either end of the sofa, they faced each other, toes touching. Kate described the hotel and the parts of Athens she'd been able to see as Charlotte nodded, listening intently. The tea gradually warmed Kate's insides, and she leaned back on the cushion behind her, letting a welcome sense of calm take over.

They listened to the sounds of Rose Street below the window. Voices of passersby and distant music from the wine bar crept into the living room, surrounding them in normality.

After a few minutes, Charlotte spoke. "Shall we eat?" She stood and gathered up the teacups. As if in response, Kate's stomach growled.

Charlotte grabbed the wine and two glasses and brought them to the coffee table. Kate then stood in the doorway to the kitchen as Charlotte served them each a large slice of quiche with a pile of green salad and thin slices of a ruby-red tomato.

"Looks fantastic." Kate smiled at Charlotte's back.

While Charlotte finished preparing their meal, Kate went to the bedroom and emptied her backpack, looking for the scarf that she had bought in Plaka. She pulled out the soft package, padded back into the living room and laid it on the table, and then settled herself back on the sofa.

Charlotte placed their plates down and picked up the gift, her eyes sparkling.

"Is this for me?"

Kate nodded and smiled as Charlotte ripped away the tissue paper.

"Oh, it's gorgeous." She wound the soft aquamarine scarf around her neck and posed, vogue-like, pacing back and forth in front of the fireplace.

Kate laughed and patted the cushion next to her. "Sit down, you mad wench. Let's eat. I'm starving."

They ate quickly and in silence, neither realizing quite how hungry they were until the last bite of crumbly pastry and creamy ham-and-cheese filling had gone.

Nodding her approval, Kate wiped the remaining crumbs of pastry up with her finger. She stacked the empty plates on the table, balanced her glass on her knee, and scooted along the sofa. Picking up her phone, she leaned into Charlotte's shoulder.

"Want to see some of the snaps I took?"

Charlotte nodded, and Kate scrolled through several photos of Syntagma Square and the guards outside the parliament building and then some of Plaka at night, glittering with tiny yellow lanterns.

"Oh, beautiful. Where was that again?"

"It's Plaka, the old marketplace. The tavernas are littered up and down the stone stairways, and the Acropolis is right behind it, so the views are amazing."

Kate moved on to a photo of her and Elizabeth outside the Panepistimiou University. Elizabeth was smiling widely and leaning her face in towards Kate's cheek as Kate snapped the photo at arm's length.

"That's a great one." Charlotte tapped her glass, to indicate that it was getting low, and Kate tipped the last of the wine into it.

"Yeah, that was a good day, all in all."

Sensing that the subject of Kate's parents was no longer taboo, Charlotte waded in.

"It was just you and your mum, though, right?"

"Yep. Dad went off to some amphitheater to take pictures, but we got together for dinner that night." She hesitated, then gulped some more wine before continuing. "Mum was great, Lottie. We talked and talked, and she was really open to the idea of you and me. The whole concept didn't seem to faze her. Like I told you when I called, she was almost relieved, which was the last thing I expected."

"I'm glad to hear it. We are pretty damn amazing, though, if you ask me." Charlotte laughed. "I think they're lucky to have us."

"I'm sure Mum would agree with you. Dad, on the other hand, probably not." Kate rose and walked to the window overlooking the street. "You'd think I'd told him I was an axe murderer or something, or had emptied their bank account to move to Mexico and join a cult." She shook her head slowly.

Charlotte watched Kate's back. Her shoulders were taut, climbing up towards her ears as she spoke.

"Mum says she is going to talk to him, but I've never seen him so closed-off before. Not with me, anyway."

Charlotte could hear the hurt in Kate's voice, and it broke her heart.

"He didn't want to touch me. He pulled away from me a couple of times. When I was leaving, it was like Mum almost guilted him into hugging me goodbye. Jesus. It was so weird."

Kate turned and sat back down on the sofa. Charlotte reached out and wound her fingers through Kate's.

"Just let things take their course. It'll all settle down. Once they get back, we'll get the dreaded introductions over with. Then, of course, they'll fall head over heels in love with me, just like you did." Charlotte tossed her hair theatrically and laughed. Seeing the concern in Kate's eyes, she reached over and tucked a strand of fair hair behind her ear.

"Just try to have faith. All will come right. They love you, Kate, and they want you to be happy, even if it's with a 'dyke.'"

The word sounded brittle. It was one that they both avoided, but the use of it broke down the remaining tension in the room. They laughed and clinked their glasses.

Kate drained her wine and then slid down, laying her head on Charlotte's lap. She was tired, not from the journey, but from breathing through so much emotion for the past few days. She had faced her fear, faced her parents, and bared her soul. Now, the rest was up to them.

CHAPTER 21

———— ◆ ————

Lake Garda stretched away from her, inky blue and immense. Elizabeth sat at a table in Limone town, drinking an ice-cold, fittingly named limoncello, a bittersweet lemon liqueur she'd first tasted in Capri the week before. Monte Baldo stood, picturesque, in the distance, as a colorful paraglider cut across the darkening sky.

The lake lapped underneath the wooden boardwalk where she sat as a spectacular yacht slipped past silently. Its proximity was such that she felt she could reach out and touch its glimmering sides. The tanned couple on board waved, so Elizabeth raised a hand and waved back, as she understood was polite in good maritime society.

She took another sip of her drink, popped a blue-green olive into her mouth, then twisted the cap off her pen, flipped a post-card over, and began to write.

Darling Kate,

Capri was a dream, so much to see. At Lake Garda now and enjoying the spectacular scenery. Home soon. Love you. M&D xxx P.S. Say hello to Charlotte.

This was the fourth postcard that she had written to Kate since they had seen her in Athens, and she expected it would be the last, as the end of their trip approached. From Lake Garda, they would go to Milan and then home.

Elizabeth checked her watch and scanned the quayside again for any sign of David, who had gone for a walk with his camera two hours before. She knew that he had more than likely struck up a conversation with someone or become so absorbed with the surreal views across the lake that he had lost track of time. She wasn't particularly worried by his lateness, but they had dinner reservations, and she was hungry.

The sun was dipping low over the lake, and the evening breeze fluttered over the water and across her bare legs. Elizabeth shivered, her skin still being warm from the sun, and slipped her cardigan up over her shoulders.

David had been very relaxed since they'd arrived at the lake four days ago. They had talked and argued their way through Florence, and Sorrento, finding common ground a few times then separating again over Kate, and how they would handle things when they got home. When they had reached the island of Capri, they agreed not to talk about it any more until they were on their way home, as the holiday was becoming somewhat sabotaged by tension and a thick atmosphere that neither of them could tolerate anymore. Once they had agreed to postpone further discussion, they'd steadily rediscovered their holiday selves and had slipped back into the comfortable and companionable days that they had hoped for on the trip.

In the back of her mind, Elizabeth was anxious about what awaited them at home and felt sure David was feeling the same. However, they had each respected their agreement not to discuss it for the moment and were enjoying the even keel they found themselves on once again.

As she stared out at the water, a waiter approached, checking her glass with his eyes.

"One more, madam?" He smiled, his tanned skin in deep contrast to the white of his shirt.

"No, thanks. I'll wait for my husband." Elizabeth gestured toward the lake. "He's taking photographs."

"Ah, very good." The waiter nodded and walked away, a tray laden with empty glasses balanced over his shoulder.

She pulled her book out of her bag and flipped to the dog-eared page she'd last read. She had always felt guilty about bending the corner of the pages over, but bookmarks irritated her. She remembered her mother telling her off for the practice, insisting that she use something to mark her place and not deliberately damage a book. She smiled at the memory as she smoothed the tiny triangle out and resumed her education on Italian wine.

Absorbed in what she was reading, she jumped when David put his hand on her back.

"Sorry. I got caught up taking pictures."

"Thought as much. It's fine. I've eaten a whole bowl of olives, but I'm so ready for dinner."

David laughed and plopped down in the chair opposite. Placing his hat and camera on the table, he stared out at the lake.

"This place is incredible, isn't it? Almost otherworldly."

Elizabeth drained her glass and nodded.

"It's stunning. So peaceful."

David looked at his wife's face as she took in the scenery. He knew that they had agreed not to talk about Kate for the moment, but Elizabeth's profile was so much his daughter's that he was compelled to mention her.

"Kate would love this."

Elizabeth pulled the edges of her cardigan closer together and shivered.

"She would."

David glanced down at the postcard and then lifted it from the table. As he skimmed Elizabeth's distinct script, his eyes were drawn to the last line. He felt his heart contract as he saw the name "Charlotte." In black and white, it took on a tangibility that was so sharp it caused him pain. He let out an involuntary gasp.

"What?" Elizabeth traced his focus down to the card and frowned.

"Is that really necessary?" David's eyes snapped to hers.

"Is what necessary?"

"Mentioning her. You don't even know her."

Elizabeth watched his face contort as he spoke. The calm lines of his smile gone, deep parentheses formed around his mouth as he pressed his lips together and clenched his jaw.

"It does no harm, does it? It'll mean a lot to Kate to have us acknowledge Charlotte's existence."

David dropped the card on the table, picked up the camera, and fiddled with the strap.

"I don't see the point, that's all. Seems odd and forced to me, having never met the woman."

Elizabeth returned her gaze to the inky water. The hairs on her arms were raised against her cooling skin, the cardigan no longer taking the chill from her shoulders.

"Let's not do this again. We agreed." She stared ahead.

David shrugged, wound the camera strap around his index finger, and watched her hair move in the gathering breeze. Why did she have to contaminate the post card that way? Did she get some twisted pleasure in rubbing this Charlotte person in his face?

Elizabeth picked up her pen and slid it back inside her bag.

"Let's go and eat. Our table is reserved for seven." She looked over her shoulder at him as she rose from her chair.

"I'm not sure I'm very hungry now." David sulked.

"Fine, well, I am. Join me if you want to, or not. Up to you." She slung her bag over her shoulder and walked away from the table into the dusk, leaving David staring out across to Monte Baldo, the camera strap twisted so tightly around his finger that the tip was turning purple.

CHAPTER 22

Kate dropped the heavy cardboard box onto the floor and felt her back muscles tense as she bent over. This was the last of her things, her past and present, all wrapped in newspaper and stacked in the hallway of Charlotte's flat. Between them, they had made two trips with both their cars, and now, after several hours of effort, she officially lived above the Rose Street Bakery.

Charlotte had gone down to the shop to grab some sandwiches, so Kate, suddenly tired, flopped on the sofa and slipped her shoes off. As she glanced over at the bay window, the dark wooden mantel above the fireplace, and the wide door to the kitchen, she smiled. There were no rough edges here, no sense of the permanent awkwardness she'd grown up with – always feeling like the fork in a drawer full of knives. This was where she fit, finally.

The door flew open and Charlotte strode in, a large brown paper bag under her arm and a steaming paper cup in each hand.

"I brought lattes, too." She grinned at Kate. "Slacking off already, are we?"

Kate laughed and stretched her long legs out, crossing her feet on the coffee table.

"Yep."

"Good for you. Let's eat, and then we can start unpacking some of these boxes." Charlotte placed the cups on the table and walked into the kitchen. Returning a few moments later with their sandwiches, a bag of crisps, and two apples, she sat next to Kate.

"Well, shall we toast?" Charlotte raised her coffee cup.

"Sure." Kate smiled.

"To us." Charlotte touched her cup to Kate's.

"To us." Kate felt her heart tear at the simple words, which Charlotte had plucked right out of her own heart.

As they ate, Charlotte chattered about where they might put Kate's things. She suggested moving some furniture around and clearing a few of her own belongings to enable Kate to put her stamp on the place. She listened and nodded, letting Charlotte chatter. Kate was happy, at peace, and excited at the prospect of not having to leave to go back to her own flat in Morningside ever again, something she'd always dreaded after spending weekends here on Rose Street. This night she could stay, and then all the nights after.

She had picked up the last of her mail from her flat before leaving, and the small pile lay next to her cup on the table. Amidst the official window envelopes, circulars, and obvious bills, the corner of a colorful postcard stuck out. Having put the last bite of sandwich into her mouth, Kate wiped her hands on her jeans and reached for the card. The picture was of a lake, immense and an incredible shade of navy. Behind it stood a graceful mountain, and a few scattered cotton clouds brought the unrealistically blue sky to life. Flipping it over, she began to read.

Charlotte chewed silently, watching Kate's face. She felt a twinge of anxiety as she waited for a reaction, some indication of the contents of the card. It was obviously from Kate's parents and, as she waited, Charlotte held her breath until Kate's face broke into a broad smile.

As she looked over at Charlotte, the beginnings of tears flashed in her eyes.

"What is it?" Alarmed, Charlotte reached over and took her hand.

"Mum says hello." Kate was now grinning like a teenager as a single tear broke loose and trickled down her cheek.

Charlotte scooped it up on her finger and then cupped Kate's cheek in her hand.

Kate was crying. Not a flimsy weep, but a muscle-wrenching, breath-stealing cry that caused her to fold over and lay her head on Charlotte's lap. Asking nothing, Charlotte stroked her hair and back until the shaking subsided.

After a few moments, Kate, sitting up, ran a hand through her hair and tucked it back behind her ears. Sniffing, she swiped at her nose and laughed, catching Charlotte's questioning glance.

"You officially exist." She held Charlotte's hand as she spoke, extending the postcard towards her.

"Well, that's progress, then." Charlotte grinned, leaned in, and kissed her. "Come on, let's unpack a couple of boxes, then you'll feel much more at home."

Kate nodded, gathered their plates and cups, and stood up.

"I've never felt more at home in my life."

CHAPTER 23

---◆---

Kate stretched her legs out towards the end of the bed. It was Sunday, and the knowledge that she didn't have to go to work was intoxicating. Charlotte had left her a mug of tea on the bedside table when she'd left for the bakery some time earlier. It sat untouched. Although parched, Kate hadn't wanted to sit up and spoil the blissful sensation, the perfection she was enjoying, of knowing that she lived here now. This was her home.

They had talked until well after 1:00 a.m. the night before as they'd unpacked a few boxes of books and clothes. Kate had sold much of her own contemporary furniture from her flat in Morningside, as Charlotte's home was already full of graceful antiques that fit the character of the place so perfectly. She had, however, brought several paintings with her, and an art deco dressing table that sat in the spare room, waiting for its new permanent position in their bedroom.

Her favorite watercolor, a view of Portree Harbor on the Isle of Skye, was propped up against the wall in the living room. Charlotte had said that they would hang it in a prominent spot when they could find her hammer.

Kate's clothes were now hanging in the wardrobe, and her shoes were stacked close to Charlotte's. The sight of them there, next to Charlotte's much smaller ones, had touched her.

Having finished a bottle of wine, they had fallen into bed and, despite their exhaustion, made love. While always tender, Charlotte had taken tome to focus on Kate's pleasure. The singular feeling of being the subject of so much love had overwhelmed her. Kate knew she was loved, both by her parents and by some of her closer friends, but this kind of love was ethereal, utterly consuming, and something she never wanted to let go of.

She knew her parents were due back within the next few days. Just the thought of them re-emerging onto the landscape of her life chipped a tiny crack in the pristine surface of the moment.

Shifting onto her side, she glanced at the clock. She couldn't remember the last time she'd lain in bed until 10:00 a.m. It was a guilty pleasure she usually denied herself. Throwing the covers back, she sat up and touched the mug hopefully, but the porcelain was cold under her fingers.

She stood up and walked to the window. As she pulled the heavy curtains back, she could see Rose Street below. To the left, a small gallery with a Georgian bay window was open, with several paintings propped up on easels outside. Next to it, a fancy paper store, selling hand-stenciled cards and customized invitations, had baskets of goods lined up on the pavement. The wine bar opposite was serving Sunday brunch al fresco and two of the tables were occupied by early birds, reading newspapers and watching the world go by.

As she watched the gentle activity, Kate tried to calculate where her parents were now. The last postcard she'd received had been from Lake Garda, so according to the itinerary that Elizabeth had left her, they must be in Milan, their last stop before making their way home. She hoped they'd had a good time, but was anxious that her unexpected visit had totally spoiled things for them. She knew it wasn't the most considered thing she'd ever done but, for once, she had gone with her gut and jumped on the plane. At least this way they'd had uninterrupted time together to think things through and, she hoped, come to terms with the new dynamic in all their lives.

As she thought about Elizabeth, she felt a pang of sadness. She had missed her mum, and the time they'd spent together in Athens remained, in her mind, some of the most honest that they had ever shared. She was looking forward to seeing her again. Her dad, on the other hand, was now the source of her anxiety. One way or another, they'd all have to navigate the changes that had taken place. He would have to accept this new face of his daughter and let her be happy. Despite her nerves, Kate wanted to believe that they would manage it, in time.

Having dressed and tidied the kitchen, she locked the flat and made her way down to the bakery. Charlotte was behind the big glass counter, serving a customer. Her mass of dark curls was subdued, for the most part, behind a wide bandana, and she wore the signature white chef's jacket with her name and the bakery logo on the pocket. Kate's heart lifted as Charlotte raised her eyes and smiled at her.

"Hey there, sleepyhead." Charlotte nodded as the customer walked away with a huge slice of lemon meringue pie.

"Sorry. I was just so comfy." Kate shrugged, grinning.

"No problem. You relax. Some of us, on the other hand, have to earn a living." Charlotte laughed and brushed a stray curl behind her ear. "Want a coffee?"

Kate nodded and, as Charlotte pressed the fragrant grounds into the espresso maker, she shuffled through the Sunday papers that were lined up on the old Welsh dresser. Grabbing the *Telegraph*, she sat at a tiny marble-topped table next to the counter and glanced at the headlines, flicking the pages over in quick succession.

Charlotte placed the steaming cup in front of her and sat down.

"What's happening in the world? I haven't had time to look this morning."

Kate shrugged. She had not taken much in, her mind still full of what was to come over the next days and weeks. She held the paper out to Charlotte.

"You tell me."

Charlotte took the paper and scanned the front page, her eyes lifting intermittently to Kate's face. Kate tried not to seem too distracted, staring out into the street, then back to the table.

"Penny for them?" Charlotte placed the paper back down on the table.

"Oh sorry. Just thinking about Mum and Dad getting back."

"Right. It's this week, isn't it?"

"Yeah. Wednesday, I think." Kate forced a smile.

"Good. We should ask them over for dinner, once they get settled."

Kate's eyes widened. Charlotte never failed to amaze her with her openness and, at times, the childlike simplicity with which she saw the world. Sure, it'd be great to have her parents invade the sanctuary of their flat upstairs, their discomfort leaching into the very fabric of the walls, contaminating the space. They could all sit awkwardly around the French kitchen table and exchange strained pleasantries, avoiding the frigging great elephant in the room. Oh yes, she couldn't wait.

"What?" Charlotte watched Kate's face contort through some secret thought process.

"You are crazy." Kate shook her head.

"Why?" Charlotte's smile faded, and she looked offended.

"It's just not going to be that simple, love. I wish it were."

Charlotte frowned.

"Sorry, Lottie, but you didn't see their faces. I mean, Dad's, at least."

"I get it, Kate. I'm not trying to make light of it, but we need to set the tone. If we're ever going to have a relationship that includes them, we have to make the first move."

Kate sipped her coffee. She watched Charlotte's face flush. She knew she'd hurt her feelings.

"You're right. I know. You see things more clearly than I do sometimes. I get so wound up with the emotion, the idea of disappointing them."

The careless words were out and, as Kate heard them, she understood the weight of what she'd said. Charlotte winced, and Kate put her cup down and reached across the table for her hand.

"Don't misunderstand me, Lottie. I'm not ashamed of who I am, of you, or of us."

Charlotte met her gaze. Letting Kate cover her hand for just a few moments, she then withdrew it and sat back in her chair.

Kate felt the conversation spiraling towards a darker place than she had intended. She needed to get them back onto a positive footing.

"You sound like a scared child, Kate." Charlotte's voice was low, ominous.

Kate was taken aback by the subtle forcefulness she heard.

"I need to get back to work." Charlotte stood up.

"Wait. Let me explain what I mean."

"Later, Kate. Let's talk later. It's OK." Charlotte patted her shoulder dismissively as she walked back to the counter. Kate could feel the frustration emanating from her fingertips.

"I'm sorry, Lottie."

Charlotte raised a hand over her shoulder as she walked into the back office.

Kate sighed. Perhaps she needed to take Charlotte's tack? If she treated the situation with her parents with a little more levity, perhaps it would take on less of a pall? If she visualized them all sitting around the kitchen table, having a relaxed conversation over a meal and a bottle of wine, then could it become reality?

Kate drained the coffee cup and walked over to put it on the counter. There was no sign of Charlotte, so she placed some cash on the counter and left.

It was a beautiful day, and she felt like walking. As the sun climbed in the sky, so the activity along Rose Street picked up. The cafés and galleries were humming, and Kate allowed herself to get lost in the flow of life. As she walked and observed, her mind went back to the conversation she'd just had.

She knew that what her parents thought of her had always

mattered to her, perhaps too much. Seeing the way Charlotte's parents had embraced their daughter's sexuality, and then Kate as her partner, had amazed and impressed her beyond words. It was obvious that Charlotte was more evolved than she was. How else could it be explained?

Here she was, a thirty-year-old professor of civil engineering, a well-traveled, informed, intelligent adult, fretting over what her dad thought about her life. Should she just give him an ultimatum? Just tell him that if he wanted a relationship with her, he had to accept Charlotte as an inevitable part of her future? The idea made her balk even as she considered it.

No sooner had she flinched at her own train of thought than Kate was ashamed of herself. Charlotte deserved better than this. She had put Kate first from the moment that they had decided to be together. Perhaps Charlotte was right, and it was time she just grew up.

CHAPTER 24

———◈———

Elizabeth sat on the leather armchair in the living room, a rug over her legs. The pile of unopened mail lay on the side table with the cup of tea David had left for her when he'd gone to the shops to fill the list that she had written.

Although it was late August, Elizabeth felt a chill in the atmosphere of the big house that she couldn't seem to shake. She wondered if she was perhaps still adjusting to the temperature change, having come from Milan, where it had been in the eighties for the last three days of their holiday. Or perhaps she was sickening with something? She had slept well, being back in her own bed, but still felt discombobulated.

Glancing out of the bay window, Elizabeth felt the deep sense of peace being in her favorite spot brought her. She loved this time of day. The gloaming, as the locals called it. The sun was almost down, but not quite. The light took on a purple hue, reflecting the dense green of the grass and the warm tones of the heather covering the gentle curve of the bank that ran between their garden and their neighbor's.

The silver River Tay, languishing at the bottom of the garden behind a low stone wall, flashed in the afternoon light. The striking view, with its gentle familiarity, and the tangy salt air that she breathed in the moment she stepped outside were why she had fallen in love with this place many years before.

Elizabeth shook her hair out of her eyes and reached for the first of the envelopes on the pile. Having gone through the inevitable heap of circulars, a few bills, several catalogues she hadn't asked for, and requests for donations from the charities they supported, Elizabeth spotted a pale blue envelope. The address was in Kate's familiar handwriting, and she turned it over and opened it, her spirits lifting. Inside was a single-sided card.

Dear Mum and Dad,

Welcome home! Hope the rest of your trip was fun? Can't wait to hear all about it.

Charlotte and I would love you to come for dinner. We can crack open a nice bottle and look at your holiday snaps. Give me a ring with some dates that might work for you and we'll get it organized.

I love you,

Kate.

As she re-read it, Elizabeth's hand shook. The word "we," and seeing Charlotte's name in Kate's hand, evoked a new sensation, one that she couldn't put into words. For years, she'd been longing for Kate to be part of a "we." She had been afraid that her clever, career-focused, and often solitary daughter might remain alone forever, a Jean Brodie archetypal academic in dusty robes and sensible shoes. The prospect had worried Elizabeth, not for the predictably selfish reasons of wanting grandchildren or the extension of the family line, but because she herself feared loneliness. For Elizabeth, the worst form of purgatory would be to be abandoned by the people she loved, be it by design or even by death, left to watch the world forget her as she withdrew into an ever-shrinking microcosm. She had no idea where this irrational fear came from, but she had lived with it for years.

She turned the card over. Why did she think there would be more? A P.S. perhaps, or a private note to her from Kate, acknowledging the deep connection they'd made in Athens. As she stared at the blank side of the card, Elizabeth imagined what words would fill it up over the coming weeks. She rose and placed it in front of the clock on the mantelpiece. She'd tackle the invitation with David later.

The river was low and calm. The late summer sun glinted on the surface, reflecting the famous metallic glow that poets and authors had written of. Her river was always there for her. Broad-shouldered and consistent like a good friend, it was something she knew she could rely on.

As she stood at the window, a woman wearing a wide-brimmed hat walked along the footpath behind the wall at the foot of the garden. Elizabeth could just see her head and shoulders as she made her way past, her head swiveling as she glanced out to the water, then back to her feet.

A walk suddenly seemed like a good idea. She could shake off this odd feeling, go and get a newspaper, and be back in time to help David unpack the groceries. Yes, she needed to get out and smell the air of home.

Having showered and dressed, Elizabeth strode along the

waterfront. The river crinkled like silver paper as the breeze folded it into gentle pleats. Gulls cawed above her, and she could smell the musty hills of seaweed lying along the banks. A man and a small boy were digging for clams in the shallows, plopping them into a tin bucket. The little boy wore bright-red wellingtons and a pair of oversize sunglasses. She could hear his peals of laughter at something his father had said, and it reminded her of the way Kate used to laugh uproariously at David's marginally funny jokes. Kate always made such a big deal about how funny her daddy was, and Elizabeth would observe, knowing it was Kate's way of showing her love for him. She'd always thought it a very astute thing for an eight- or nine-year-old to do.

She wondered what Kate was doing today. She would give her a ring later and let her know they were back. When it came to the invitation to dinner, she'd have to come up with a way to approach that with David that would not cause too many ructions. The thought of the card on the mantel made her uncomfortable, but underlying that was also a twinge of excitement. They were going to meet Charlotte. Elizabeth had a mental picture of her, and from Kate's description, she sounded lovely. But Kate was far from unbiased, and Elizabeth was looking forward to forming her own opinion. Getting David on board would be the next challenge.

As she walked along the path, the only blots on the sunny landscape were a few fluffy clouds and some carelessly abandoned dog mess on the pavement. Spying the post office ahead, Elizabeth breathed in the familiar salty air. It felt good to be home. This was her place, her space in the universe, where she wholly belonged.

Their trip overall had been wonderful, despite the rocky start, and both she and David had found time to relax, regenerate, and reconnect. Their differing positions on Kate's situation had necessitated their mutual focus and honesty with each other. The conversations had generated passion, anger, and fear, all emotive and enlivening sensations. She felt as if they were firmly back in the same arena, even if at opposing edges.

Despite the tension and arguments, they had somehow found their way back to each other, and regardless of her frustration at the way he was handling Kate's revelation, Elizabeth was determined not to let that closeness slip away again.

The time since David's affair had been sore on her soul, lonely and interminable. Now, even with all the questions and challenges before them, she believed that they were going to be all right. They all were.

CHAPTER 25

David pulled into the driveway. The sight of the river always gave him pause, and he would often sit in the car, turn off the engine, and just stare. He hoped Elizabeth was feeling better, as she'd seemed so quiet when he'd left earlier. He doubted it was jet lag, as the time difference from Italy was only an hour, but there was something going on with her that he hadn't been able to pin down. He knew the holiday hadn't been as idyllic as he'd hoped, and the whole business with Kate had disrupted things, but despite all that, he felt closer to Elizabeth than he had in a long time.

She had begun to let him back in, and even if it was tinged with anger and frustration, they were finally communicating again.

As he leaned over to look out the windscreen, he saw her pass the kitchen window. She lifted her head and spotted him in the car. Raising a hand, she waved, then stuck her tongue out.

The small trademark gesture touched him, and he waved back. Perhaps she was over her malaise?

He reached into the back seat and grabbed the shopping bags, heavy with two Angus sirloin steaks, fresh fruit, salad, vegetables, and milk. He had enjoyed the food that they'd eaten while away, especially in Italy, but it was good to come home to some of his favorites.

David pushed the button on his key fob and heard the customary bleep as the car lock engaged. The stones of the driveway crunched under his feet as he approached the front door. He had always wanted a driveway with gravel, ever since he'd been a little boy and had visited Hampton Court with his parents. He had fantasized about having his own roundabout one day, where he'd drive in a full circle, leaving a low, sleek car of some kind at the door of his home. There was something quintessentially decadent about that picture, and while he hadn't managed to create the roundabout, he did have his stones.

Elizabeth was in the kitchen, and he could hear the radio. That was a good sign, as she switched it on when she was in a good mood. He'd sometimes find her bopping around as she chopped vegetables, and then she'd blush and turn the volume down when she saw him watching her.

He put the bags on the table and walked up behind her. She was peeling potatoes at the sink.

"I got some lovely steaks. Thought we could open that Beaujolais we got from the wine club before we left." He leaned in to kiss the side of her face.

Elizabeth nodded as his arms circled her waist.

"Yep – good idea." She continued with her task, not turning her face to meet his pursed lips.

As his mouth made awkward contact with her hair, David felt a tiny stab of hurt. Had she done that intentionally? Stepping back, he disengaged himself from her waist and began to unpack the groceries.

"Shall I pour you a glass?" He lifted two glasses down from the cabinet and reached for the bottle opener in the drawer.

"Sure." Her back was still turned towards him, and as he uncorked the wine, David tried to read the muscles, sinew, and bone of her frame to get a sense of what was going on in her mind.

The deep aubergine-colored liquid flowed into the glasses, and as he watched, David was transported back to Lake Garda. They'd had the most marvelous Bardolino while sitting on the sun terrace of their hotel. They'd eaten a mound of olives, local goat cheese, and bruschetta. Along with the wine, the conversation had flowed freely. He wanted to get her back to that open place, to that level of connection they'd reached. Why was it that as soon as they'd got home, he'd seen her shutters coming back down, her eyes taking on that distant look, and her answers sliding back towards monosyllabic? Was he just imagining it? Perhaps he was just paranoid.

Elizabeth ran her hands under the tap and lifted the bowl of potatoes onto the counter. As David placed a glass of wine at her elbow, she let go of the deep breath she hadn't been aware she'd been holding and turned to look at him. In his face, she could read his obvious concern. A flash of pity made her smile at him.

"What's wrong?" She lifted the glass and sipped. "You look worried."

David swallowed his mouthful and shook his head.

"No – I thought something was wrong with you." He shrugged.

"I'm fine. Just tired and ready for dinner." Elizabeth let her eyes slide to the window as a tiny sparrow landed on the sill. She loved to scatter breadcrumbs on the long wooden sill, then sit with her morning coffee and watch the finches, sparrows, and sometimes robins enjoy their breakfast. There was nothing out there for the birds to eat. She needed to fix that.

"I'll start the steaks whenever you tell me, sensei." David winked, trying to reintroduce the banter that had made her laugh on holiday. Elizabeth smiled and nodded, then turned back to the stove.

David watched her back and felt his anger rise. He gulped more wine, then put his glass on the table.

'What's going on?" His voice was low.

"Nothing. I'm just thinking through everything that's happened. Mulling things over." Elizabeth continued to clatter pans, filling one with water.

"Are we going to go through all *that* again?" David could hear a buzzing in his ears. There was a familiar tightness in his throat. This was a bad sign. He needed to breathe, get control.

"Through what again?" She turned to face him.

"The whole Connie thing. I thought we'd gotten past that." David slumped into the chair and reached for his glass.

"Seriously, Dave? I wasn't talking about that." She shook her head walked over and sat opposite him at the table. "You need to get over that. I have." Elizabeth lifted her glass and leaned over, inviting him to touch his to hers.

David stared, momentarily confused. Seeing her open

expression, he lifted his glass and clinked the crystal goblet against Elizabeth's.

"Cheers. Here's to being home and to the future of this family." Elizabeth was smiling.

David felt a warm surge of relief that he didn't have to face the firing squad again. Underlying that veneer of a truce, however, he remained confused as to what she'd been referring.

Seeing his blank expression, Elizabeth tutted in frustration.

"I was talking about the holiday. Kate showing up. Everything." She waited for her point to register.

David swallowed. Yes, of course, the whole Kate situation. He had, in his usual miraculous way, been able to put that to the back of his mind. It was a talent he'd developed as a bank manager when he'd had to disengage from his feelings of pity or guilt over calling in bad debts or not furnishing loans to bad risks. It drove Elizabeth mad that he could compartmentalize this way, but it was the only way he knew of to cope with things that were to any extent difficult.

"Right." He managed to squeeze out the word.

"So have you given it any more thought?" Elizabeth eyed him over her glass.

"No. I haven't, actually. I think we need to just let the dust settle and see what happens." He stood, picked up the wine bottle, topped up his glass, then sat back down.

Elizabeth watched him, seeing the slow, deliberate movements, the eyebrows reaching for the ceiling, and the mouth working silently on itself. He was avoiding the issue. Classic David. She pushed the glass away from herself and sat back in the chair. This was probably not the best time to tell him about Kate's card, but for some reason, she couldn't help herself. There was a tiny part of her that was enjoying his discomfort with the whole thing, and despite her fleeting guilt, she knew she was going to go for it.

"Well, we don't have long to wait. They want us to go to dinner." The words out, Elizabeth felt lighter.

CHAPTER 26

Charlotte walked past the table again. It was the fourth time she had checked the place settings in the past twenty minutes. The French linen napkins that she had brought back from Avignon, where she had attended a patisserie course two years ago, were perfectly pressed. Arrows of sunlight bounced off the crystal glasses, sending shards of rainbow colors across the warm wood surface of the table. The vase of tightly packed hydrangeas that she had bought at the farmer's market sat in the center, and she leaned in and turned it around, reorienting the pink and white blossoms for the umpteenth time. Her stomach was knotted and her hands sweaty.

Turning back towards the living room, she glanced at the clock. In just two hours, Kate's parents would be here, in her home. No, in her and Kate's home. After the lunch rush was over, she'd left the bakery in the capable hands of Mungo and Chloe and had come upstairs to prepare. They were her only staff and were integral to the success of the business.

Mungo had worked for her since she had opened the bakery. He was a diffident, lanky, hardworking local lad in his late twenties who had a knack for baking. He lacked confidence in his abilities, and Charlotte had taken him under her wing, determined to help him develop skills around his passion for food.

Chloe was a twenty-six-year-old French graduate student who had come to Edinburgh from Paris for a year, three years ago. She had fallen for the capital city and, despite her affluent lawyer-parents' protestations, had made a life for herself in Scotland. She and Kate had developed a good working relationship, and the customers loved Chloe's open, friendly manner.

Charlotte had decided to make Kate's favorite for dinner, her trademark coq-a-vin, with dauphinoise potatoes, sautéed fresh asparagus, and then a deadly, decadent chocolate mousse for dessert. Kate always said that she defied anyone to be unhappy after eating Charlotte's chocolate mousse. She smiled to herself, hoping Kate was right.

A good sauvignon was chilling in the fridge, and two bottles of Burgundy that she had been saving for a special occasion sat on the sideboard. The smell of garlic seeped out from the oven, and as she inhaled its sweet fragrance, she caught sight of herself in the mirror over the fireplace.

The cream silk blouse complemented her fair complexion, and she'd taken extra care with her makeup. Not too much rouge, just a touch of mascara and a swipe of nude lipstick. She had pulled her long, dark curls back from her face with a gold clip, and the large hoop earrings Kate had bought her for Christmas glinted at her jaw line. Was it too "gypsy"? Should she go with the pearl studs instead? She reached a tentative hand up and touched one of the earrings. Did it matter? She doubted it.

Kate was due home from the university in half an hour, which would give them some time to talk before the Fredericks arrived. Kate had been like a cat on hot tiles that morning, and while Charlotte had done a good job of keeping her calm, her own insides were quivering now. What if it all went wrong? What if they hated her? How would Kate cope? A flurry of angst-ridden questions filled her head as she turned her back on her reflection. *Enough, Charlotte Macfie.* They were all adults, and this shouldn't be such a big deal in this day and age. After all, her own parents had embraced Kate immediately, and she'd quickly become a fixture at Sunday lunches and on Thursday movie nights at Charlotte's childhood home in Morningside. Elsie and Duncan had adored Kate. All that Charlotte was asking for from Elizabeth and David was acceptance. She could live without the adoration. After all, she still had her dad and Kate for that.

The phone rang, jarring her already jangling nerves. Charlotte grabbed it.

"Hello?"

"Hi, love, it's me." Kate sounded breathless. "Everything OK?"

"Yes, all set. Where are you?" Charlotte felt her stomach relax at the tone of Kate's voice. All seemed to be well.

"I'm just leaving work. Do you need me to pick anything up on the way home? Wine? Valium?" Kate laughed.

"Oh, ha ha. You were the one climbing the walls this morning. What's with the cocky attitude now? Have you been drinking?" Charlotte giggled.

"No. I'm just being upbeat. You know, sending out positive vibes and hoping the universe is listening."

Charlotte nodded and glanced back at the table. There was a

beeping sound, and then Kate spoke again.

"Oh, hang on. Mum's calling me. Stay on the line." Kate's voice was gone, and the only sound in the room was the ticking of the clock on the mantelpiece. Charlotte ran through several potential scenarios – Kate's boss was calling to say that she needed to stay late for a faculty meeting. A student had a problem with an assignment and had requested a late tutorial. The Dean wanted her to attend some last-minute reception or other. After a few moments, there was a click, and Kate was back.

"So? Who was it?"

"Mum. She says Dad's not coming." Kate's voice was flat. The lilting quality and bubble of her previous optimism gone, she sighed into Charlotte's ear.

"Why?" Charlotte asked the idiotic question she already knew the answer to.

"She says he's not feeling well. It's pathetic, Lottie. Do they think we were born yesterday?" Charlotte could hear the threat of tears in Kate's voice.

"No, sweetheart. Don't cry. Think of it this way. Your mum *is* coming. Right?"

Kate sniffed. "Yes."

"Well we're fifty percent there then, aren't we?" Charlotte held her breath. Her heart was pattering wildly, and she tried to picture Kate's face, visualizing the way she chewed on her bottom lip when she was processing something. After a few moments of silence, she could bear it no longer.

"Kate?"

"Yes. I'm here. You're right. Sod him. Mum's coming, and she said she was looking forward to meeting you. Let the silly old bastard stew." Kate forced a laugh.

"Don't say that, Kate. He'll come around. If it takes him longer, then so be it." Charlotte flopped down on the sofa. She needed to keep it together for Kate. This was going to be a pivotal evening in their lives, and she had every intention of it being a success, with or without David Fredericks in attendance.

Charlotte hung up the phone and walked to the table. She gathered up one set of cutlery, lifted the shimmering glass, and flopped the placemat and napkin over her arm. Seeing the remaining three place settings, she smiled. In this case, three would not be a crowd.

CHAPTER 27

———◆———

Elizabeth leaned back into the cushions on the low sofa in the living room of the flat on Rose Street. She had been pleasantly surprised by the décor, a clever combination of French country chic and local antiques which she knew, based on her daughter's penchant for beanbag chairs and linear, Ikea-type bookshelves, had to be Charlotte's touch. For some reason, she had expected a cold, contemporary environment, so the warmth and eclectic nature of this home pleased her.

Her wine glass was half full, and her shoes were tucked under the coffee table, where she'd kicked them off after dessert. Charlotte had prepared a spectacular meal, and Elizabeth had even managed to pry the recipe for the chocolate mousse from the petite chef her daughter hadn't been able to take her eyes off all evening.

Charlotte had been prettier than Elizabeth had imagined. The small frame, the classic Celtic combination of dark hair and blue eyes, the wide mouth and strong jaw line all reminded Elizabeth of her own mother.

Charlotte had been a confident hostess. She'd circled the table, serving food and filling glasses while chatting easily about her business, her family, and her travel in Europe and Asia. She'd asked Elizabeth insightful and earnest questions about her own life, Kate's childhood, David, and their recent trip, commenting on the postcards and the scenery of Greece and Italy that they'd shown.

Throughout the evening, Elizabeth had been intrigued to see Kate, her strong-minded and vocal daughter, taking a back seat, allowing Charlotte to showcase her culinary skills. It was clear that the tiny woman was in her element.

Elizabeth had watched as Kate's eyes followed Charlotte around the warm flat. A soft glow on Kate's cheeks indicated the combined effects of the wine, the crackling fire in the grate, and, Elizabeth was sure, the extent of her daughter's happiness. It was good to see her looking so at home, so comfortable in her own skin. Elizabeth couldn't remember the last time she'd felt her daughter exhale, let herself relax, and just be.

"Mum. Want a top-up?" Kate hovered with the wine bottle.

"Gosh, no. I'd better not." Elizabeth reached over and put her hand over her glass. "I have to drive."

"Why don't you stay, Mrs. Fredericks?" Charlotte popped her head out from the kitchen door.

"Call me Elizabeth. Please?"

Kate's head snapped up and she looked startled, but then she nodded at Elizabeth.

"Stay, Mum. It's a long drive back to the house, and the

spare room is made up. I think I even have a new toothbrush somewhere." Kate placed the bottle on the table and, beckoning Charlotte into the room, sat down opposite her mother on the Persian carpet in front of the fireplace.

"You could have some limoncello if you stayed." Charlotte was smiling and waving a tall, opaque glass bottle at Elizabeth. She placed it on the table, then picked up her wine glass and sank cross-legged onto the floor next to Kate. Kate leaned in towards Charlotte and laid a hand on her knee.

Elizabeth felt a jarring in her stomach. She realized that this was the first physical contact the two young women had had all evening. Despite her delight in finding Charlotte a charming and intelligent companion for her daughter, Elizabeth had not anticipated how she'd feel about this new aspect of her daughter's life. Visions of them kissing each other, lying in the big four-poster bed she'd seen in the room overlooking the street, assaulted her. Suddenly uncomfortable, Elizabeth pulled herself upright on the sofa.

"I really should be going."

The two young women watched her reach under the table to retrieve her shoes.

"Are you sure, Mum? It's no trouble." Kate looked disappointed.

"Yes. I'd better make tracks. Besides, your dad won't sleep unless I'm there." Elizabeth shrugged and stood up.

Kate and Charlotte followed suit and the threesome walked towards the front door.

"I'll walk you to your car." Kate reached for her coat as Elizabeth slipped on her own.

"That's OK, sweetheart. It's right around the corner." Elizabeth slid her handbag over her shoulder.

"Thank you both for a wonderful evening. Charlotte. So good to meet you." Elizabeth extended a formal hand as Charlotte walked forward, stood on tiptoe and wrapped her arms around the taller woman's shoulders.

"It was a pleasure, and I'm so happy to have met you too."

Elizabeth dropped her hand and tentatively returned the smaller woman's embrace. Charlotte felt so small compared to Kate, like a bird she might crush in her arms if she wasn't careful. And yet this was a strong young woman, in many ways even stronger than her own daughter.

"Well, goodnight." Elizabeth turned back towards Kate, who now stood in the open door with her coat on. "You don't have to come down."

"I'm walking you to your car. Come on." Kate put her arm across her mother's back and led her to the staircase.

As the pair descended the stairs, neither spoke. The gentle syncopated thunking of their heels on the wooden stairs was the only sound as both mother and daughter contemplated the evening.

Kate broke the silence.

"So. What do you think?" She eyed her mother as they emerged into the brisk Edinburgh night.

Elizabeth noted that the bakery windows were dark but the wine bar opposite was busy. The door swung out into the street as a young couple emerged, laughing. Inside, the light glowed a soft yellow, and Elizabeth could hear a guitar. As they turned left and walked away from the flat, the rest of Rose Street hummed with the evening activity that Kate had described to her.

"She's wonderful. Honestly. I like her." Elizabeth searched her daughter's face. Kate broke into a broad smile and linked her arm through her mother's.

"She *is* wonderful, isn't she?"

Elizabeth squeezed Kate's hand and her heart lurched with pleasure as Kate laid her head on her shoulder.

"Thanks for coming, Mum. It means the world." Kate's voice was full.

Elizabeth swallowed over her own walnut of emotion as they walked on.

"I'm sorry about Dad not coming, love."

"Yeah, it was a disappointment. He's not ill, is he?" Kate lifted her head and looked at her mother's face.

"It's complicated." Elizabeth shrugged. "He's struggling, Kate, but he'll get there. I have every faith in him."

Kate stepped over a crack in the pavement and waited under the street light as her mother located her car keys.

"I hope you're right. Because he's hurting no one but himself by staying away." Kate's voice was low, tinged with irritation.

"Let it go for now. OK?" Elizabeth slid into the driver's seat and looked up at her elegant daughter. "Tonight was lovely. Let's leave it at that for now."

Kate nodded and closed the door. Elizabeth wound down the window and reached for Kate's hand.

"She's a delight, Kate. You are good together."

Kate's smile was back and she patted her mother's hand.

"Text me when you get home. OK?"

Elizabeth nodded, closed the window, started the car, and pulled away towards home. As she drove away, she watched Kate in the rearview mirror. Was it her imagination, or did her daughter's willowy frame have a new, more confident presence against the night?

CHAPTER 28

David stared at the clock on the cooker. It was 11:15, and Elizabeth still wasn't home. He turned and padded through to the living room with the mug of hot chocolate he'd just made. He didn't know if he wanted it, but it seemed the thing to do this late at night. He'd put the dishwasher through its cycle, emptied the dryer of clothes, finished the crossword, and watched three marginal programs on television. He just wasn't used to being home without his wife. She filled the gaps that his own lack of imagination left around him.

He glanced at the TV guide on the arm of his chair. He'd looked at it a dozen times but regardless of how much he stared the evening's entertainment remained unchanged and he was uninspired by all of it. David flopped down into the chair sending a wave of hot liquid over the edge of the mug and onto his thigh.

"Jesus" he yelped, standing up and lifting the mug higher to avoid any further spillage. "That's bloody hot." He grumbled as he swiped at the stain on his trousers and made his way back to the kitchen.

The hot drink thrown down the drain he washed the mug and sat it on the draining board. The kitchen clock said 11:29. He was tired and wanted to go to bed, but he also wanted to wait until Elizabeth got home. He didn't like her driving back from Edinburgh at night, and he'd told her so. But, as she had so eloquently put it, she wouldn't have had to make the drive alone if he had not been such a stubborn idiot about meeting Charlotte.

At the thought of Elizabeth in a room with Kate and that other woman, David felt himself cringe. He supposed that it did make him look like a narrow-minded bigot, not showing up. He had never thought of himself as either narrow-minded or bigoted before, but perhaps he was?

As he dabbed the corner of a wet tea towel on the dark chocolate stain, David felt a twinge of guilt. He should have gone to support Elizabeth, if nothing else. Staying home had been a mistake, and he knew it.

"Are you seriously asking me to tell Kate that you're not feeling well, at this late stage?" Elizabeth had stared at him earlier that evening. She'd stood in the hall with her coat on, holding a bunch of stargazer lilies tied with a hessian bow. The scent of the flowers had been overpowering, and David remembered how odd it had felt to notice the cloying smell while arguing with his wife about meeting his daughter's partner. Once again, David cringed.

Kate had called them three times that week to confirm that they were going to dinner. He had spoken to her once, then had quickly handed the phone over to Elizabeth. The subsequent times she'd called, he had recognized the number and left Elizabeth to answer it, taking himself out of the room as she confirmed the time with Kate and talked about what they could bring. He'd known all along that he wasn't going to go but had waited until the last minute to back out. It was a cowardly move. There was no denying it.

He walked back into the living room and turned off the lamps at either end of the sofa. The curtains were drawn already, so he turned towards the stairs. Just as he started up them, he heard a key in the lock.

"Hello. You're back late." He watched Elizabeth close the door behind her, hang her coat on the rack, and run a hand through her hair at the hall mirror.

"So how was it?"

Elizabeth didn't turn to look at him but leaned in towards her reflection as if checking a blemish on her chin. She took a deep breath, then slid her feet out of the pale blue high heels.

"It was a super evening. The flat is gorgeous. Charlotte had made a wonderful meal, and all in all, it was lovely."

"All in all?" David tried to keep the hopefulness from his voice.

"It was lovely." She met his eyes full on. "The whole thing."

David cleared his throat and shuffled his feet on the bottom stair.

"If you're wondering whether you were missed or not, to be honest, I don't think you were." Elizabeth flashed him a glare, then dropped her eyes, apparently feeling bad for the snipe.

"Well, good. I'd hate to have spoiled the lovely evening with my absence." David spoke huffily and turned to go back upstairs.

"Is that it? Are you really going to leave it there?" He could feel Elizabeth staring at his back.

"What do you want me to say?" He swung around to face her. "That I regretted it? That I ran down the driveway chasing your car so I could come with you?" He stepped back down the stair and then walked past her into the dark living room. "As a matter of fact, I did feel bad about it once you'd left." He spoke quietly, over his shoulder.

Elizabeth followed him into the room and turned on the floor lamp behind her chair. He was tired, but this conversation needed to take place, and it was clear that Elizabeth was not going to wait until morning.

"Don't you want to know anything about Charlotte?" She sat down in the armchair, the outline of her face silhouetted against the lamplight glowing behind her. Even without seeing her face, David knew the expression that lay there. It would be a combination of disappointment, frustration, and irritation. Yes, he could see it in his mind's eye.

"Do I have a choice?" He collapsed onto the sofa and scratched futilely at the stain now drying on his trouser leg. He knew he sounded like a child, but for some reason, he couldn't stop himself.

"She is charming. Attractive, clever, industrious, well-traveled, a marvelous cook, and she adores Kate. That is patently obvious." Elizabeth leaned back in the chair. "She wasn't exactly what I was expecting, but I liked her, Dave. She is a real person."

David shrugged and pulled another cushion behind his back. He wasn't so much uncomfortable as discomfited.

"I suppose that's good. I mean, that you liked her." He put his feet up on the coffee table. "How was Kate?"

"She was more relaxed than I've seen her in years." Elizabeth pushed herself up from the chair, padded over to the sideboard, and poured herself a brandy. She shook the bottle at David, who nodded in response. Once she'd sat down again, David sipped the amber liquid she'd handed him. He felt the welcome burn slide down his throat and into his chest. It seemed to take some of his guilt down with it, and he felt able to ask more questions.

"So what's the place like? Where she lives?"

"Where they live, you mean? It's a lovely flat above Charlotte's bakery. There's a beautiful fireplace in the living room and original hardwood floors everywhere. It has high ceilings and big bay windows overlooking the street. It must've been built around the eighteen hundreds, I'd say. You'd love it. There are lots of original features." She sipped her brandy.

David listened, visualizing each of the rooms as Elizabeth talked on. She described the galley kitchen with the copper pots hanging from a drying rack on the ceiling and the French country décor in the lounge. She went on to describe the dinner they'd eaten and the wonderful wine choices. She talked about Kate and her ease around Charlotte, her obvious happiness. At this, David squirmed again.

"So I'd like to have them over next weekend. Maybe Sunday lunch?" Elizabeth waited for a response.

David heard the words skirting his consciousness but didn't let them sink in until Elizabeth prompted him for a response.

"David?"

"I think it's too soon." He pushed himself up from the sofa and walked across to the fireplace. Picking up the poker, he thrust it into the fire, breaking up a small piece of cold, charred wood that lay in the grate.

"Too soon for what?"

"To have her *here*. I mean Charlotte." Saying her name made his tongue feel heavy.

"Why?" Elizabeth wasn't letting up at all.

"Because I'm not ready to meet her yet. That's why." He replaced the poker in the wrought-iron stand and turned to face his wife. "If you push me, Liz, you know it will only make things worse."

Elizabeth stood up, picked up the two empty brandy bowls, and headed out into the hallway. David followed her, not sure if they were finished talking.

She stood at the sink rinsing the paper-thin glasses. Her head was bent over, and he sensed her concentration on the task.

"Liz?" He addressed her back.

"What?" She snapped.

"Did you hear me? I'm not ready to …"

"I heard you. I'm just trying to work out how to respond." Her whole frame was supporting an imminent explosion of anger. He could see it in her raised shoulders, her tilted hips, the way her feet were planted on the ground and her toes clenched on the ceramic tile floor. David braced himself.

"I think it's time you stopped beginning your sentences with 'I' when it comes to discussing Kate. How about that?" She turned and glared at him.

He opened his mouth to protest and she raised a warning hand.

"I'm not listening to it anymore." She threw the tea towel onto the countertop and walked past him. "I'm inviting them here a week from Sunday, so be here or be somewhere else. It's up to you. I'm going to bed."

CHAPTER 29

———◆———

Kate flipped the damp cloth at Charlotte's backside. Charlotte yelped and jumped out of the way. The dishes were all clean and back in the cupboards, and each of the women had a tall, frosty glass of limoncello that they sipped on as they circulated around each other, tidying the last of the wineglasses away.

"So, how do you think it went?" Charlotte scanned Kate's face.

Kate felt giddy.

"Fantastic. Really, love – it was just about as good as it could have been." Kate slid onto a kitchen stool at the side of the counter. "She loved you. She loved the flat. She loved the food. She loved *you*." Kate beamed.

"You already said that." Charlotte walked over and wrapped her arms around Kate's neck. "Your mum is wonderful. From what you'd told me in the past, I was expecting the inquisition, but she was so open. She really listened to me, asked me thoughtful questions, and looked me in the eye. God, it felt good to just be in the same room as someone in your family." Charlotte laughed and kissed the end of Kate's nose.

Kate raised her lips and kissed Charlotte. She could feel slender fingers in her hair and taste chocolate and lemon. She stood up, taking Charlotte with her. They laughed their way into the bedroom, where Kate gently dropped Charlotte onto the bed before lowering herself down next to her.

Kate stared at the canopy above them. Charlotte's breathing was slow and rhythmic. She was facing away from Kate and her legs were entwined in the duvet, while her top half shone luminous in the lamplight. Kate reached over and lifted the covers up over Charlotte's shoulders, then slipped from the bed and pulled on her robe. She tiptoed into the living room and opened the curtain a sliver, just enough to see the street below. The amber streetlights glowed, reflecting off the wet cobblestones. She guessed at the time and then padded into the kitchen to check the clock on the cooker: 4:39.

The surfaces were clear, the butcher-block chopping boards Charlotte loved were stacked neatly, and the glass-fronted cupboard showed muted outlines of the crystal glasses they'd used that evening.

As she opened the fridge to grab some milk, Kate noticed the container of leftover coq-au-vin. Charlotte had excelled herself with every detail of the dinner, and Elizabeth had seemed impressed by everything she'd seen and heard.

Kate poured milk into a tumbler and reached for her phone. There was a text from her mum.

Home safe. Please thank Charlotte again for the delicious dinner.

Loved meeting her. Can you both come to lunch Sunday after next? 1-ish? Love you x

Kate swallowed a mouthful of milk and read the message again to make sure she was seeing it properly. She'd been so disappointed that her dad had been a no-show at dinner, so this invitation to come to the house seemed fast on the heels of Elizabeth meeting Charlotte. Had her father relented and agreed to meet Lottie? Or had Elizabeth bullied him into it? Either way, the prospect of David and Charlotte being in the same room was both terrifying and exciting. She would text her mum in the morning and, once she had spoken to Lottie, would confirm the lunch. The sooner they got the first meeting out of the way, the sooner, she felt sure, her dad would take to Charlotte, just as her mum had.

CHAPTER 30

Elizabeth watched David's car disappear down the driveway. He was heading to visit a friend who had just returned home from hospital after a knee replacement.

It had been two weeks since her dinner in Edinburgh, and things had been strained with him since then. Kate and Charlotte had come for Sunday lunch the previous weekend, and David, to Elizabeth's embarrassment and frustration, had gone to play golf rather than join them.

The lunch had gone well. Kate had been relaxed, cracking jokes and gently teasing her mum about the predictable menu, testing the newfound closeness they'd found over the past few weeks. Elizabeth had once again noted and appreciated the shift in Kate's manner towards her, enjoying the new, kinder dynamic between them. She had even felt comfortable enough to tease her daughter back without the usual sense of trepidation.

Kate had seemed to particularly enjoy seeing Charlotte in her parents' environment. Charlotte had loved the house and been so taken with the view that she asked if they could walk along the river after they had helped Elizabeth clear away the dishes.

The three women had put on their heavy coats and walked all the way to the town, taking time to browse in the antique shops and boutiques along the way. When Charlotte spotted Visocchi's Café, she bought them all gigantic ice cream cones. They had passed the cones between them, tasting each other's choices, as they wandered home along the river wall.

Elizabeth then made them coffees and they sat in the living room, sipping the frothy lattes, browsing through the Sunday papers, and watching the trickle of yachts sliding by on the early evening tide.

Realizing that she was staring blankly through the darkening window towards where David's taillights had disappeared, Elizabeth sighed and threw her cloth into the sink. It had been an almost perfect Sunday with the girls, the only blot on the landscape being David's absence. When she'd challenged him, he had insisted that his golf game had been arranged weeks in advance. Elizabeth, knowing this to be untrue, had covered for him with Kate and Charlotte as best she could, but it was obvious that they had both seen through her charade. Noticing the exchange of eloquent glances between the two young women as she explained David's absence, Elizabeth was instantly angry with herself. She was not in his camp on this stance he was taking, so she'd made a resolution never to take responsibility or make excuses for him again. The last thing she wanted was for Kate and Charlotte to think she condoned his behavior. She did not. If he made this kind of childish stand again, he was on his own.

The phone rang in the hall, jarring her from her train of thought. She hoped it was Kate, as it had been three days since they'd spoken. They were talking almost every day now, and to Elizabeth, the novelty of this level of contact was still shiny and thrilling. She picked up the handset and walked into the living room. Hitting the answer button, she flopped into her chair.

"Hello?"

"Hi, Mum. It's me." Kate's voice was bright.

"Hi, sweetheart. How're you?"

"Fine. Busy but fine. How's your week going?"

Elizabeth smiled. It had been such a long time since Kate had asked about her week that it took her a few moments to gather herself.

"It's going well. I've been working in the garden, as usual, getting things ready for the winter shut-down." Elizabeth lifted her feet up onto the coffee table.

"Got any bridge games coming up?"

"Not until next week. Thursday's game has been canceled, as Nancy isn't well." Elizabeth wriggled her toes inside her slippers. Her feet were cold. The weather was changing, and the autumn was closing in, ready to turn this corner of eastern Scotland into a collage of copper, bronze, and auburn. October could be a fickle month in Broughty Ferry. Some years, they'd been able to sit on the patio and have their pre-dinner drinks, and others they'd been huddled at the fire with their sweaters on. She hadn't thought of lighting the fire for months, but today it felt like a good idea.

"Sorry Nancy's ill, but it's actually quite good timing. I wanted to know if you were free on Thursday afternoon to come to Aberdeen with me? I've got to go up to the university to give a guest lecture."

Elizabeth let Kate's words sink in and waited for the catch, the pebble under the heel that would normally have come with an offer like this.

"I thought maybe we could grab some lunch and then do some shopping?" Kate sounded genuinely hopeful. "I really want some new boots, and Lottie has given me a list of things she needs from some kitchen supplier up there."

Elizabeth was elated. Kate wanted to spend time with her, without any persuading, complaining, or self-pitying jibes required from Elizabeth's side.

"Is Charlotte going, too?" Elizabeth crossed her fingers and, while she would have been quite happy to see Charlotte again, felt a simultaneous rush of hope that she'd get to spend the time alone with her daughter.

"No. She can't leave the bakery that day, as Mungo is off. He's going on a pastry-making course in Glasgow for a couple of days."

Elizabeth smiled broadly in the empty room.

"That's lovely for him. Charlotte is very good to send her staff on training courses like that. She's a good manager, Kate." Elizabeth nodded. 'It's important to make people feel valued."

"So can you come?" Kate asked again.

"Oh, yes. I'd love to." Elizabeth, still smiling, was suddenly overcome with the notion that she should ask if David was invited. She swallowed. "Do you want Dad to come, too?" The words out, she wished she'd stopped them in her throat.

"No." Kate's response was abrupt. Then her tone softened again. "I thought we'd just have a girls' day."

"I love that idea." Elizabeth, selfishly pleased, placed her feet back on the carpet and pushed herself out of her chair. "Lunch is my treat, though. That's the deal."

"OK, that's great. We'll have fun. The lecture will take about an hour and a half, so you could scout out some good lunch places if you like, or do some boot-reconnaissance." Kate laughed.

"I'll be fine. I'll wander around and find us a nice restaurant."

"Brilliant." Kate sounded happy. "I'll pick you up at eight-thirty, if that's OK? It's a bit early, I know."

"That's perfect. I'll get Dad set up with his meals for the day, then I'm all yours."

Elizabeth walked to the window and looked out at her river. She visualized the two of them singing in the car, watching the scenery changing around them, the way they had when Kate was a child.

"Wonderful. See you Thursday, then. Love you."

Elizabeth felt her breath catch in her throat at the throw-away statement from her daughter.

"I love you too, sweetheart. See you then."

After a few seconds, she realized that Kate still hadn't hung up. She could hear her breathing.

"Kate?"

"How is he?" Her voice seemed distant.

"He's fine, love. Just being Dad. You know?"

"Yeah – I figured. OK, see you Thursday." Kate was gone.

As she placed the phone back in its cradle, Elizabeth replayed the conversation in her mind. Kate had asked her to have a girls' day out, no David. The idea that she had usurped David as the accessible (she wouldn't say favorite) parent would take some getting used to. It had been over twenty years since she'd occupied that position.

As soon as Kate had turned seven, David had taken on full hero status, and from that point onward Elizabeth had gradually become the mundane disciplinarian. Dad was kind and fun, and Mum was boring and bossy. That pattern had defined the dynamic among the three of them most of the time, and David had done nothing to alter its course, obviously comfortable with the arrangement.

As she walked back into the kitchen to put the kettle on, Elizabeth marveled at how the tables had turned. David seemed to be flitting about on the periphery of their little family unit, as she and Kate became closer and closer. She wondered how he was feeling, not being the center of his daughter's attention or affections anymore. She knew how much it must hurt. After all, she'd been the outsider all these years. Now she was inside looking out at his discomfort. The difference being that she, despite her occasional wish to let him swim in his current misery, could not let him make a fool of himself much longer. No. She knew that she would help him through this. Being a bonded family was the most important thing, and the sooner David realized that Charlotte was now part of that family, the better for all concerned.

CHAPTER 31

—◈—

David parked his car, turned off the ignition and pulled on the handbrake. He knew exactly how many clicks he needed to hear before he was comfortable that the car was secure on the gentle slope of George Street. He twisted the rearview mirror towards himself and took in his reflection. His wiry hair was combed back, and his eyes, despite the dark crescents that the recent sleep deprivation had caused, looked their usual blue. He was still slightly tanned from the summer trip and from helping Elizabeth in the garden. The color in his cheeks was ruddier than usual, which he put down to his nerves.

He ran a hand over his thinning top and sighed. It wasn't as if it mattered how he looked, and he certainly didn't care what Charlotte would think anyway.

He had picked this day because he knew Kate was lecturing, and he'd told Elizabeth he was golfing in Perth. He had left the house before breakfast, as was his usual pattern before eighteen holes, and the drive to Edinburgh had taken him just over an hour.

He had written down the address but guessed that there weren't many bakeries on the famous Rose Street. Everyone in Edinburgh knew the pretty, cobblestoned, pedestrianized street, thick with galleries, pubs, chic wine bars, and eateries owned by celebrity chefs. In his university days, he and several classmates had participated in The Rose Street Challenge, involving a drink at every establishment along the length of the street. As he remembered the ensuing colossal hangover, David smiled. Even if nothing else might impress him about Charlotte, he had to admire the prime location of her business.

Letting himself out of the car, David rummaged in his pocket for change for the meter. Sliding several coins into the slot, he calculated that he'd have an hour and a half before he needed to be back. That should be plenty of time.

It was cold. The autumn temperatures and biting wind made him glad of his heavy jacket and gloves. It always felt colder in Edinburgh than in Broughty Ferry. Perhaps it was the river that tempered things, but the climate at home was gentler on its residents than the capital's was.

He always enjoyed being in this city, and ever since completing his degree here, he'd felt it belonged to him.

As he walked down the hill towards Princes Street, his stomach rumbled. He needed to find somewhere to have breakfast, then he'd make his way over to Rose Street. He had no idea if Charlotte would be in the bakery this morning, but he hoped he'd be able to get a look at this person who was causing all the upset in their lives. At the thought of the as-yet faceless woman who had turned his sensible daughter's head, he felt his stomach tighten. She had better be something pretty damn special to account for all this worry and upheaval.

Turning down a side street, David saw a blackboard sitting out on the pavement. He hoped it was advertising breakfast, and as he approached, he was not disappointed. The chalky handwriting promised a full cooked breakfast of haggis, two eggs any style, toast, and unlimited coffee or tea for 6.99. It felt like a bargain at this particular moment.

Removing his gloves, he pushed his way through the heavy door and scanned the room for a table. It seemed that the majority of customers were lined up at the counter, waiting for their breakfasts to go. A couple of tables were occupied, so he chose one in the far corner, near the back of the room, and settled himself. There was an abandoned copy of the *Herald* on the next table, so David leaned over and pulled it towards himself. Sliding out of his coat, he hung it on the back of his chair and looked around.

The waitress, a young woman in dark jeans and a white T-shirt, was clearing dishes from another table. She nodded at him as she passed with a heavily laden tray.

"I'll be with yuh in a tick." She smiled.

"Thanks." David smiled back, noticing the spidery dark tattoo that stretched from under her jaw line down the side of her neck and then disappeared inside the collar of her shirt. It looked like Japanese or some other character-based Asian language. What would possess a young woman who was otherwise attractive to do that to herself? David shook his head, nonplussed. He'd never understood the fascination with tattoos. Marking oneself permanently that way was insane, to his mind. What if she woke up one day and thought better of it? What would she do on her wedding day, posing for her pictures in a long white gown with a black jigsaw puzzle of characters on her neck, marring the ensemble? What would she feel like as a mother if her own daughter came home one day decorated like a menu from a Chinese restaurant? Thinking through all the future scenarios in which the girl might regret her choice, David felt a jolt to his middle. What if Charlotte had tattoos?

The café had seen better days. It was dimly lit, with a few tightly packed tables and mismatched chairs, and as he lifted the menu from the table, it felt sticky under his fingertips. This was not the sort of place Elizabeth would frequent. She'd have glanced in the door and then suggested they move on. David decided he liked its seediness. It suited his mood and the day.

As he read through the list of available morning fare, he felt another flash of guilt for having lied to his wife. Despite his past behavior, he didn't want to get back into the habit of deceiving her, but when he had planned this, he had been unable to come up with any other way to get around it. He needed a few hours to himself, and golf was the only plausible excuse.

His closest friend and golf partner, Mike, had been furious when David had asked him to provide a false alibi. David had felt awful telling Mike that he was planning a surprise for Elizabeth, and that there was no evil agenda at play. Mike had finally agreed to support his story, but had threatened that if there were any negative consequences for either of them, he'd drop David in it faster than you could say Jack Robinson.

David admired Mike's strength of character, and as he'd been the only one of his friends who had known about his affair with Connie, he could understand Mike's reluctance to get involved in any deception on David's part – especially as Mike's wife Clare was on the bridge club committee with Elizabeth, and the two of them frequently met in town for coffee.

The waitress was back.

"What can I get yuh?" She held a small pad and pen, and her short, white-blonde hair was slicked down to her head. Her brown eyes were set wide in her round face, and as she spoke, David tried not to stare at the tattoo.

"I'll have the full haggis breakfast with scrambled eggs and a pot of tea, please."

"Right-o." She wrote on her pad, then turned and walked away from him. David watched her go and wondered if, when the food came, he'd be able to force it down his tightening throat.

Forty-five minutes later, he pulled on his gloves and left the café. He was full and felt fortified, ready to face the enemy. Rose Street was only a five-minute walk away, so he'd have plenty of time to get to the bakery, take care of business, then make it back to his car before the meter ran out.

The early morning streets were busy with suit-clad workers making their way to offices and shops. The sky was heavy with clouds, and David shivered as he picked up his pace. He should have brought his big golf umbrella, but it was in the boot of the car along with his clubs, the equipment innocent and yet oddly complicit in his lie.

Rose Street had a steady flow of people heading in both directions. David dodged a young man who had his head intently dipped towards his phone, his thumbs seeming to work a tiny, invisible keyboard. A middle-aged woman followed close behind, talking loudly into a headset that was hung over her ear. As he watched her pass, David patted his pocket, checking that his own phone was where it should be.

On his left, he saw a gallery with a landscape of a Highland scene propped up on an easel in the broad window. Next to it were two bay windows, their old-fashioned paned glass panels overhanging the wall beneath. A glass door with a dark wood frame was set in the middle of the bays. Above the door, the sign, suspended from an intricate wrought-iron frame, read simply, "The Bakery."

David slowed his pace and headed to the opposite side of the street. Stepping into the doorway of a yet-unopened stationery shop, he looked across the way. So this was where she worked?

Elizabeth had said the flat was directly above the business. Lifting his chin, he looked up above the shop front. These buildings in New Town all dated back to the reign of King George III, and by the look of the stonework and architraves, David estimated this one at around 1800. Elizabeth had been right about that when describing this place. Perhaps some of his obsession with architecture had rubbed off on his long-suffering wife? No. He couldn't think about Elizabeth now, or he'd lose his nerve and not go through with this. He needed every muscle, sinew, and nerve to be focused on walking through that door, finding this Charlotte person, and telling her to leave his precious daughter the hell alone.

CHAPTER 32

Charlotte slid the tray of scones from the oven.

"Watch your back." She addressed Mungo's hunched shoulders as she walked behind him, the tray heavy with warm, golden rounds. "These look great, Mungo."

The young man shrugged, avoiding her eyes, as she playfully nudged him aside.

"Take a compliment for once, will you?" Charlotte shook her head.

"Thanks," he muttered into his concave chest as he continued to work beside her.

She was doing her best to build Mungo's confidence. She hoped that at some point, as a result of the professional pastry-making courses she was sending him on and the encouragement and tips she was providing daily, he might be capable of taking on more responsibility. The more successful the business became, the more she needed a real sous-chef, and she hoped Mungo would take up that gauntlet eventually.

The Bakery was busy with the usual pre-work crowd, and this was the second batch of fruit scones they'd sell before the customary pre-lunch lull. When things quieted down, she planned on dashing upstairs to the flat, calling an equipment supplier in Perth, then putting her feet up for an hour with the paper. Mungo and Chloe could handle the lunch prep perfectly well without her.

It was a grey day, but so far there had been no rain, which was good, as during heavy downpours, water would sometimes puddle on the flagstone inside the front door and soak the doormat.

She glanced out the window, watching the activity on Rose Street. She loved this corner of Edinburgh and was grateful daily that she had bought this place when she had. She would never have been able to afford it now, with the way property prices had increased over the past few years.

The doorbell jingled as another customer came in to join the line at the counter. Chloe was doing a good job of keeping on top of the orders. She made the coffees, lattes, fresh juices, and teas while Mungo assembled the hot rolls and sandwiches in the kitchen. He slid each plate through the long service window towards Chloe and then tapped the small concierge bell to indicate that the next order was ready. While hectic at this time of day, it was a well-oiled machine, and Charlotte was proud of the way her small business ran.

She lifted her gaze from the tray she held and looked through the service window. The customer who had just walked in was a newbie. She hadn't seen him in here before, but as she watched him gazing around the bakery, there was something familiar about him. A tall man, he looked to be in his sixties with thick, wavy grey hair that was thinning on top. He wore a heavy brown coat and twisted his gloves nervously in his hands as he waited his turn. As she watched him, the turn of his head and the line of his jaw stirred something in Charlotte.

For some reason, she wanted to see him up close, so she quickly transferred the remainder of the warm scones to the cooling rack, tossed the baking tray into the stainless steel sink, and wiped her hands on her apron.

She walked back around Mungo, who was assembling two bacon rolls, and stepped in behind the counter next to Chloe.

"How're you doing?" She placed a hand on Chloe's back. The young girl nodded.

"Fine. *C'est bon*." She indicated the line coming to an end, with the grey-haired man being the last customer waiting.

"Why don't you go and help Mungo with the last few orders? I'll take over here for a bit." Charlotte looked down at the computer terminal. The new POS system had been installed a few weeks earlier, and while it had made the flow of ordering smoother, it had brought its own set of issues with its operational complexity. "I've got to get better with this thing anyway." She stuck her chin out towards the terminal, laced her fingers and cracked her knuckles while crossing her eyes.

"Hmm. It's a bit of a pain, but once you get used to it, it's great." Chloe smiled, pushed her blonde fringe away from her eyes, and touched her fingertips to her freckled forehead, delivering the little salute that always made Charlotte laugh. "All yours, *patron*."

Charlotte looked up as the grey-haired man approached the counter.

"Can I help you?" She smiled.

"Um, yes. I, um. Are you? I mean I'd like to…" the man stuttered.

"Yes?" Charlotte saw his eyes flick to the dark blue scroll of her name embroidered on the left breast pocket of her chef's jacket.

He cleared his throat. He appeared to be struggling with something. After a few moments, Charlotte tilted her head to one side and smiled again.

"Do you need some help deciding?"

Finally he spoke.

"I'd like a scone, please. What kind do you have?" The man raised his hand and coughed behind it, as if covering his embarrassment at his own indecision.

"Fruit, plain, treacle, blue cheese and bacon, and the specialty of the house, stem ginger, which would be my recommendation. They are fabulous." Charlotte watched him scanning the contents of the glass display case that separated them.

"I'll take two ginger ones, please." He raised his eyes to hers, hesitated, then spoke again. "Is this your business, Charlotte?" Again his eyes were on her jacket pocket.

"Yes, it is, as a matter of fact." She nodded. "First time you've been here?" She watched his face. His jaw was ticking, as if he was gnawing on the inside of his cheek.

"Yes. First time." The man nodded and reached into his trouser pocket for his wallet.

"Well, welcome. I hope we see you again." Charlotte handed him the paper bag with the scones and took the five-pound note he held out. "It's always nice to see new faces in here."

He wouldn't meet her eyes now.

She turned to the terminal and pressed a few buttons, hoping for the cash drawer to open. Nothing happened except for a series of annoying beeps, then a green light flashing a message on the screen – "Incorrect entry."

"Damn. Sorry, I'm still getting used to the new system." She looked over her shoulder apologetically. The man was standing with the bag held in both hands high up under his diaphragm, like an anxious child guarding a precious packed lunch.

Turning back to the register, she tried again. This time, the screen prompted her to "enter quantity of goods," which she did; then she pressed "conclude sale." To her relief, the drawer opened, and she reached in and retrieved the change. As she turned back to the counter, all she saw was the back of the man's dark coat as he walked out the door.

She called after him. "Excuse me. Sir. You forgot your change."

He stopped in the outside entryway as the glass door closed behind him. He seemed to be leaning against the doorframe, as if catching his breath. Was he ill or something?

Charlotte walked around the counter with the money still clasped in her hand and headed for the door. The man looked over his shoulder, and as he saw her approach he raised a hand and patted the air, as if to say "stay where you are – everything's under control." Charlotte stopped in her tracks and caught her breath. That movement, that placatory gesture, was so familiar.

The man turned to face her through the glass door, and she raised the coins mutely. He shook his head, and through the glass, she heard his muffled voice.

"Keep it." Then he turned and walked briskly away.

Charlotte stared after him as he disappeared from view,

heading towards George Street. How odd was that? She shook her head and went back around the counter, depositing the cash into the tip jar. His face, that gesture, where had she seen the man before? As she picked up a tray and began gathering cups and plates from two of the tables that had been occupied, it struck her. It was Kate's gesture. She did that with her hands all the time, to tell Charlotte to calm down, to relax, to stop worrying. She swallowed as the realization of what had just happened washed her in a thin film of sweat.

CHAPTER 33

———◆———

Kate slid her leather folder into her desk drawer. The lecture had gone well today, and she felt exhilarated by the students' obvious interest in the material she had presented on suspension bridge technology. There had been a good turnout, perhaps thirty master's students, and the dean had slipped in towards the end, giving her the thumbs-up from the back row.

Kate was a good teacher. She had the ability to connect with the students without patronizing them or expecting to be their friend. She never socialized with them, despite several invitations each term to join them at various pubs or concerts. Instead, she hosted an annual gathering at her home with beer, wine, finger food, and a good mix CD that she had a friend who played guitar in a local nightclub compile for her. She always dreaded the evening but then usually enjoyed herself, despite her trepidation.

As she dragged a brush through her hair, she watched herself in the gilt-framed mirror behind her desk. She supposed this year the gathering would be at the flat above the bakery. The thought of if made her smile, but then she felt anxious at the idea of her students invading her and Charlotte's space with their inquisitive eyes, probing questions, and unending curiosity about her closely-protected private life outside of the lecture halls.

She threw the brush into her bag just as her phone rang. Glancing at her watch, she saw that it was 5:50. It was probably Charlotte checking on how it had gone today and asking what she wanted for dinner.

"Hi, sweetheart." Charlotte's voice was warm.

"Hi, love. Just finished. I should be home in twenty." Kate tucked the phone under her chin, picked up her bag, and slid one arm into her coat.

"Sounds good. I'm making lasagne for tonight."

"Perfect. Want me to grab some wine or are we set?" Kate took the phone back into her hand and shrugged her coat up over her shoulders.

"We're fine. We've got some Bordeaux left from Saturday."

"OK. See you soon, then." Kate blew a kiss into the mouthpiece and hung up.

The roads were busy, but she made good time. Within half an hour of the call, she was bounding up the stairs two at a time to the flat. She let herself in and was instantly washed by the scents of garlic, cheese, and the piney logs crackling in the fireplace.

"Hi. I'm back," she called into the living room. Vaughn Williams was playing on the CD player, and Charlotte was nowhere to be seen.

"Lottie?"

The bedroom door opened, and Charlotte came out wearing a

pair of leopard-skin leggings and one of Kate's T-shirts.

"Hello, you." Charlotte smiled at her as she wound her arms around Kate's waist. "How did it go?"

Kate pulled her close and kissed the top of her head.

"It was good. The dean popped in. Seemed that all was to his liking."

"Great. Of course it was to his liking. Listen, dinner's almost ready. Want to have a quick bath first?" Charlotte pulled back from Kate's embrace and looked up at her.

"That'd be great. These shoes look good, but they kill me after a while." Kate looked down at the black high-heels she wore.

"I'll run it for you." Charlotte was walking towards the bathroom. "I'll pour you some wine and we can chat while the lasagne rests."

Within a few minutes, Kate was lowering herself into the hot foamy water. She lay back and rested her head on a hand towel that Charlotte had rolled into a tight sausage and left on the ledge for her. The water lapped over her breasts and shoulders, making her skin tingle.

Charlotte walked in with two glasses of red wine. She placed one on the ledge behind Kate's head and then lowered herself onto the bath mat, resting her back against the wall.

Kate twisted around and picked up the glass. She sipped the wine and felt the luxurious heat of the liquid in her throat as she swallowed.

"So. I had a visitor today." Charlotte sipped her wine.

"Here, or at work?"

"At The Bakery."

Kate pushed herself up a little and focused on Charlotte's face. She looked flushed. Not excited exactly, more agitated.

"So who was it?" Kate probed, her interest piqued.

"I think it was your dad." Charlotte sipped more wine, then set the glass down carefully on the ground next to her.

"What?" Kate sat up abruptly, sending a wave of water over the back of the bath. "What do you mean? Was it Dad or not?"

"Calm down. I just said I thought it was him. This guy came in. Early sixties, tall, grey-haired. He was acting oddly, kind of uncomfortable. He asked if the bakery was mine, then bought two ginger scones and left without his change." Charlotte licked her lips. "He kept looking at my name on my chef's jacket, like he wanted to be sure it was me." She shrugged.

"But you know what my dad looks like, Lottie. Don't you? You've seen photos of him." Kate put her wine glass back on the ledge and reached for the soap and flannel. Charlotte pushed herself up from the floor and took the wet cloth from Kate's hand.

"I've seen a couple of snaps, but seeing someone in the flesh is different. Especially if it's the first time you've met them." Charlotte sounded huffy, and Kate felt bad at the sharp tone she'd used. She needed to sound less accusatory.

"Yeah. You're right. But if it was him, what was he doing coming to The Bakery announced?" Kate leaned into the pressure of Charlotte's hand as she rubbed her neck and shoulders with the soapy cloth.

"Casing the joint? Checking me out?" Charlotte laughed, then dipped the flannel back into the bath to rinse it. Serious again, she continued. "He seemed to want to say something, then changed his mind. He bought two scones he didn't want rather than talk to me." Charlotte wrung out the cloth, handed it back to Kate, and then bent to pick up her wineglass. "I'm going to check on the lasagne."

Kate stood up, the water cascading into the tub from her lean body. She grabbed a towel from the rail and wrapped herself up. What the hell was her dad up to? She padded into the bedroom and pulled her phone from her handbag.

It rang four times before Elizabeth picked it up.

"Hi, sweetheart. What's up?" Her mum's voice was upbeat. "I'm so looking forward to tomorrow."

"Yeah, it's going to be good. Listen, what was dad doing today?" Kate cut straight to the point.

"He was playing golf with Mike. Why?" Elizabeth sounded confused.

"I dunno. I might be wrong, but I think he came to the bakery today. Charlotte said she thought she'd seen him."

Elizabeth was silent for a few moments.

"He told me he was in Perth. Is Charlotte sure it was him?"

Kate pulled the towel tighter around herself and sat down on the edge of the bed. She felt bad for her mother. Her father had developed quite a skill for being untruthful a few years ago, and despite all the repercussions of his idiotic transgression, here he was reliving those mistakes and just as Elizabeth had begun to trust him again.

"Look, Mum, don't say anything to him. It's just a bit creepy, to be honest. I mean, if he went to all the trouble of covering up where he was going, driving all the way into Edinburgh, then walking into the bakery without having the balls to introduce himself to Lottie, to be honest, it's a bit pathetic." Kate heard the disappointment in her own voice.

Elizabeth was quiet again. Kate presumed she was gathering her thoughts.

"Mum. What do you think he was thinking?"

"I have no idea, love. But I can tell you that I will get to the bottom of it." Elizabeth sounded furious. "Tell Charlotte not to worry. It won't happen again."

"Lottie is fine. It's just sad that he's behaving this way. I just can't believe he's being so rigid, letting this come between us. We were so close…"

"I know, love. I don't know what to say." Elizabeth's voice was low.

"It's not your fault, Mum. I just wish things were how they used to be between him and me." Kate swallowed.

Elizabeth confirmed that she would be ready by 8:30 the following morning and hung up the phone. Kate threw the damp towel on the floor and pulled on a tracksuit just as Charlotte called to her that dinner was ready. It was clear that she needed to talk to her father, and she planned on confronting him tomorrow when she dropped her mum off on the way back from Aberdeen. This nonsense had gone too far.

CHAPTER 34

———◆———

E lizabeth was waiting for David when he walked in the door at 6:45. She made a herculean effort to control herself when asking how his golf had gone, waiting for him to bluff his way through an explanation of the lay of the course and the score. Instead, seeing her pinched face, David had crumbled, instantly admitting where he had actually been.

"What the hell possessed you?" Her voice was shrill, accusatory.

"I thought I could go there, see her for myself, and tell her just to back off."

Elizabeth's mouth fell open, her jaw slack with both shock and disbelief.

"Are you confusing yourself with a gangster from some old film?"

"No. I just wanted to see what all the fuss was about, that's all. I thought that if I was face-to-face with her, I could catch her off guard. I don't know. Maybe rattle her a little, let her know Kate is not alone in the world." He hung his head. "I wanted her to know that Kate has a family."

Elizabeth watched him shrug his coat off, drape it over the banister and head for the living room. She felt sorry for him as she watched his shoulders curve forward as he shuffled across the carpet, defeated.

She stood in the hall for a few moments until she heard the whisky decanter chinking. She focused on regulating her breathing and gathering her thoughts. Did he really think he could scare Charlotte away? Was he that naïve?

She walked into the living room to see him staring out of the window. The river was iced with a layer of white-topped waves, and David sipped at the heavy crystal glass in his hand.

"Dave. Talk to me." She walked over to him. Her shoulder brushed his, and David turned to look at her.

"She is tiny." His face was blank.

"What?" Elizabeth waited for him to make sense.

"Charlotte. She's tiny. She has such big eyes, and all that curly hair. Not what I expected at all." He sipped his drink again. "I couldn't do it."

Elizabeth's heart ached for him as she watched his poor tortured face, contorting with the memory of the day. She reached out and wound her fingers through his.

"She's gorgeous, isn't she?" She leaned her head against David's shoulder. "Like a little Gaelic wood nymph."

David nodded.

"I don't know what I was expecting. Perhaps some tattooed scary creature with bad teeth." David shrugged and looked down at Elizabeth. "I'm a fool, Liz."

Elizabeth squeezed his hand.

"That bakery is wonderful, too. It's cozy. It was very busy, and in a great spot. I bought some scones."

"You did what?" Elizabeth couldn't help herself as a single, sharp laugh escaped her. "Scones?"

"Yes, don't laugh. I was all set to pull the protective father act, then when I saw her, I was totally disarmed."

Elizabeth stared back out of the window, picturing David standing awkwardly in the bakery buying baked goods and generally fumbling his way through the meeting. Sometimes he really was his own worst enemy.

'If you wanted to meet her, why didn't you say so?" Elizabeth released his hand and, taking his empty glass, went to refill it.

"I didn't want to meet her. Well, not in the same way you did." David ran his fingers over his hair and then shoved both hands into his pockets.

"I was curious, but not because I wanted to get to know her. I wanted to dislike her, find fault. I was looking for ammunition to help turn Kate away from her." He shrugged, his bone-deep fatigue seeming to throb around his back like a smoky-black aura.

Elizabeth was conflicted. She felt his genuine pain and confusion and wanted to be able to comfort him. On the other hand, she was staggered by his obtuse stupidity and his belief that he could influence Kate with his twisted idea of protection. David was floundering for the first time since he'd become a parent. She was witnessing it, and could not believe that he could be so wrong and yet still believe he was in the right.

"You have to let it go, Dave. They are together. Charlotte is a good person, and they are in love. It's as simple as that." Elizabeth pressed the newly filled glass into David's hand. "The sooner we get used to it, the better for everyone."

David took the glass, lifted it to his lips, then hesitated.

"I can't accept that. It's far from simple."

She watched him hold the glass below his mouth, then lean it against his chin.

"It *is* as simple as that, Dave. You must accept this. If you don't, you risk losing Kate forever."

He finished his drink in silence, watching the sun sink into the river and the dark of night sweep across the window. She had no idea what time it was, but Elizabeth was suddenly overcome by a heavy weariness.

"I'm too tired to eat. I'm off to bed. Can you shut up the house?" She patted his back.

"Yep. I'm not hungry either. I'll be up in a bit." David turned to face her. "I know I'm a big disappointment, but I just can't take this in." His face hung, the lines around his eyes and mouth more deeply etched than she remembered.

"I know, love, but you'll have to find a way. That's all there is to it."

David smiled weakly as she left him at the window.

Elizabeth took her time in the shower and in going through her bedtime regime. She creamed her face and neck and then cleaned her teeth as she listened for David coming to bed. Finally, she heard him moving around in the bedroom. She had yet to tell him that she was going to Aberdeen the next day, and the memory of his tortured face once again made her feel guilty that she was going to spend time with Kate, alone.

She pulled on her robe and walked into the bedroom. David was lying, fully clothed, on top of the duvet, staring up at the ceiling. He turned to face her, propping himself up on one arm.

"Are you done in there?" He nodded towards the bathroom.

"Yep – sorry. Took a while." She smiled at him.

David pushed himself up from the bed and walked towards the bathroom.

"Listen, Dave, I'm going to be out all day tomorrow. I'm going to Aberdeen." Elizabeth pulled back the duvet on her side of the bed.

David turned around.

"What for?"

"I'm going with Kate. She's lecturing up there, and then we're going to do some shopping." As she said the words, she saw his face twitch as if she'd slapped him.

"Did she ask you to go?" His eyes glittered and his face sagged as he spoke.

For a moment Elizabeth considered lying, saying that she'd asked if she could go along, then thought better of it. There had been enough lying.

"Yes, she did. She thought it might be fun for us to have a girls' day."

Elizabeth slid into the bed and pulled the heavy quilt up around herself.

David nodded, turned, and silently walked into the bathroom. Elizabeth swallowed over the nut of pity that was stuck in her throat, picked up her book, and settled back onto her pillows. She knew that David was in hell at the moment, but she had no intention of leaving him there. She intended on talking to

Kate about it the following day. Between them, they would come up with some way to get David on board with the parameters of this new family they were all going to be a part of. Elizabeth felt confident that with her help, David would get there.

CHAPTER 35

———◆———

Kate sped along the road towards Broughty Ferry. It was a bright morning, and the gentle sweep of the River Tay was guiding her towards her parents' house. She was looking forward to the day. Not so much to the lecture itself, as it was always nerve-racking addressing a group of students she didn't teach on a regular basis, but to the time alone with her mother. The past few weeks had been enlightening, and she had learned much about Elizabeth that had surprised her.

She had known that her mother had suffered over her father's deceit. She didn't know until recently, however, just how cripplingly depressed Elizabeth had been after she and David had appeared to reconcile their differences. Kate had since learned that it was common for people to fall into a depression after the worst of a situation was over. The knowledge that her mother had been so bone-deeply sad made Kate hate herself for her lack of empathy towards Elizabeth at that time.

This new relationship that she and her mother were building was precious, and Kate hoped that their developing closeness would somehow compensate for the years of distant disapproval that had existed on both sides.

To Kate's delight, Elizabeth had begun to forge a relationship with Charlotte, too. Her mother had been in to The Bakery twice since being at the flat for dinner. She'd bought things to take home, then had chatted to Charlotte while she baked.

Lottie had sat Elizabeth at the long stainless-steel counter in the kitchen and given her a warm chocolate croissant straight from the oven. Elizabeth had said it was the best croissant she'd ever eaten, even compared to those she'd had in Paris. It made Kate smile to think of the two most important women in her life forming a genuine friendship. It meant everything to her that they admired and respected each other, as much as she loved them both.

As she had left the flat in Edinburgh that morning, Kate had hugged Charlotte and said she'd be in touch from Aberdeen. Charlotte had given her the name and address of the equipment supplier on a sticky note and Kate, laughing, had slapped it to her forehead as she'd walked out the door.

"Don't worry, I won't forget." She'd turned back to kiss Charlotte and then headed for the stairs. "I'll phone you when we're leaving for home."

Charlotte had called after her.

"Love you, you nutter."

Seeing her turn coming up, Kate indicated, then pulled the car into the driveway and cut off the engine. The sight of the house always flooded her with childhood memories and today she saw herself at the age of twelve, building a snowman in the back garden with the neighbors. Smiling, she made her way to the front door and rang the bell.

When Elizabeth opened the door, she was dressed in a long cream-colored wool coat. She had on pale-blue leather shoes, and her hair was neat and firm with spray. Her trademark mulberry-colored lipstick was flawless, and Kate felt a jolt of love for her mother, recognizing the effort she had gone to in order to look her best for their outing.

"Love the shoes, Mum. Are those the ones you got in Athens?" Kate hugged her mother, smelling the familiar light musk perfume Elizabeth liked to dab behind her ears.

"Yes. They're so comfortable. More so than they look."

Kate scanned the hallway, but her father was nowhere to be seen.

"No Dad?" She eyed Elizabeth's face.

"He's not up." Elizabeth rolled her eyes.

Kate felt a flash of disappointment but in the same instant decided not to let it spoil her pleasure in the day to come.

The first stage of the drive to Aberdeen was easy. They talked about Kate's upcoming lecture and the possibility of her teaching at the university more often. The dean of the engineering school had asked if she would be prepared to be included in the curriculum as an adjunct professor for the next academic year. Kate had told him that of course, she'd have to discuss it with the dean at Edinburgh, but that if the timing worked out, she'd be interested.

"It could be quite fun, coming up here twice a month. A

change of scenery, some new faces." Kate kept her eyes on the road and nodded, more to herself than to Elizabeth.

"Yes, it would be wonderful. And quite a feather in your cap, sweetheart, lecturing at both colleges." Elizabeth took in her daughter's profile as Kate focused ahead. "I'm so proud of you." Her voice was thick with emotion.

Kate turned to look at her mother. The face that had often looked distant was now so full of warmth that Kate caught her breath. Whatever else her revelation about Charlotte had brought about, the expression on Elizabeth's face now made it all worthwhile.

As she soaked up her mother's obvious joy in the moment, Kate suddenly heard her name, then felt Elizabeth's arm coming up across her chest as a disembodied scream filled the interior of the car.

She turned back to look at the road just as the cab of an articulated lorry punched through the central barrier as if the thick metal was nothing more than a toothpick.

Time slowed down. Kate could hear her own breathing and feel her heart thumping in her chest. As she watched, the trailer behind the cab jackknifed. Swinging out across two lanes, the two sections formed a right-angled open jaw that there was no way to avoid.

Kate dragged her head back to look at her mother. Elizabeth stared at the road ahead. Her mouth slowly contorted into a strange grimace, and whatever she was shouting was distorted, her voice stretched in time as if some celestial DJ had pressed his fingers down on an old vinyl LP, preventing the sound from coming out at the intended speed.

The lorry crabbed towards them, and Kate heard her mother

shouting again. She tried to reply, to reassure her that she had it under control, but the steering wheel had become lead in her hands, and as she pressed her foot down on the brake pedal, it felt like sponge under her weight. As she steered in slow motion, trying to control her own skid, the small car glided out, passenger side first, towards the oncoming metal V of the lorry.

The impact was thunderous. Metal against metal, scraping, tearing, the sounds were unearthly and high-pitched. Kate's head flew sideways, her temple bouncing from the blossoming side airbag, and then her head slammed back over her left shoulder. Her ears were ringing and her face quivered as the car folded, yielding to the side frame of the trailer.

Kate's eyes were closed. She tried to open them, but the lids were too heavy. She could taste blood in her mouth and felt something hard and sharp, like fragments of gravel, lying on her tongue. As she took a mental inventory of her body and the strange sensations that were cascading over her, there was a metallic sound. It reminded her of the clatter of a dropped dustbin lid, spiraling in ever decreasing circles until it finally came to a stop on the ground.

Kate filled her lungs and felt a stabbing under her rib cage. Forcing her eyes open, she saw the side of the trailer towering over them through the gaping hole where her windscreen had once been.

She turned her head towards her mother. Elizabeth's head lolled to the left side, dangling at an awkward angle. Her left arm was draped across her lap, and a crawling crimson stain marred the front of her pale coat.

Kate swallowed, then gagged on the broken teeth that she had been holding in her mouth. She spat into her right hand and threw the bloody detritus onto the floor of the car.

"Mum?" Her voice sounded echo-like, distant. "Mum, are you OK?" Kate felt something warm trickle down the side of her head. She was dizzy and nauseous. The light around her began to dull. She must not pass out. She needed to make sure her mum was all right.

Kate tried to lean over and check her mother's pulse, but the seatbelt held her trapped, constricting her now aching middle. Her left arm wasn't working. Why wasn't her arm working? Fumbling with the clasp with her right hand, Kate released the belt. Her body fell slightly towards her mother's unmoving form.

She twisted at the waist, reached over, and grasped Elizabeth's wrist. With the simple movement, a tearing pain in her side made her scream out loud. Kate leaned back against the headrest, taking short, shallow breaths. The blackness was coming again. She focused on pushing it back. Not yet.

As the caustic smell of burning rubber caught in her throat, she swallowed and tried to speak again.

"Mum?"

Elizabeth was silent. The hair hanging over her face was now matted with blood, and she made no response as Kate reached over and shook her.

Kate felt her throat closing. This was so confusing. How had they got here? Where was her dad? Charlotte. What about Charlotte? Why wasn't her mother answering her?

She lifted her right hand to her temple and felt the sticky mess that was now running steadily down her cheek and onto her lap. Her head was pounding with such intensity that she could hear every valve in her veins contracting and releasing, pumping the blood that was feeding and intensifying the headache. If she could just stop the pain for a few minutes so that she could concentrate. The pulsing was pushing her eyes closed again. So heavy, so tired.

CHAPTER 36

———◆———

Charlotte stood behind the glass display case in The Bakery. She was giving a customer her change when the telephone next to the register behind her rang. She looked around for someone to answer it, but Mungo was assembling a triple-layered strawberry gateau in the kitchen, and Chloe had gone to take delivery of some flour sacks at the back service entrance.

There were no other customers waiting, so Charlotte turned her back on the café, walked over, and picked up the heavy receiver.

"Hello. The Bakery. This is Charlotte."

A crackle of static on the line caused her to wince and pull the phone away from her cheek. Tentatively, she put it back to her ear.

"Hello? This is Charlotte, at The Bakery. Can I help you?" She waited for a response.

"Hello. My name is Eleanor Harrison. I'm calling from A&E

at Aberdeen Royal Infirmary. Are you Charlotte Macfie?"

Charlotte felt her stomach contract. Did she say A&E?

"Yes, I'm Charlotte Macfie. What's going on?" She laid her hand flat on the marble counter at her side, feeling the reassuring cool stone under her fingertips.

"There's been an accident involving Kate Fredericks. You were listed as the emergency contact on the phone that was found. Are you family?"

"Yes." Charlotte responded on a reflex. She felt the room begin to shrink and turned her back to the wall. She slid down its surface until her bottom made contact with the floor and then leaned her head back and pressed her eyes closed.

"What kind of accident?" Her voice came out as a low, disembodied growl.

"A traffic accident." The woman paused, then continued. "The vehicle Ms. Fredericks was in was hit by a lorry. She is in intensive care."

"Oh, my god." All the air was sucked out of Charlotte's lungs with the words. She could not see clearly. Her heart began to clatter in her ears, and she felt sweat beading on her upper lip. She must not panic. She needed to focus, listen, and hear what this woman was saying.

Charlotte consciously slowed her erratic breathing down by filling her lungs. She then blinked several times, trying to clear her vision.

"How badly is she hurt?"

"She has a head injury and is unconscious. She has a broken arm, three fractured ribs, and a ruptured spleen. She's out of surgery now."

Surgery? Charlotte swallowed, waiting for more.

"Would you be able to come to the hospital?"

Suddenly mobilized, Charlotte swiveled onto her knees and pushed herself up from the floor. Kate needed her. Just as she began to rally, a vision of Elizabeth's happy face floated into her mind and she pressed her hand firmly down on the counter.

"What about Elizabeth? Her mother was in the car."

There was a pause, silence for what seemed like eons. Finally, the woman spoke.

"The passenger, yes. Mrs. Fredericks. There was a driver's license in her bag, but we didn't find a phone or any contact information for her husband. We need someone to..." The woman's voice faced.

"To what?" Charlotte's throat constricted as the voice on the other end of the phone halted again. Her stomach twisted as she prepared herself for the blow she sensed was to come. She needed to know.

"You said you needed someone to do something. What do you mean?" she whispered.

"Someone needs to identify her. I'm afraid the passenger, Mrs. Fredericks, was dead on arrival at the hospital."

Charlotte felt bile fill her mouth. Her legs began to shake, and there was a tinny ringing in her ears. As she turned to face the service window, Mungo, as if sensing her need, lifted his head from his task and met her eyes. Seeing her expression, he dropped the spatula, thick with whipped cream, and trotted out of the kitchen and around to the back of the counter.

As she listened to the weighted silence on the line, Charlotte's eyes widened and sticky tears made their way down her cheeks.

She shook her head to clear the woman's words. Dead on arrival. Dead on arrival. Surely she had not heard that?

"Ms. Macfie? I'm terribly sorry, but do you have any contact information for Mr. Fredericks?" The woman coughed, and Charlotte then heard her cover the mouthpiece of the phone and speak to someone near her. The conversation was muffled, but she could make it out. The woman asked if there were any other instructions. A male voice in the background replied, "Just ask her to come here. There's paperwork to be signed, and we need to know if there's a living will."

Charlotte grabbed Mungo's extended arm. Meeting his questioning look, she bent over at the waist and vomited over both his and her own shoes.

CHAPTER 37

———◈———

Having opened the door to the dark uniforms of two Tayside police officers and to the nightmare that this day had delivered, David now sat on the sofa in the living room. The female officer had made him sweet tea that, in a cruel twist, she had brought to him in Elizabeth's favorite mug.

They had asked if he had a relative who could go with him to Aberdeen. David had not answered, just shaken his head. His family was in that car. All of his family was in that car.

He lifted the mug to his mouth but was shaking so much that he dropped it, a dark stain creeping across the pale carpet as he watched, numb and unmoving. He stared down at the mark as it seemed to turn blood red. He closed his eyes and swallowed.

"Is there anyone we can call, Mr. Fredericks?" The young male officer sat opposite him, his black hat dangling from his hands between his open knees. His blonde hair was military-short, and his sympathetic brown eyes scanned the room as if a forgotten family member might be lurking behind a piece of furniture.

David found his voice.

"No. No other family." He shook his head and watched the female officer dab at the tea stain with a towel she'd carried in from the kitchen. As she wiped at the mess he'd made, David saw that it was the towel they'd brought back from Athens. The blue line drawing of the Acropolis on a white background was now bruised with brown, the Greek and English words for Parthenon scrunched up in the young woman's hand.

"A friend, then?" The male officer tried again. "There must be someone?"

Mike's face came to David's mind, and he lifted his gaze from the carpet and nodded.

"A friend. Mike Jenkins. Lives in town." David nodded listlessly towards the river.

"Right, then. Where can we get his number?" The young man was on his feet.

David indicated the phone table in the hall.

"It's in the blue book, in the top drawer."

The policeman walked out into the hall as David leaned his head back on the cushion and closed his eyes. Perhaps if he pressed them closed tightly enough, when he opened them again this would all have gone away. The black-clad officers, the tea stain on the carpet, the knife point pressing up under his sternum, the noise in his ears like rushing water, all an illusion.

He heard the young man speaking into the phone in a hushed tone. He didn't care what he was saying. What he'd already said to David, just a few minutes ago, could never be unsaid. No words would ever hold as much power over him again. *Your wife has been killed in a car accident. Your daughter is in a coma.* He might as well have said to David, *your life is over.*

The female officer returned with another cup of tea.

"Try to drink it, Mr. Fredericks." She smiled down at him. "It might help."

He wondered how old she was. Was she younger than Kate? Kate. His beautiful daughter was in a coma. His beloved wife was dead. Gone.

As he swallowed the tea, tasting nothing, David recalled the last words he'd shared with Elizabeth.

She had made his coffee that morning, as usual, and he had watched her pull on her best coat. She was obviously excited about her day out, pacing along the hall fifteen minutes before Kate was even due to arrive.

He had decided to take his coffee back to bed, not particularly wanting to see Kate, so had kissed his wife on the lips, lingering a few moments longer than he would have ordinarily.

Elizabeth had kissed him back, her eyebrows rising, perhaps at the unexpected intensity of his mouth. True to form, she had sensed his insecurity and had wrapped her arms around his neck.

"Have a good day. Give my love to Kate."

"You're a silly old goat, David Fredericks." Her clear blue eyes had melted his last ounce of reserve, and David had buried his face in her neck.

"I know I am. But I have you to sort me out, don't I?" He had straightened up and then pecked her on the tip of her nose.

"Yes. Lucky for you, you do," she'd replied, winking.

Hearing Kate's car in the driveway, he had pushed Elizabeth gently towards the door before retreating up the stairs.

The male officer came back into the room. He nodded at his partner and sat back down opposite David.

"I spoke to Mr. Jenkins. He's going to be here in about half an hour." He scanned David's blank face.

"Will you be OK until then, or would you like us to wait with you?" The female officer had been standing at the window, but now she moved closer, placing a hand on David's shoulder as she spoke.

"I'll be fine." He wanted them to go. He needed them to go, to get out of this space where he and Elizabeth had exchanged their last words, their last kiss, where their last shared breaths had mingled. These strangers' presence was contaminating the air that still held the musk scent of his wife's perfume. No one else should be breathing that in but him.

The two officers walked down the hallway towards the front door. The man turned and replaced his hat.

"We're very sorry for your loss, Mr. Fredericks." He lowered his eyes, and then they were gone.

David closed the door. His hand looked ghostly against the dark wood, and his feet felt like lead inside his slippers. It was both ludicrous and infuriating that his entire life had fallen apart, and yet his slippers looked exactly the same. The carpet under them was exactly the same. The wallpaper, the sideboard, the phone table, the banister at the stairs – all unchanged, and yet nothing would ever be the same again.

CHAPTER 38

---◆---

Mike had been mercifully silent for most of the journey. When he arrived at the house, he had hugged David, telling him how sorry both he and Clare were. He had washed up the teacups and then waited in the living room while David had changed his clothes, packed a small overnight bag, and locked up the house.

As David left the house, he had wondered if there was any point in locking the doors. Was there any point in anything anymore?

David stared out the window as the A90 rolled noisily under the car.

"You all right, Dave?" Mike looked straight ahead.

"OK." That was all that David could manage.

The two friends fell back into silence as David once again lost himself in thought.

They had told him that Kate was unconscious, that she had a head injury, some other broken bones, and had been operated on for a ruptured spleen. She was alive but in critical condition. What did that really mean?

As the trees and shrubs, the grassy banks and metal road signs sped past the window, David willed his daughter to hang on, to wait for him to get there. The rhythm of the road sounds and the light moving around the blurry objects that they passed combined in his senses, creating a chant that repeated over and over in his head. *Hold on, my Kate, hold on. Hold on, my Kate, hold on.* If he could just get to her, everything would be all right. He was her father, and he'd make it all better. That was his job.

The memory of deliberately distancing himself from her and his petulant behavior over the past few weeks brought hot shame to his face now. If he could just get there in time, he'd make it right. He would fix things. He wouldn't let her down again.

He couldn't stand to lose Kate. The purgatory of that, on top of losing Elizabeth, would be his end.

CHAPTER 39

Charlotte ran a hand through her knotted hair. She had been at Kate's bedside for three hours, and now she needed to get a drink and use the bathroom. Her rucksack, which she'd thrown some clothes and a toothbrush into as she left the flat, sat messy and incongruous in the corner of the otherwise pristine room inside the ICU.

Kate lay motionless, propped up on two pillows. She was intubated, and the breathing apparatus ticked as it forced air in and out of her chest. Another monitor beeped consistently, and her heart rate glowed, the green numbers harsh against a black screen, at the side of the bed. Her left arm was in a cast and her head wrapped in bandages.

As Charlotte watched Kate's smooth eyelids, she held her breath and prayed for movement. A simple flicker, a blink, there had to be something.

The bandage around Kate's head covered most of her skull.

A few strands of pale blonde hair stuck out comically over her left ear, and the sight of them made Charlotte's eyes fill again. Despite all the bandages, tubes, and monitors, she thought Kate looked peaceful.

She reached out and gently squeezed Kate's long fingers. The way they were lying on the cream-colored blanket reminded Charlotte of a ballet dancer gently curving her fingers into a cup, as if to cradle a baby bird.

The nurse had told her that she should talk to Kate, make contact and let her know that she was here. Charlotte had been afraid to touch her, scared that she might inadvertently cause more hurt. But after a while, she had been brave enough to wrap her fingers softly around Kate's limp hand and rub her thumb back and forth across the soft skin.

The room was frigid and smelled of bleach. The long window across from the bed showed a flinty skyline, and Charlotte scanned the buildings, wondering which of them was the university. Which was the place Kate had been heading to when this fetid wormhole had opened up and swallowed her.

She turned her gaze back to the bed. At least she was here with Kate. As her insides roiled, Charlotte recognized that in sharp contrast to her own feelings, there was a sense of peace in the room. Swallowing over a walnut-like knot, Charlotte wondered how long the peaceful veneer would last against what was inevitably to come.

She knew that David was on his way from Broughty Ferry. The thought of officially meeting this man here, today, under these circumstances, brought a new lump to her throat. He had lost his wife. There was nothing more devastating than that, and having lived through it with her own father when her mother had passed away, Charlotte knew the road ahead for David was going to be painful and challenging. She was very much afraid that her relationship with Kate, and her presence here, would be seen as a liberal scattering of salt in his already gaping wound.

She had called her own father before leaving Edinburgh. When she'd told him about Kate and what had happened to poor Elizabeth, he'd wanted to go with her to Aberdeen, but she had refused, knowing that she needed to be alone. As she continued to stroke Kate's hand, her phone buzzed in her pocket. It was another text from him, checking on her. She disentangled her fingers and replied, assuring Duncan that she was fine.

Charlotte stood up and pressed her fists into the small of her back. She had been awkwardly twisting over the side of the bed, trying to avoid the tubes and IV lines as she made contact with Kate. Now she was afraid to leave the room to get a drink in case Kate woke up and she wasn't there. The demands of her bladder, however, outweighed her concern, but for some reason she could not understand, the thought of using the small bathroom behind her was uncomfortable.

"I'll be right back, sweetheart. I'm not leaving you," she whispered, and she patted Kate's leg through the thin blanket.

Stepping out into the corridor, she saw a nurse behind the long desk where she had checked in when she'd arrived. Charlotte walked over and cleared her throat.

"I'm just going to the ladies and then to find something to drink. I'll be about ten minutes." She scanned the fresh face in front of her. The young woman nodded and smiled.

"You take a wee break. I'll keep an eye on her. The cafeteria is down towards orthopedics." She pointed to her right.

"Thanks." Charlotte nodded. "I won't be long."

From what she had seen so far, the hospital was enormous. The corridors were long, their surfaces squeaky underfoot, and row upon row of identical doors leading to other departments and multiple staircases meant that Charlotte had to concentrate on where she was going so that she'd be able to find her way back.

After what seemed like an age, she spotted the sign for the ladies' room. Grateful and relieved, she pushed the heavy door open, hoping there would be no one else inside. There was no way she could muster a polite smile or greeting should she come across anyone else at the moment.

Catching sight of herself in the mirror, she stopped. Her hair was wild, dark curls spiraling mutinously away from the crown of her head. Her skin was grey, and her pale eyes looked huge in her pinched face. How was it possible that Kate, this marvelous, natural blonde, Amazonian braniac she had fallen in love with, could love that odd little face back? Charlotte gasped and swallowed fresh tears. Kate would not leave her now. She couldn't leave her now that their life together was truly beginning.

She washed her hands and smoothed her hair, tucked some strands back behind her ears, and then remembered Elizabeth. She was dead, broken, lying in the cold morgue, waiting for David. Once again, her heart went out to him. What could be more hellish than having to confirm that the person lying on an impersonal hospital table was indeed your loved one? She couldn't even imagine. When – not if – Kate woke up, she would have to tell her that her mother was gone. It was particularly cruel that now, just when Kate had begun to realize that Elizabeth loved her and accepted her for who she was, that newfound closeness with her mother would be brought to such a brutal close.

Having found the cafeteria, Charlotte walked back along the labyrinth of corridors, hoping she was heading in the right direction. She'd bought herself a coffee and two bottles of water. She hadn't eaten anything since four that morning, but there was no way she would be able to force any food down right now. Her stomach ached with emptiness, but not from hunger.

Ahead of her, she saw the sign for the ICU. Relieved, she picked up her pace, smiling at the nurse who still sat at the desk as she approached. As she passed, in the corner of her eye she saw the young woman stand up and raise a hand, as if trying to catch her attention. Not stopping in her progress, Charlotte proceeded into the room.

A man was sitting in her chair. His long back was covered by a dark coat, and a shock of wavy silver hair was brushed back tidily over his ears. His large, tanned hand covered Kate's paler one, and as Charlotte stopped in her tracks, she noticed his back quivering. She wasn't sure if he was crying or if it was just from the effort of breathing. She stood still, frozen, suddenly unsure of her right to be there, of her place in the room. No sooner had the thought entered her head than she pushed it down. She was Kate's partner. She had every right to be there.

She tiptoed over to the small table that sat against the wall and placed her coffee cup down. The plastic water bottles crackled as she sat them on the surface, causing the man to start and turn his head towards her. She cringed at the noise she'd made and raised her eyes to meet his. They were Kate's eyes, wide-set, soft, blue and questioning.

David Fredericks sat in front of her. His face was haggard. Under normal circumstances, Charlotte's instinct would have been to wrap her arms around his sad frame and offer him some comfort. Instead, she stopped the impulse, pulled her shoulders back, and steeled herself for what she suspected was the unpleasantness to come.

He stood up slowly and, facing her, pulled the flaps of his coat together across his broad chest. Charlotte felt herself shrinking as he assessed her, his mouth pressed closed and his disapproving expression saying all that he wasn't able to voice.

They stood and looked at each other, mute, suffering. Charlotte saw the raw pain in his face. He wore it like a mask. She felt her resolve cracking. She needed to make the first move. That much was obvious. He was drowning, and she could throw him a rope. Extending her hand, she stepped towards him.

"David. Mr. Fredericks. I'm Charlotte. I'm so sorry about your wife."

David watched her advance and immediately shoved his hands into his coat pockets, standing his ground.

Charlotte felt her nerves kick up a notch. She dropped her hand and stopped moving forward. She couldn't believe he would blank her now, not in this horrendous situation. There had to be more depth to Kate's father than this, surely?

David remained still and silent. Only his eyes moved, tracing her outline, her hair, her face, and her clothing. What was he thinking? Seeing him now in front of her, she was in no doubt that this was the man who had come to The Bakery that day. His jaw ticked in the same way it had when he'd stood at her counter, stammering over which scones to buy and then asking her if she owned the business.

Charlotte was overcome with the sudden desire to back away from him. Rather than injured, he looked angry now, his sadness eclipsed by what seemed like a bone-deep fury that he was struggling to keep down. Why had she spoken first?

She squirmed under his penetrating gaze. He had still not said a word. This was becoming excruciating. A few feet behind him, wired up to tubes and beeping machines and struggling for her life, was a woman they both loved. Could he not see past his ridiculous prejudices and take that in?

She couldn't stand his cold scrutiny any longer. Her own anger rising, she dropped her gaze and cleared her throat. Just as she was preparing to speak again, another man walked into the room carrying two paper cups.

"Oh, sorry. I didn't realize there was anyone else here. I'd have brought you a drink." The tall, thin man carefully placed the steaming cups on the side table next to Kate's bed. He wore a raincoat and heavy brown brogues, his hair was sandy-colored, and his eyes, a friendly hazel, smiled at her.

"That's OK," she replied, smiling back, grateful for the perfectly timed distraction. "I just got myself something." She nodded behind her to the cup she'd brought in herself.

"Oh, good. My name's Mike Jenkins. I'm a friend of David and …" The man hesitated, then turned to look at his friend. Seeing David snap his head towards him, Mike turned back to Charlotte and continued, "Of David and Elizabeth's." He reached his hand out to her and Charlotte grasped it in hers.

"I'm Charlotte. I'm…"

Behind Mike, David stood with wide eyes. His mouth had fallen slightly open and everything about his tense stance was asking her for something. Instantly she knew what it was that he wanted.

"I'm a friend of Kate's." The words stuck in her throat like barbed wire, but glancing over at David, what she saw in his face was unmistakable relief. He returned her gaze and gave her an almost imperceptible nod. She saw gratitude seep into his eyes, and while it pained her to deny her true relationship with Kate this way, it was what needed to be done.

She released Mike's hand and turned to retrieve her coffee. It was going to be a long night.

CHAPTER 40

D avid couldn't get the picture of Elizabeth out of his mind. Her face had looked so normal, so clean and unchanged. In the car on the way up to Aberdeen, he had been imagining her battered and ravaged by the crash, her face torn, her beautiful eyes like black holes, and her hair matted with blood. They had told him that her neck had been broken by the impact. Instantaneous death was what they'd said. Painless. Merciful. What the hell did they know?

The hospital had kept her in a small room inside the morgue, and David had been accompanied by a pathologist and a police officer when he'd gone in to identify her body.

The pathologist was in his mid-fifties, a short, bald, whitecoated, TV-drama caricature type that he knew Elizabeth would have smirked at had she seen him on one of her favorite medical dramas. However, he'd been kind and respectful and had asked if David would like to be alone with his wife. David had responded with a silent nod.

When the white sheet had been pulled back, David steeled himself for the worst his imagination had lined up for him. To his relief, her lovely face remained intact. Her skin, when he reached out and touched it, was still soft if cold. Her eyelids lay heavy across her usually expressive eyes, and he saw traces of the brown shadow she had so carefully applied that morning.

There had been no sign of blood on her head or shoulders, the only visible sign of damage being a small plum-colored bruise that shadowed her left temple. Her hair was brushed back from her forehead and splayed out on the sheet beneath her. He'd been in no doubt that someone had painstakingly cleaned her up, combing her hair and wiping away any visible traces of the means of her death. He was as sure of that as he was grateful to whomever it had been.

Now, as he stood in Kate's room staring at this small, dark-haired woman in front of him, with Mike between them as an oblivious buffer, his heart was racing. Charlotte looked so pale, so thin and waif-like; and yet, rather than sympathy, he felt overwhelming resentment towards her. He pictured slapping her little face, screaming at her to get out of the room and just leave him with his daughter. How dare she presume to be here? How dare she talk to him, to offer condolences? She barely knew Elizabeth and knew nothing about him or his pain. How could she empathize with something she had never experienced – a lifetime together with someone being torn away, a marriage that had lasted through turmoil and mistakes being gut-wrenchingly terminated. His relationship with Elizabeth had produced Kate, the only remaining light in his life. Who the hell did Charlotte think she was to be sorry for him?

Mike turned towards David and smiled nervously.

"Shall I leave you two alone for a wee bit?"

David and Charlotte responded like a well-rehearsed duo.

"No." Charlotte said.

"No." David echoed.

Mike nodded, seeming to be confused by the urgency of their matched tones. He pulled a second chair over to the bedside and gestured towards it.

"Please, sit down," he said to Charlotte as he handed David a cup of coffee and pressed his friend down into the other chair.

David acquiesced under Mike's guiding hand. He lifted the cup to his lips. His hands were shaking as he sipped the bitter liquid and felt it burn his tight throat as he swallowed.

Mike coughed and turned to Charlotte.

"So, how do you know Kate? Do you work at the university, too?"

Charlotte sat on the edge of her chair, her own cup held in front of her. David noticed her eyes swivel towards him at Mike's question, and he glared at her, hoping she could interpret his silent warning.

"No. We're friends, but not from work." Charlotte lowered her eyes to the floor and sipped her drink.

David felt his diaphragm relax. At least she had had the decency not to embarrass herself, and him, by saying something inane about being Kate's girlfriend. Surely, in the face of all this tragedy, that little drama had lived out its course? Perhaps Charlotte would just fade away now, this elfin woman who clung to his daughter like an unwelcome limpet. Perhaps now that Kate was in trouble, this woman would show her true colors and head for the hills?

David reached out his free hand and wrapped it over Kate's. She was cool to the touch, but not as cool as Elizabeth had been. At the memory of his wife, passive, still, serene as she lay down in the basement as if waiting for dawn to break so she could wake up, David screwed up his eyes. He felt the pain in his head, on his scalp, under his skin, in his bones and teeth. It was making him catch his breath.

Obviously seeing his struggle, Mike placed a hand on David's back. David felt the strong pressure of sympathy, and it was all he could do not to shrug his friend off. It was all right for Mike, he would go home to Clare tonight. His life had not shattered into a million slivers of hell that he would have to walk barefoot over every day for the rest of his life.

David filled his aching lungs and willed himself to accept the small gesture of support his friend had offered. After all, Mike had been good enough to drive David here and accompany him down to the morgue, where he'd then waited in a small, windowless room nearby until David re-emerged.

David opened his eyes and looked at his daughter. Her mouth was obscured by the breathing device, and her head was all but covered in bandages. She didn't look like herself, and yet it was unmistakably Kate. He needed her to open her eyes, raise a hand, see his face, and breathe on her own.

"Kate? Darling. It's Dad." His voice sounded brittle, rattling inside his head.

He squeezed her hand again and willed her on with every cell in his body. *Open your eyes, Kate. Just open your eyes.*

217

CHAPTER 41

———◆———

Three days had passed, and Charlotte and David had reached an agreement that they would take turns at Kate's bedside. David took the night shift, from midnight to five in the morning, which allowed Charlotte to rest until she took over from him between five and noon.

The hospital would not allow either of them to sleep in Kate's room, but they had been given the use of a narrow bed in an empty room in the orthopedic department, where Charlotte had lain each night, spending much of the time awake and staring at the ceiling.

She and David split the afternoon hours between them. As one of them left and the other entered the room in the ICU, their time with Kate handed over like a precious baton, their exchanges remained curt, often monosyllabic. It distressed Charlotte that this was the situation, but despite her several attempts to connect with David, he had made it clear that he had no interest in her or in anything she had to say. She imagined that she could taste his resentment, smell it in the air each time he looked at her.

During her agreed-upon time slots, Charlotte had barely left Kate's room.

Kate was stable but had made no visible progress as regards waking or breathing on her own. The neurology consultant had told Charlotte that the first few days were critical in terms of brain injuries and the ability to gauge the potential for recovery. At this point, they knew that there was still some brain swelling, which was cause for concern. She had also told Charlotte that some patients with Kate's type of injury would wake up after a few days and be completely normal, suffering no significant aftereffects. Others could take weeks or months to come around and then might experience memory loss, disorientation, loss of sensation or weakness in their limbs.

The consultant had said that Kate's brain activity was good, so she was hopeful that there would be no permanent damage. However, she followed up by saying that there were no guarantees when it came to the brain.

Three of the first critical days had passed since the accident, and Charlotte was counting the hours, mumbling encouragement to Kate and to herself like a mantra, waiting, hoping, and praying for some sign that Kate was coming back to her.

Her morning stint was coming to a close, and she could sense David hovering in the hallway.

She squeezed Kate's hand, leaned over, and kissed her forehead through the bandages.

"I'm going to go now, sweetheart. I'll be back in a few hours. I love you, Kate."

David stood in the doorway. He was disheveled, his hair needed a comb, and his sweater had food stains on the front. From what she could surmise, he had brought only one change of clothes and was in desperate need of some fresh ones. She, at least, had thought to grab several shirts and sets of underwear, knowing that she could get by with the jeans she was wearing as long as she could change the rest of her clothes regularly. She had taken to washing a couple of things through each morning and hanging them in the small bathroom in Kate's room. She was careful to remove them before she switched with David, anxious that he not be assaulted by her personal clothing, thereby adding insult to injury.

He nodded at her as she passed. He was holding a newspaper, a plastic-wrapped sandwich from the cafeteria, and a small bunch of carnations he'd apparently bought at the hospital shop. They were an unnatural shade of pink, and as he carried them at his side, Charlotte thought it apt that they drooped their ugly heads towards the floor.

She nodded back at David, taking in his appearance. He was a stubborn old fool, but she couldn't help but feel sorry for him. If only he'd open his eyes and his mind, they could help each other through this.

Before she could stop herself, Charlotte turned back.

"David?"

He swiveled on his heel, as if shocked by the sound of her voice.

"Yes?"

"Is there anything I can do? I mean, to help with arrangements for Elizabeth?" She swallowed. This could be a can of worms, but if she didn't keep trying, things would never improve between them.

His face was moving in a strange way; his lips were pursed, and he blinked so rapidly that she wondered if he was going to pass out. Charlotte stood still, watching him work through whatever internal conflict he was dealing with. Suddenly, he lifted the flowers and jabbed them towards her.

"What could you possibly do?" He hissed. "You barely even *knew* my wife." A single fat tear brimmed over the bottom of his right eye, and he swiped it away with the back of the hand still holding the carnations. He narrowly missed Charlotte's face with the flowers as they swung out towards her. She stepped back, drawing her chin in towards her chest to avoid being struck. This was the last straw.

"I know that she was a wonderful, caring woman who loved her daughter unconditionally. And I know she wouldn't want this." Charlotte's palm slid back and forth between them.

She regretted the words as soon as they were out. She knew mentioning Elizabeth would provoke him, create more anger and vitriol, but she had reached her threshold for taking abuse from this man.

David gasped. He took a step back and glared at her. As she watched his features twisting, as abruptly as it had sparked into life, the fire seemed to go out of his anger. He took on a distant look, and his shoulders slumped as he dropped the flowers back towards the floor. He looked broken, exhausted.

"David, are you all right?" Charlotte took a small step towards him.

Rather than back away from her as she'd expected, he shook his head. As he raised his eyes to hers, she saw them full of tears. Charlotte held her breath.

"You're right." He spoke quietly, but with the words, a sob

escaped him, then another almost primal burst of pain followed. Charlotte stood transfixed, unsure what to do. She was hurting for him. Should she wrap her arms around him? Would he tolerate her sympathy now, when he had so brutally rejected it before?

As if answering her silent questions, David gave in to his grief. Seeing his legs begin to buckle, Charlotte hooked her arm through his, led him into the room, and then helped him into a chair. As he gulped and sobbed, she lifted the flowers and food from his hands and placed them on the bedside table.

"Stay here. I'll be back in a minute." She patted his quivering back, turned and left the room.

Charlotte trotted along the corridor towards the cafeteria. Her mind was racing as she bought two cups of tea and a packet of Kit-Kats. She made her way back to Kate's room, running through various scenarios in her mind. Perhaps David would have thought better of his epiphany and have settled back into his anger by the time she got there? Perhaps he'd have disintegrated and she'd find him in a heap on the floor? He could have closed the door to start his shift, locking her out of both the room and any further interaction.

As she rounded the final corner, she saw that the door was still open. Relieved, Charlotte slowed her pace and walked into the room. David had put the flowers in a vase on the bedside table and was sitting on the far side of Kate's bed, his hand over hers. He was leaning in and whispering to her. Charlotte couldn't hear what he said, but as she approached, he sat up and met her gaze.

"Here's some hot tea and there's something for later." She placed the Kit-Kats on the table. Embarrassed at her choice of biscuits, Charlotte felt her face flush.

"Thanks." David nodded and accepted the cup she held out

to him.

She nodded back at him and, holding her own cup in front of herself, made to walk away. This was a definite truce, of sorts, and she'd accept its terms. However basic, this was progress.

"You could stay for a bit, if you're not too tired?" David's voice was rough, as if from disuse, as he lifted the steaming cup to his lips and blew on the surface of the dark liquid.

Charlotte started at his unexpected invitation, then felt a release of some of the pent-up tension lingering under her diaphragm. Had he just asked her to stay? Letting this new development sink in, she took a deep breath and then nodded.

The second chair sat close to the wall, so she reached over and dragged it to the bedside. Settling herself, Charlotte sipped her tea and looked down at Kate. She'd had a little more color in her face when Charlotte had come in that morning, and, while it might be her imagination, despite there being no visible signs of change, she felt that Kate seemed more present in the room,

"Don't you think she looks different today?" Charlotte kept her voice low as she scanned David's face. "She has more color."

David looked at his daughter, then ran a hand over his messy hair.

"You could be right." He nodded. "I asked the doctor if they could see any improvement, but it seems it's a waiting game." He shrugged.

Charlotte gave him a half smile. She didn't want to push things, but it felt like a bridge was forming between them. If all they could do was talk about Kate's condition, then that was enough for now. Kate was the commonality between them, perhaps the only thing that they would ever have in common.

The two sat in silence. Charlotte's fatigue was forgotten, and before long, she realized that two hours had passed. Her back ached, and she needed to use the bathroom, but she was reluctant to stand up and risk cracking the film of peace that had settled over her and David. She shifted in the chair.

David turned to look at her. He seemed to be taking in her face, her hair, and her clothes as if it was the first time he'd ever seen her. Charlotte felt herself blushing under the not unkind scrutiny.

"Why don't you get some sleep?" David's eyes were on her face. "It's almost two. I can stay a while longer, then I'll leave you alone for a bit, before I come back tonight." He nodded towards Kate as he spoke.

Charlotte felt the prickle of tears. These were the first kind words that she had heard from David since all this had happened. She had been letting his pain-induced fury wash over her, trying to take it in her stride, but his harsh unkindness and aggression towards her had been eating away at her. Now that he was offering an olive branch, she felt the tenuous grip on her emotions slipping. She hadn't cried yet. She'd been so focused on the practical elements of this situation that she had not allowed herself to succumb.

Charlotte felt David's eyes on her as she struggled to control the surge of fear that was making its way up into her chest. The wall of pressure at the back of her throat finally gave way, and she folded at the waist. Her forehead on her knees, she felt her face contort into an ugly grimace. She stayed there, afraid to sit up or be vulnerable once more to David's potential disdain.

Her jeans were soon damp against her thighs, and as she tried to stop the force of her crying, she was unable to fill her lungs.

Just as the sobs began to subside, she felt a hand on her back. The contact caused her to gasp. She lifted her head and saw David standing behind her. He rubbed his hand across her shoulders, and she rocked slowly, receiving this small and yet significant gesture of caring and – dare she hope? – acceptance.

CHAPTER 42

David watched as Charlotte walked away from the room. She had cried for over twenty minutes, and with each tearing sob, he had felt his guilt at his treatment of her stab him. As Charlotte had given way to her own pain, he had imagined Elizabeth watching him, shaking her head in disappointment at his lack of empathy.

Charlotte saying so emphatically that Elizabeth would not have approved of his behavior had snapped something inside him, and he had fallen headlong into a vat of his own shame. Charlotte was right. Of course she was right. This was the time that Kate needed him to be a father. She needed him to be there for her and for the people she loved. If Charlotte was someone Kate loved, then surely, somewhere inside him he could find the ability to give this woman the benefit of the doubt? Symmetry or no, this was his new reality, and he must find a way to make it bearable.

Mike had called him the day before and offered to come back to Aberdeen with some clean clothes for him. He had told Mike not to bother, but remembering his friend's kindness, David looked down at his sweater. He had spilled tomato soup on it the day before and hadn't even bothered to sponge it. Elizabeth would have been shocked, telling him to get cleaned up before anyone saw him or thought that his wife didn't care about him. His throat tightened at the thought of her scolding him with a smile on her face. The face he pictured was the one he'd watched across the living room, the one that he'd seen asleep on the pillow next to him, the familiar profile he'd taken in as she soaked up her favorite view of the river – not the face downstairs underneath the white sheet.

As he squeezed his eyes shut, David reached for Kate's hand. Here, at least, he was grounded. He could feel her pulse under his fingers, and that tiny beat would have to be enough to sustain him for now.

Today he knew he had to deal with Elizabeth's funeral arrangements, and he dreaded it with every cell in his body. The idea that she would be transported back to Broughty Ferry in a windowless van made his stomach churn. He knew that she'd wanted to be buried in the cemetery close to the river, and he was glad that they'd discussed their wishes with each other a few years earlier when they'd registered their wills with their solicitor.

David had always assumed that he would go first. He had never imagined that he would be left to take care of this for his wife. God forbid he needed to do it for Kate, too. As the notion flashed into his mind, David felt as if he might vomit.

He sat up straight and took a deep breath. Outside the window, the day was bright. The sky, a stretch of blue dotted with a few thin clouds, seemed incongruous to the atmosphere inside this room. The beeping machines and flashing monitors had faded into the background, and all David could hear was the swish of air going in and out of his daughter's lungs. That was the only sound in the universe.

A nurse padded into the room, checked Kate's pulse, then adjusted the IV bag.

"How's she doing?" she asked David.

"The same." He replied, holding tight to Kate's wrist.

"Well, hang in there. She's young and strong." The nurse smiled.

David nodded. Despite knowing the woman's kind motivation, he felt a surge of anger at the obvious platitude. He bit back his retort, with Elizabeth's voice coming to him. *If you can't say something nice, say nothing at all.*

Charlotte had offered to help him with the funeral arrangements. He knew that she wanted to be supportive, but he felt that this was something he needed to do alone. He was glad that they had found a way to be in the same room together, albeit for small stretches of time. He knew that it was her compassion that had formed the bridge between them. Despite his bad treatment of her, she hadn't given up, and that had to say something about her as a person.

The funeral would be in three days, and in order to get everything done, he knew he'd have to go home. He was afraid to leave Kate, but there was nothing else he could do. Elizabeth couldn't wait.

CHAPTER 43

———◈———

Charlotte squeezed the water out of her T-shirt and draped it over the rail in the small bathroom. This was the fourth day that she had been at the hospital, and she was worried about the bakery. Mungo had said that everything was going fine but, contrary to her long-term plans for him, this had been a true baptism by fire as regards him taking on more responsibility. She had been calling often through the day, but the last time she'd spoken to him, she'd sensed his growing anxiety about when she was coming back.

As she hung a pair of damp socks over the rail next to the T-shirt, she imagined Kate being transferred and ensconced in a sunny room at Edinburgh Royal Infirmary, an easy trip from The Bakery and from their home. Was it terribly selfish of her to think of the convenience of that?

She looked at her reflection and shook her head. She was in a state. She longed for her own bed, to soak in the bathtub, and to dry herself with a towel that didn't feel like sandpaper. No sooner had she entertained the thoughts of home than she felt guilty. How shallow she was, when Kate was lying in a coma with no options open to her other than to be right where she was.

Her phone vibrated in her pocket. Pulling it out, she saw The Bakery number.

"Hi. What's up?" she whispered, then recognized the irony over her concern about the volume of her voice when Kate was unconscious. Hospitals had a way of hushing loud voices, much as churches could.

"Just checking in." Mungo sounded distracted, and she could hear music and voices in the background.

"Everything OK?"

"Yeah. Fine. Do you want me to re-order coffee? The supplier called this morning and I wasn't sure if you wanted me to go ahead or what." His voice faded.

"Yes, definitely. Just tell him to send the usual amount for the week. If he wants to talk to me, you can give him my cell number." Charlotte looked at herself in the mirror. She noticed a smudge under her left eye, so she leaned in and wiped at the mark with her finger.

"OK." Mungo's voice sounded flat.

"I'm sorry to be away this long, Mungo. It's just that we don't know how long she'll be…" Charlotte swallowed the end of her sentence.

"Look, boss, it's OK, honest. We're busy, but Chloe is coming in a couple of hours early to help me with prep, and when we get desperate, we're using a few day-old things for the breakfast crowd, just to give us time to get the fresh batches out for lunch."

He sounded characteristically unsure of himself as he shared the information.

Charlotte felt a bubble of indignation at the back of her throat. She never used day-old anything. It was a policy of hers that everything should be baked fresh on the day. As she struggled with how to let Mungo know she was not comfortable with his decision, she closed her eyes and pushed down the instinct to complain. He was working wonders without her, so she had to give him leeway to cut some corners if need be.

"No problem. If you want to lower the price on the morning items, that's fine, too. I'll leave that up to you." She smiled at her reflection, pleased that she was empowering him despite her initial reaction to his decision.

"All right, we'll see how it goes." He sounded brighter, her words seeming to give him back his confidence.

"I'm waiting to speak to the doctor, then I'll call you this afternoon. I should have a better idea of when I can come back once I've spoken to her." Charlotte nodded at her reflection as she spoke, as if reassuring herself that she'd have some news that day.

Mungo wished her well and hung up. It was time she gave him a raise, maybe even promoted him sooner than she'd planned. He'd earned it.

She walked back into the room just as a nurse came in to check Kate's vitals. The IV bag was almost empty, so as she watched, the nurse hung a new one, checked Kate's pulse and blood pressure, and then straightened the light blanket over the long, non-responsive thighs.

It seemed as if Kate were melting into the bed. She was losing weight, and each day, as the nurses tucked the clean sheets and blanket around her willowy form, Charlotte felt she was seeing more sharp edges of bone protruding through the flimsy covers.

Charlotte nodded as the young woman left the room. She wondered what the medical team was saying while they ate their lunches in the break room. Were they talking about the poor disheveled woman who was waiting for her lover to wake up? Were they thinking it was sad to watch her waiting for a sign of something that might never come? Perhaps they thought it odd that she and Kate's father seemed to be so distant from each other, so formal? As she felt another twinge of pain in her lower back, Charlotte exhaled. She didn't care what they thought so long as Kate opened her eyes and saw her sitting there. However long that took.

David had told her that he would be going home that afternoon to make arrangements for Elizabeth's funeral. She had once again offered to help him, but he'd told her how important it was for him to take care of it alone. Charlotte had accepted his response and backed off, understanding that she was approaching thin ice. She appreciated their newfound truce for what it was and had learned from previous experience not to create any waves, especially when it came to Elizabeth.

David was due to come in any minute and spend a few hours with Kate before heading home. Mike was coming to pick him up and drive him back, and David had said he hoped to return to Aberdeen within forty-eight hours. He planned on spending one more day with Kate before returning to Broughty Ferry for the service.

Charlotte settled herself in the chair next to the window. She laced her fingers through Kate's and began to sing a low lullaby. She rocked as she sang, and the words, igniting memories of her own mother's comforting presence, brought fresh tears to her eyes.

David was in the doorway. He looked flustered. His face was red and his hair more unruly than when she'd seen him earlier that day. He wore his coat, and in his left hand, he carried a clear plastic bag. Bigger than a normal shopping bag, it touched the ground next to his foot. He said nothing, his eyes piercing blue in their intensity.

"David. Are you OK?" Charlotte stood and walked towards him.

He looked manic as he shook his head, working his lips hard against each other as if struggling to keep some painful secret.

She reached him and placed a hand on his arm.

"What's going on?"

David leaned in towards her and dropped his head as the bag bulged on the floor.

"Her things. Her coat. The shoes." David's voice cracked, his face crumpled, then his knees buckled and he fell to the floor. The bag, loosed from his grip, gaped open at the top, and Charlotte caught sight of the cream wool coat and on top of it, a single blue high-heeled shoe.

"Oh, David." She slid down onto the floor next to him, pushed the bag away with her foot, and as her throat began to constrict, she lifted his tattered head into her lap.

CHAPTER 44

———◆———

The pub was dark inside and smelled of cigarettes. The surface of the bar was tacky under his palm as David emptied the glass of whisky Charlotte had bought him. She'd gone outside to make a phone call, and as he waited for her, he stared at his reflection in the mirror behind the rows of half-full bottles.

He didn't recognize the person he saw there – haggard, grey-skinned, crazy-haired, and slouching over a glass. Embarrassed, he smoothed his hands over each ear, then pulled his sweater down at the back, sitting up straighter. It had been an hour or so since he'd collapsed in the hospital, and while his insides were still quivering, he felt somewhat revived by the change of scenery and the drink.

Charlotte had been a rock. She had taken charge, closing the door to Kate's room, helping him up and into the chair, and then taking the bag with Elizabeth's belongings and tucking it out of sight in the bathroom. She'd wet a flannel and wiped his face like a child's, then instructed him to stay put while she figured out where the nearest pub was.

Slains Castle was where the taxi driver had dropped them. It wasn't too far from the hospital, and yet to David it had felt like a different country as they'd walked inside the old Gothic church building on Belmont Street.

The vampire-themed decor, which the bartender informed them was inspired by Bram Stoker's *Dracula*, had even sparked a nervous exchange of laughter between himself and Charlotte.

Having ordered their drinks and two sirloin steak dinners, Charlotte had sat next to him at the bar, her legs barely reaching the crossbar of the tall stool. David thought she looked childlike next to his own lanky frame. However, despite her tiny build, this woman had proved herself to be strong, compassionate, and brave in the few days he'd spent time around her. She was obviously devoted to his daughter, and no matter how hard he tried to disapprove, David found himself warming to her. The way she had just handled his breakdown had been discreet, calm, nonjudgmental, and effective. Whatever else transpired, he was grateful to her for that and would never forget it.

As he pushed his empty glass towards the bartender, nodding to accept a refill, the door opened and Charlotte came back in, along with a gust of frigid air. She slipped her phone into her coat pocket as she climbed back up onto the stool next to his.

"Everything OK here?" she asked, lifting her glass of wine to her lips. "No one sucking on your neck or anything?" She smiled at David.

He shrugged and accepted his refilled glass.

"Seems I'm not very tasty-looking."

Charlotte laughed and lifted her glass to him in a salute.

He touched his glass to hers, then swallowed a mouthful of peaty, twelve-year-old Macallan, enjoying the enlivening burn of its passage down his throat. This superior twelve-year-old whisky would not have been something he'd usually have chosen, but today it was more than warranted. What reason was there to be circumspect now?

He watched as Charlotte sipped her wine. Her hair was tied up at the back of her neck, with just a few dark tendrils curling around her ears. Her pale blue sweater hung loose around her body, and her jeans were tucked into brown suede boots which seemed to accentuate the smallness of her feet. She wore a ring on the middle finger of her left hand that he hadn't noticed before. Catching the glint of gold as she placed her glass back on the bar, David's breath caught in his throat. Blinking to clear his vision, he focused on the ring. It was the one he and Elizabeth had given Kate on her twenty-first birthday. A white gold band with a square-cut topaz, the smoky stone looked dark against Charlotte's pale skin. Before he could stop himself, David reached out and lifted her hand.

Charlotte's face paled under his silent gaze. She squirmed on the stool and pulled her hand back.

"I'm sorry, David. It was with her personal things in the hospital. I'm just wearing it for safekeeping until she wakes up."

He could see fear in her face as she spoke. He wasn't sure whether it was fear of his reaction to her wearing the ring or of the notion that Kate might not wake up. He felt ashamed that he had made her so nervous of him.

"It's all right. She'd want you to wear it, I'm sure. Better it's safe with you than in some bag in her room." David nodded.

They ate in silence, and after their coffee cups were drained, Charlotte asked the bartender to call them a taxi. She reached into her bag for her purse, but David patted the air, indicating that he was paying. Charlotte caught the gesture and nodded her assent.

The taxi bumped across the university campus back towards the hospital. David watched the stone façades changing as they passed, and wondered halfheartedly what era the buildings were from. There was a good deal of wonderful architecture in Aberdeen, and he'd been here once in his twenties to visit, among a long list of A-Class architectural wonders, the North of Scotland Bank building, designed by local architect Archibald Simpson. He remembered the feeling he'd experienced as he'd stood across from the building on the corner of Castle and King Streets. He'd felt both exhilarated and subdued at the same time. The perfect, symmetrical, pillared façade, wrapping itself around the corner of the two streets, was simplistic in its grandeur and had brought a lump to his throat. Sighing, he closed his eyes. That was back when people knew how to design buildings.

Charlotte shifted next to him. She'd been keeping an eye on the time for David so that he would be ready for Mike when he arrived. She glanced at him, then turned her head and looked out the window.

"Are you sure you're going to be all right, going home, I mean?"

He knew what she was saying, and the thought of opening the door to the house and walking into the reality of its emptiness was weighing heavily on him.

"I'll be all right. I have to deal with it sometime." He shrugged.

"I can come back with you, just to help get the house set up for the reception. I could take care of the food and stuff and then I'll leave you to it. I won't intrude." She turned to face him, her eyes brimming with sympathy.

David considered the idea for no more than a moment. If she were at the house and someone came by, how would he explain her? Who could he say she was? How would her presence make sense? No, there was no way he was ready for that. He shook his head.

"No. But thanks. I'll be fine."

She nodded and turned back to look out the window. He heard her sigh but chose not to acknowledge the subtle sound of her disappointment.

Kate's room seemed even colder than usual. As David rubbed his hands together, he wondered why it was necessary to keep it at such a glacial temperature. He sat next to the bed and held her hand in his.

"I'm going to pop home today, love. Just for a night or so. I've got some things to do at the house, but Charlotte will be here with you. You'll not be alone, and I won't be gone long." He kissed the back of the slender fingers. "You just rest now, and I'll see you soon."

David swallowed hard as he rose and walked around the bed towards the door. Would this be the last time he'd see his daughter alive? No. He had to banish that thought from his mind if he was going to get through the next day or so.

Charlotte stood out in the hallway, having given him time alone with Kate to say goodbye. He lifted the overnight bag that he had brought with him, and the two walked down the long corridor towards the exit.

Having reached the door, David turned to Charlotte.

"You'll call me if there's any change? Anything at all?"

She smiled up at him.

"Of course I will. Don't worry."

He nodded, and just as he was about to walk away, Charlotte rose on her tiptoes and kissed his cheek. Her mouth was warm and dry on his face, and the contact was both unexpected and shocking. David jerked back, on a reflex, then instantly regretted his reaction when he saw the hurt cross her face.

He reached out and touched her arm.

"Sorry. It's just that everything hurts at the moment." He scanned her face and was relieved to see understanding in her eyes.

"I get it. No worries. Just take care and let me know how you are, if you need anything."

David walked out into the chilly evening. Spotting Mike's silver car parked in a visitor's spot, he made his way over towards his friend. As they pulled away from the hospital, David saw Charlotte standing in the doorway. She raised a hand and waved before turning back inside.

CHAPTER 45

The darkness was thick and chewy. Kate felt her bones soft, heavy. What was she lying on? Her eyelids felt like lead, not responding to her request to lift. It was easier to keep them closed for now, as she was too tired to fight them open.

She was aware of a smell, like toast. Was she hungry? What time was it? Her legs ached as if she'd been on a long run, and yet she couldn't feel where they started or finished. The muscles were loose but tight at the same time, and even although she asked her feet to move, they resisted her. She was tired. More tired than she ever remembered feeling before. If only she could get her eyes to open, then she could check the time.

There were noises close to her. She could hear a familiar voice, too soft to discern. It was low, song-like, lulling her back to sleep. Mum? Charlotte? She wanted to listen. Wait. Don't sleep again. The voice felt good, like a blanket over her aching, non-existent body. Why was she so cold? There was no weight of covers on her.

Was she in the right bed?

There was another voice, stronger this time and to her left side. This one was deeper toned, a man. Was it her dad? Open up, eyes, damn you. Something was filling her throat, and a weight across her mouth kept her still, as if she were pinned to the surface below her. What was in her throat? Perhaps if she swallowed, it would go away? Now swallowing was not happening either. What was wrong with her body? She was too tired.

The man's voice halted, and the softer voice took over again.

What was that whooshing noise? Louder than the voices, it almost obliterated the soft undertone of whomever was talking to her. Shhhh. Let me listen to the voices.

There was pressure on her hand. She felt pressure. Could she press back? She wanted to press back. No. Her arms were gone. There was nothing there but space and weight. God, she was cold.

The whooshing sound came again, and with it a disconcerting lifting of her chest. What *was* that in her throat? She wanted to lick her lips, but her tongue was pressed down underneath something heavy, so it remained idle, flat.

The gentle voice stopped. All she could hear was the whooshing, taking over everything. If it had sounded like the ocean, it would have been comforting, but this was more like a set of old fireside bellows. It was loud and annoyingly close to her. Where had the voices gone?

She focused all her energy on listening. Beneath the whooshing, she heard the two voices now. The man, it was her father, was saying that he was sorry. What was he sorry about? Where was her mother? The softer voice was there too, saying that it would be OK. Damn, the bellows were loud. Perhaps if she tried to open her eyes again? No, no light was coming in. She could hear beeping now, too, high-pitched and consistent like an alarm clock. Beep, beep, beep. Then the voices were gone. She was alone with the pressure in her throat, the whooshing, the odd sensation in her chest, the soft limbs and uncooperative eyelids. Why was she so cold?

CHAPTER 46

———◆———

The cafeteria was busy with the usual early evening traffic. Many of the customers looked like bedraggled family members, bored, killing time between visits at bedsides, much like Charlotte did herself.

She looked around at the activity. Life was going on, moving forward. People were buying sandwiches, fruit, hot chocolate, and packets of crisps. They were eating, drinking, and laughing, acting as if something deep in the core of the planet had not shifted. Did they not know that the love of her life was lying in a coma?

To her right, two tables away, a man sat with his head in a book. A dry-looking Danish pastry lay on a grey-white plate in front of him, and a mug of something hot steamed at his right hand. He raised his eyes from the book, possibly sensing that he was being observed. Scanning the room, he connected with Charlotte's stare and nodded in acknowledgement of her small, awkward smile. Charlotte dropped her gaze, hoping he wouldn't think she was staring or being intrusive.

He lowered the book and smiled. She guessed that he was in his mid-fifties. He had kind brown eyes and a thatch of salt-and-pepper hair and wore a heavy Arran sweater. A ring glinted on his left hand, and spotting it made Charlotte relax. No propositions to field here.

"Waiting for someone?" he asked her, then took a sip of his drink.

"Yes. Well, not exactly." Charlotte shrugged and pushed the empty plate in front of her away. "My partner – is in a coma." The words sounded surreal as they floated towards this stranger.

Empathy clouded his face.

"I'm sorry to hear that. How long? I mean, how long has he been here?" The man closed his book and laid it on the table.

"She – has been here four days. A car accident." Charlotte watched his face as he registered what she'd said.

"Was she badly hurt?"

"She has a head injury, some broken bones, and a ruptured spleen." Charlotte heard the crazy-sounding words surround her. They didn't seem to relate to Kate or her life.

The man sat back in his chair.

"Do you feel like some company?" He gestured towards the chair opposite him.

Charlotte considered the offer for a few moments, then stood up. Taking her coffee mug with her, she walked over and joined him.

"Thanks. I'm Charlotte." She extended a hand.

"John. Nice to meet you." He shook her hand.

"So who are you waiting for?" she asked as she sat down.

"My wife. She had surgery this morning. She's asleep now, but she'll be able to come home in the morning." He nodded as he spoke.

"That's great." Charlotte felt a surge of jealousy. Go home tomorrow. What would it be like to say those words about Kate?

"I hope it was nothing too serious?" She sipped her tepid coffee.

"A lumpectomy."

Even the words felt heavy to Charlotte. Her new companion settled back against the chair, and his eyes swept the room behind her.

"Oh. Sorry. I didn't mean to intrude." She cleared her throat.

"No, it's fine. It's good to talk to someone. We've kept it quiet – not told our daughters. It's what she wanted." His mouth turned down at the corners as he spoke, and Charlotte's heart was tugged towards him, as if it was tied to a gossamer thread that he held the end of.

"I'm sure it will turn out to be nothing." His voice lifted at the end of the sentence, posing a question rather than stating a fact.

"I'm sure it will, too." Charlotte nodded her agreement. "They're probably just being cautious."

They exchanged stories. John asked her more about Kate and how Charlotte was coping with being away from home and her business. She asked him about his daughters and their new granddaughter, and John showed her several pictures. In one of them, he and his wife, Sheila, held the baby up between their cheeks. His wife had a long, narrow face, and her dark hair was scraped back in a ponytail. Her nose and cheekbones, like Kate's, were scattered with freckles. She was smiling broadly, and John was laughing into the camera lens.

"Oh, she is gorgeous." Charlotte cooed over the baby.

"Yes, she's an angel. We've been married thirty-three years." John, presuming she was talking about his wife, looked down at the photograph.

"That's wonderful." Charlotte smiled. "The baby is adorable too," she added, watching realization dawn on his face.

"Oh, yes." He laughed. "Poppy is a doll. Keeps her parents and her grandparents on their toes."

The two soon settled into an amicable silence. He lifted his book, and she scrolled through the emails on her phone. The cafeteria gradually emptied around them, and then Charlotte checked her watch. It was eight o' clock and time she got back to Kate.

She slid her phone back into her pocket.

"Well, I'd better be getting back. Can't have Kate waking up and me not being there."

"Right. I'm sure she'll be back with you soon. Be strong." John reached across the table and patted her arm. "She won't want to leave you, I'm sure of it." He smiled.

Charlotte felt the familiar tightness in her throat. She didn't want to cry. This man didn't need her problems to deal with when he had plenty of his own. She swallowed.

"Well, why would she?" She held her hands up at her sides, presenting herself as a prize.

The two exchanged a smile, then she wished him and his wife well. Whatever cells or knots of tissue that formed the lump that Sheila had found, she hoped they were harmless. This kind man deserved to live out the promised lifetime with his wife, as poor

David had deserved to with Elizabeth, and just as she did with Kate.

CHAPTER 47

———◆———

David stood at the window. The river was sparkling and topped with white frills as it rippled across his view. The trees bent away from the wind, and the November sky stretched above, heavy with the promise of colder weather to come.

The last guest had left, and the kitchen was full of empty wineglasses, teacups, and platters with the remains of the food from the reception. Elizabeth's funeral was over, and now that the house was empty once again, David found the silence claustrophobic.

Several neighbors and friends had offered to stay to help him clean up, but he couldn't stand any more pitying glances or platitudes about the tragedy of it all. He knew they meant well, but sympathy was more than he could bear.

Charlotte had called that morning to check on him and let him know that there had been no change in Kate's condition. This was day seven since the accident, and while she had shown no signs of waking, her vital signs and brain activity remained stable.

He wondered what his daughter was seeing inside her heavy sleep. Was it true that comatose patients could hear activity around them and were aware of their loved ones' presence? He hoped so. In the same instant, he hoped that Kate hadn't been aware of his absence for the past two days. He'd been back to Aberdeen to see her before coming home to Broughty Ferry for the service, and he had been somewhat surprised when Charlotte had genuinely welcomed him when he'd walked back into Kate's room in the ICU.

Charlotte had asked if she could come to Elizabeth's funeral, but after discussing the logistics, they had agreed between them that it would be best if she stayed at the hospital in case Kate recovered consciousness. However, to his surprise, he realized that he would have appreciated Charlotte's company on this difficult day.

He turned away from the view. Elizabeth's ability to stare at the river, for hours sometimes, had never failed to amaze him. She'd said she found the movement of the water calming, soporific. Today it was nothing more to him than a sharp reminder of what he had lost.

As he walked across the room, David caught sight of the stain on the carpet where he had spilled the tea a few days earlier. So much had happened since then, and yet, amidst the sorry chaos, he'd also been standing still, holding his breath, waiting for what remained of his family to open her eyes and say his name.

David worked methodically clearing the kitchen, stacking the dishwasher, drying the glasses with the special cloths that Elizabeth kept for the purpose, and replacing the dishes on the

Welsh dresser that sat against the wall. He filled the dustbin with paper napkins, leftover food, and empty wine bottles, then pulled the over-full bag out of the bin and tied a knot in it. Elizabeth had often complained about his ability to see past the overflowing bin, shoving one last teabag in rather than admitting defeat and taking it outside.

The plastic bag weighed heavy in his hand, reminding him of the one he'd been given a few days earlier in the hospital, containing Elizabeth's clothes, handbag, and the blue shoes. As he thought about her delight over the shoes, memories of their blissful evening in Athens flooded his mind, the steps in Plaka, the chilled retsina wine, the Acropolis, ghostly and floodlit behind them as they talked and laughed over dinner. They had become close again, the past forgiven. Their trip had helped heal any remaining rifts between them, and he had felt sure that his Elizabeth was back.

He carried the bag outside and stuffed it into the already full bin. The sour smell of the canister threatened to turn his stomach, so he quickly closed the lid and headed inside to shower the day from his body.

David lay still. The sheets had not been changed since the last time he and Elizabeth had slept in the bed together. Her nightdress hung on the hook behind the bathroom door, and the book she had been reading sat on the bedside table, the bookmark that he had bought her from Lake Garda protruding from between the pages. He reached over and picked it up, flipped it open to the page that was marked, and scanned the words. It was about a young woman who had been helped to escape her brutal life as a slave on a Southern plantation, the underground railroad, and the families who had assisted her. He read a few pages, then replaced the bookmark where it had been and closed the paperback.

As he leaned across to put it back on the bedside table, he was aware of a faint almond scent on Elizabeth's pillow, a hangover from the cream she rubbed into her face and neck at night. The smell was like a slap. He rolled facedown onto the pillow and filled his lungs. His whole body hurt, was weary from grief and weak from lack of nutrition. As he breathed in the scent of his wife, David pressed his eyes closed and moved through a slideshow – seeing the images of their time in Greece and Italy, remembering exchanged glances, and then, finally, imagining the sound of the ocean until sleep claimed him.

The phone rang, jarring him to the bone marrow and sending his heart into overdrive. David sat bolt upright in bed and stared into the darkness. He was on the wrong side of the bed, Elizabeth's side. The window and the door to the hall were dark, so it wasn't yet morning. As his muddled thoughts settled, the phone continued to ring. Kate. It must be about Kate.

Throwing himself across the bed, back to his own side, David reached out and grabbed the phone. Before he could speak, he heard a breathless female voice.

"David. It's Charlotte. She's awake. Kate's awake."

CHAPTER 48

Kate looked around the bright room. It was sparsely furnished and glacially cold. She had asked for an extra blanket but still shivered under the light cotton covers. She turned her head and looked out of the long window. The sun was rising amidst a pink and blue sky that was strung with spidery clouds.

She could smell food, hospital food, cloying and meaty. The tray with the watery scrambled eggs that the healthcare assistant had brought her sat untouched under a cover on the thin movable tray table that hovered over her hips.

Charlotte had left the room to get her some dry biscuits that she could dunk in her tea. Lottie always knew what to do when it came to food, and when she saw Kate's reaction to the eggs, she'd suggested some digestives instead.

The removal of the breathing tube had been nothing short of agonizing, and her throat smarted with each swallow. She couldn't tell the difference between the pain of the raw tissue and the cutting pain of the knowledge that her mother was gone.

The first question Kate had asked when she had opened her eyes and seen Charlotte at her bedside was, "Where's Mum?" Charlotte had hesitated, tried to deflect, but Kate had had such a deep sense of foreboding that she'd pressed her. As Charlotte explained what had happened, Kate had seen the image of her mother in the car with her head dangling to the side and her coat stained with blood. She'd known then, before she'd succumbed to the darkness, that Elizabeth was dead. She realized that now.

Kate closed her eyes as tears slipped over her top lip. After all the years of bitterness, estrangement, and conflict, she had found her way back to her mother, only to have her ripped away. She let the sadness seep into her bones, breathing it in and floating in it. She heard their happy voices on the drive to Aberdeen, singing "Ten Green Bottles" in the car, joking with each other about the traffic and the music on the radio, and talking about how they would win David over – get him to open his mind to Charlotte. The images filled her mind as she ached from the inside out.

Elizabeth had been so happy that day. They had talked as honestly as Kate could have wished for, and she had felt over-whelming acceptance emanating from her mother. The thing she had longed for the most had finally been there, open, blatant, and bountiful.

Kate gulped through her tears. Despite her deep sense of loss and regret that they wouldn't have any more time together, what she was most grateful for, right at this moment, was that she and her mother had reconnected over the past few weeks and had become the friends they should always have been.

Charlotte walked into the room carrying a packet of shortbread and the newspaper Kate had asked for. The loss of an entire week was disturbing to Kate, and she seemed anxious to catch up with what had happened in the world while she had been sleeping.

"Here, sweetheart. This was all I could find." Charlotte placed the newspaper and biscuits on the tray. "Do you want me to open them for you?" She gestured towards the shortbread, and Kate nodded.

"Yes, please." Kate's voice was husky and disjointed.

Charlotte tore the tartan wrapping and placed a single finger of shortbread in Kate's right hand.

Most of the life-support monitors had been removed, which meant that there was now more room for Charlotte to move around the bed. She watched as Kate dipped the biscuit into a mug of tea, then lifted it to her mouth.

"Is it OK?" she asked as Kate chewed slowly. Her face was so thin. The blue eyes, David's eyes, were huge in their sockets and the cheeks sunken and pallid. Kate's skin sat atop her bones like a sheer curtain, and it hurt Charlotte's heart to see her struggle with even this simple meal.

"Your dad is on his way. He'll be here in a couple of hours." Charlotte smiled as Kate swallowed, a grimace indicating that it hurt her to do so.

Kate nodded and laid her head back on the bank of pillows.

"Good. Is he coping? The funeral was yesterday?" Kate's eyes filled again as she spoke.

"Yes. It was yesterday afternoon. I wanted to go, but we both decided that I should stay here with you." Charlotte watched as Kate closed her eyes and bit down on her lower lip.

"I'm so sorry, my love. I'm so sorry." Charlotte scooted the chair closer to the bed, leaned over, and clasped Kate's hand. "What can I do?"

Kate blinked, seeming to want to clear her foggy vision, and squeezed Charlotte's hand.

"You're doing it. Just be here. Be with me."

"I'm not going anywhere, sweetheart.

Three hours later, David strode into the room. Charlotte noticed that he was pale. He was wearing his heavy coat and carrying a travel bag. Tossing the bag onto the floor, he leaned over the bed and gently placed a hand on each of Kate's shoulders, kissing her bandaged head.

"Hello, darling girl. You're back with us." His voice cracked as he stooped over his daughter, and Charlotte heard the heartbreak in his words.

"Hi, Dad," Kate whispered against his cheek. "How are you?"

David stood up, ran a hand over his hair, shrugged out of his coat, and draped it over the back of the empty chair.

"I'm fine. More to the point, how are you?" He sat down and leaned in towards the edge of the bed.

"Sore. Tired. I have the headache from hell and a throat like chopped liver, but otherwise, I'm great."

David nodded and laid a hand on her shin.

"Dad, I'm so sorry." Kate reached for his hand. "About Mum."

David shook his head and kissed the back of her hand.

"It was a tragic accident, darling. No one is to blame." His voice faded as Kate sniffed and wiped at her eyes.

"How was it – yesterday?" Kate shifted her hips in the bed.

"Fine. Nice. Everyone came. She'd have been happy." David shrugged and turned to look out the window.

"I'm so sorry I wasn't there." Kate sniffed as fresh tears rolled down under her jaw. "I loved her very much." Kate was watching his face.

"I'm the one who's sorry, love. I don't know what to say. I just…"

Kate shook her head, reached up, and placed her fingers on his shoulder.

Feeling as if she was intruding, Charlotte stood up and cleared her throat.

"I'm going to pop outside for a bit. Get some fresh air." She laid her hand on David's back and smiled down at Kate. "You two catch up, and I'll be back shortly."

David turned to look at her, and she saw the gratitude in his eyes. She leaned over and kissed Kate lightly, then left father and daughter to each other.

Kate looked over at her father. His face was worn, with lines deeply etched around the mouth, and his complexion was yellowish. She watched as he talked about the funeral and the reception afterwards. She listened to his voice, picturing the people he mentioned, the many handshakes and kisses on the cheeks he'd had to endure alone. Her heart ached as he described the silence in the house. She couldn't imagine how difficult it must have been for him to deal with all that by himself.

"It feels so odd, Kate. The house is like a shell now. I can't see myself being there without her." He shook his head.

"You'll need to take some time to let everything settle down,

Dad. If you decide you don't want to stay there, then fine, but it's too early to make that decision at the moment."

David scanned her face.

"Yes, I know. I need some time."

As she watched him wearing his suffering like a lead overcoat, Kate recalled Charlotte touching him on the shoulder as she left the room. She hadn't asked Charlotte how things had been between her and David. There had been so many other things to talk about. Now, she began to realize that while all this pain had been circulating, her father and Charlotte had been forced to communicate, in one way or another. They'd been in the same room, sharing time with her, presumably helping each other, maybe even forming some kind of tenuous bond.

David stood and went to the window.

"It's so bloody freezing in here." He turned back towards her, swiping at his eyes.

Kate nodded her agreement.

"Dad. Can I ask you something?"

"Sure, darling. Anything."

"How's it been with you and Charlotte?" Kate watched his face, expecting the customary closed mouth, hardened jaw, and warning flash from the eyes.

David sat down next to her and leaned back in the chair.

"It's been – unexpected." He nodded to himself as much as to Kate, then picked up her hand and held it in his own.

CHAPTER 49

———— ❖ ————

Kate had been awake for two days, and the consultant had said she was making good progress. She had been moved out of the ICU and into a ward, had been up and walking, and now spent a few hours each day sitting in an armchair at the side of her bed. Her appetite was returning, and Charlotte had been running into Aberdeen, trying to find her nutritious things to eat that she could cope with.

She had left Kate with David and dashed back to Edinburgh for a night to check in with Mungo, do laundry, and gather some clothes for Kate to come home in. The hospital estimated two to three days until they would release her, and Charlotte couldn't wait to get her out of there and back onto home ground.

Having spent the night in her own bed, Charlotte got up at 3:00 a.m., went down to The Bakery, and started on the morning routine. As soon as she started mixing the dough for the morning rolls, her body on autopilot working with the raw ingredients, the magnitude of the past few days laid its full weight on her. After all the worry and burdens she'd been carrying, the simple acts of mixing, kneading, and cutting were clearing her troubled soul.

How much she had missed this accustomed part of her day over the past week. The feel of the dough, cool and pliable, its creamy color, and its heft under her hands were grounding. She could smell the ovens warming and feel their heat behind her as she worked. Vaughn Williams floated through the kitchen, and she smiled as she massaged the gluey mixture, flouring, folding, pushing it against the cool resistance of the counter. This was her normality. She was happy here at The Bakery, so lucky to have the ability to work at what she was passionate about, and the crowning glory on her happiness was Kate, who had made everything more valid just by staying alive.

Having gone over the set-up, ordering, and prep for the day with Mungo and surprising him with the news of his promotion, she checked on Chloe to make sure the young woman could cope on her own for a couple more days. Chloe had reassured her that she was doing fine. She even said she'd been enjoying helping Mungo, and if Charlotte was not mistaken, Chloe had blushed when she talked about the monosyllabic, lanky sous-chef. Charlotte had often wondered if there was perhaps some chemistry between the two of them, and now her suspicions were being confirmed. She liked to think that they might be as happy as her and Kate someday. Chloe had said she must not worry about anything, just focus her energy on Kate and getting her well.

After hugging Chloe, Charlotte ran upstairs to shower the flour from her hair and then quickly packed a bag for herself and for Kate. Satisfied that she'd thought of everything, she locked the flat and trotted down the stairs towards the street, excited that the next time she was on these steps Kate would be with her, coming home.

Around forty miles into her journey, back to Aberdeen, Charlotte scanned the A90 searching for the spot that had changed all of their lives. She wondered if there was anything to see, any remaining signs of the crash. She half expected to see debris, twisted metal, skid marks in the lane, a broken barrier – and yet, even as she thought about it, she knew that all evidence of what had happened had been cleared away days ago. While there was no visible proof anymore, that split second in time that could never be taken back held such a weight of consequence. Shuddering, she focused on the road and turned up the radio.

By the time she got back to the hospital, it was mid-afternoon, and David was reading the newspaper to Kate. He had bought her an e-reader, but Kate was finding it hard to focus on the screen, so Charlotte and David had reverted to reading the daily headlines to her.

It was obvious that Kate was uncomfortable, feeling out of touch with the world. The day Charlotte had left for Edinburgh, Kate had dictated an email to her boss that Charlotte had typed up and sent. The dean had responded, saying the faculty all wished Kate a speedy recovery and sent their deepest condolences on the loss of her mother. Kate had seemed relieved at the response, obviously concerned that her absence could potentially jeopard-ize her position. Charlotte had reassured her that they thought too much of her than to be anything other than supportive.

As she approached them, both father and daughter raised their heads and smiled at her.

"Hi, you two. How're you getting on?" She placed the small suitcase on the floor at the edge of the room and walked over to kiss Kate. "You've got a lot more color in your cheeks." Charlotte moved a stray lock of hair from Kate's forehead. The heavy bandages had been removed, and the dark bruising on her temple that crept up into her hairline was visible.

"Dad's been keeping me busy." Kate smiled.

David folded the newspaper, stood up, and stretched his back.

"These damn chairs are murder on the back." He bent forward at the waist and groaned. "I think I'll go for a wee walk. If that's OK?" He looked down at Kate, then over at Charlotte, as if waiting for a consensus on his departure.

Charlotte nodded as Kate replied.

"Sure, Dad. Take your time. Thanks for today."

David patted Kate's foot through the blanket, picked his coat up from the back of the chair, and walked out of the room.

"How was the drive?" Kate accepted the glass of water Charlotte held out to her, sipping carefully through the straw.

"Fine. It was weird, passing that section of the A90. I was looking for something, I don't know, some kind of sign." Charlotte shrugged.

"Yeah. I can't imagine driving there again. Not for a long time." Kate shuddered as she handed the glass back to Charlotte.

Charlotte settled herself in a chair and opened the bag of scones she'd brought from the bakery.

"Mungo sent you these. They're blue cheese and bacon."

Kate smiled. "My favorite."

After eating, Kate had fallen asleep. An hour had passed, and

Charlotte was reluctant to wake her, but not knowing when David would be back, she wanted to talk to her about how things had been going with her father. Just as she was considering coughing, Kate blinked her eyes open.

"Hi, sleepy."

"Hey. Has Dad come back yet?" Kate shifted up in the bed.

"Not yet."

"Can you help me into the chair, Lottie? I want to talk to you."

Charlotte felt a jolt to her stomach. That was never a good sign, and in her experience, it often meant the beginning of a difficult conversation.

"Sure – what's up?" She stood up and helped Kate out of bed and into the seat.

Kate relaxed back into the armchair as Charlotte tucked a blanket over her thighs.

"Dad and I have been talking, and we think, if you agree of course, that I should go back to the house for a couple of weeks, just until I get my strength back." Kate spoke deliberately, as if she were talking to a toddler who needed to pay particular attention.

Dismissing the condescending tone, Charlotte focused on the content of what Kate was saying. She heard the words and then replayed them in her mind – back to the house. At least Kate hadn't said "back home," but even so, it still cut Charlotte to think that Kate would want to be anywhere other than their own home while recovering.

"Um. Can I ask why?" Charlotte hoped she didn't sound too petulant.

"It's just that you need to work, and Dad is around all day now. He can take care of me. It'll give him something to think about, and it'll give you time to focus on The Bakery. I feel so bad that you've had to take time away from it because of all this." Kate blinked and held her hands out at each side of the chair.

"I've coped fine. Mungo's been a star. The business hasn't been hurt, Kate, but *you* have. I want to take care of you, make a fuss of you. I want you to come home – to *our* home." Charlotte searched Kate's face for more information.

"Look, the thing is, Dad needs me at the moment, Lottie. He's devastated about Mum and I just think that it might be better if…" Kate's words faded.

Charlotte closed her eyes. Of course, it was about David. She should have known that Kate would put him first. Despite everything, it was obvious that Kate still cared more about her father's acceptance than she'd let Charlotte believe. Did she think this was a way to win back his favor? Did she not see that by giving in this way, she was admitting that her ties to him were stronger than her relationship with Charlotte? After everything that they had been through, was David going to win?

Before she could edit the imagined dialogue, or develop a suitable précis, Charlotte blurted out her fear.

"Your dad and I have found a way to work together, Kate. He was foul to me to start with. It was tough, but we figured it out. I know it's going to be hard for him, but I don't understand why you have to move back there. It's like admitting defeat after everything we've been through. I just don't see why I should take a back seat again." One heavy tear brimmed over her eyelid, and Charlotte wiped it away angrily as she stood up.

"Lottie, calm down. You're not understanding me." Kate

pushed herself up from the chair and stood unsteadily at the end of the bed. "I'm not moving back there. I'm just going to let him take care of me, as part of his own healing. He can't stand being alone in the house, and I think it's the least that I can do." Kate hesitated. "I was driving, Lottie. Do you understand that? *I* was driving."

As Charlotte saw Kate's knees giving way, she darted across the floor and caught her under the arms.

"Sit down, sweetheart. It's fine. Whatever you want to do is fine. We'll figure it all out." The words were like marbles in her mouth as Charlotte pushed a pillow behind Kate's back and handed her a tissue from the box on the bedside table.

Kate was gulping down her sobs, and the sight of her struggle crushed Charlotte with guilt over her selfish outburst. Of course Kate needed to be there for David; he had lost his wife. This wasn't about her and Kate, or even about David winning some unspoken competition. This was about family doing what it does best. If they were ever going to be family, this had to happen.

Kate was breathing less heavily, filling her lungs slowly and exhaling through her mouth. Once the sobs had subsided, she looked up at Charlotte.

"Dad told me that you were remarkable."

Charlotte, startled by the statement, widened her eyes.

"He said that you'd taken charge, sorted him out when he fell apart," Kate continued. "He said you might be tiny but that you were stronger than you looked." She pulled her mouth into a half smile. "He also said that you were devoted to me."

Charlotte let the words float around her. David had said all that? Was she hearing things? Unable to respond, she just nodded, biting down on her lower lip.

"You've made an impression on him, Lottie. I think we're all going to be OK." Kate looked like a child promising her best behavior in exchange for the gifts she hoped for. "You can come over to the house whenever you can get away. We can spend time at the river and take walks into town. You can cook for us. It wouldn't be for long, maybe two or three weeks. Lottie?" Kate was pleading now.

Charlotte swallowed over the remaining grains of her objection. It was obvious that Kate needed this badly. Charlotte could see that not only was she doing this for her father, but also as a way to assuage the mistaken belief that she had perhaps been responsible for Elizabeth's death. Thinking of Kate putting herself through that self-inflicted torture made Charlotte's stomach hurt. She needed to be there to stop that thought process. She would be the bigger person here, and whatever Kate needed was what she, Charlotte, would provide.

"Of course. Don't listen to me. I was just looking forward to taking care of you in our home. But I get it. Your dad needs you." She sat down on the edge of the bed. "I can come over often, and now that Mungo has taken on more responsibility, it's easier for me to get away during the week." As obvious relief flooded Kate's face, Charlotte mustered a smile. "It'll be good. The three of us spending time together."

As she said it out loud, Charlotte hoped that the universe was hearing her words and taking them to heart. She hoped that the tenuous friendship that she and David had crafted would stand the test of them caring for Kate together. When they were back on his territory, would he be as amenable as he had been recently? When he had Kate back, would he welcome Charlotte into their home?

The thought of the beautiful house where Elizabeth had hosted them a few weeks ago on that peaceful Sunday filled her memory. It would be overwhelmingly sad to be there without Elizabeth, and when she put her own disappointment aside, she could understand why David might be dreading that scenario.

"Thanks, love. I hoped you'd understand." Kate's face was regaining its calm equilibrium. "We'll make it work, and it won't be for long."

Charlotte nodded, leaned over, and kissed Kate.

"Whatever you need, sweetheart. It's going to be fine."

CHAPTER 50

David paced outside the door of Kate's room. He had overheard her telling Charlotte that she was going to go back to Broughty Ferry, and while he was happy about it, he felt a flash of guilt over the knowledge that Kate was making the decision more for him than for herself. The truth was that he was dreading being back at the house, and even if it was only for a couple of weeks, having Kate there would soften the impact of the emptiness that waited for him there.

Charlotte had sounded upset, and while he wouldn't dissuade Kate from the decision, he could understand Charlotte's reaction. If he were a good father and selfless human being, he would insist that Kate go home to Edinburgh, but at this moment in his life, he was giving himself a get-out-of-jail card on perfect parenting. He needed Kate's company, and having her there to take care of could be his salvation.

He coughed loudly, then tapped on the doorframe.

"Can I come in?"

Charlotte turned to look at him and seemed startled by his presence.

"Come in, Dad." Kate pulled the blanket that covered her legs to the side and held her hand out to Charlotte, who stepped forward and helped her stand up. "I've talked to Lottie about me coming back to your place for a while." David turned to look at Charlotte, who seemed to be avoiding his eyes. Another momentary surge of guilt forced him to be more effusive than he might have been ordinarily.

"I hope you know that you are welcome there anytime?" He pushed his hands deep into his trouser pockets and jingled the coins he carried there. "We've plenty of room."

Charlotte nodded and kept looking straight ahead at Kate.

"Thanks, David. As long as Kate's happy and can rest and heal, that's the most important thing."

He thought Charlotte sounded tired, not defeated, but as if she had conceded a point in a chess game. He shuffled his feet, suddenly feeling awkward in the room.

"Well, why don't I go and get us some snacks? What would you like?" He spoke to Charlotte's shoulder.

"Not for me, thanks." She held onto Kate's hand and helped her get back into bed.

"Sure? Kate, do you want anything?" He cringed as he heard the forced jollity in his own voice.

"No, thanks, Dad. I think I'll have a nap for a bit." Kate settled back against the pillows, and Charlotte tucked her under the covers, gently brushing a lock of hair away from her forehead.

Seeing the way Charlotte treated his daughter, as if she might shatter into a thousand pieces, tore at his heart. Charlotte was a good woman, and Kate was lucky to have her. He had been lucky to have Elizabeth, but he had put a crack in their relationship that had almost been fatal. Had it not been for Elizabeth's forgiving nature, he could very well be a lonely old fool right about now. As it was, he still had his daughter and this woman she loved. In the big scheme of things, he recognized that despite the loss of his best friend in life, he was still a lucky man.

Kate closed her eyes and seemed to sleep instantly. Her breathing became audible, slow and steady. Charlotte busied herself with unpacking the clothes she'd brought for Kate, placing them in the slim drawer at the top of the bedside cabinet. As she moved around the room, being careful not to make a noise, David sat down on the metal chair next to the bed.

"I didn't mean to cause a problem," he whispered as Charlotte slid past him and tiptoed around the end of the bed. She looked over at him and nodded.

"I just thought it might be more restful for her at home." No sooner had he said the words than he recognized his mistake.

"Kate has a home, David. It's in Edinburgh. She wants to go back to Broughty Ferry for a while, and that's fine with me, but she has a home." Charlotte's voice was soft, but her eyes were bright, as if she was holding back tears.

"I know that." He nodded, matching her whisper, and linked his fingers into a knot between his knees. "Elizabeth told me how lovely your flat is." He lengthened the olive branch and waited for her to accept it.

"Yes, it's a good place." Charlotte stood by the window and looked out at the Aberdeen skyline. "We've made it ours."

David swallowed hard. *Ours* was a concept he had yet to fully absorb. Kate had made a home with Charlotte, and Broughty Ferry was now in her past. At some point, he was sure he'd have to visit their place in Edinburgh, but for now all he wanted was to try to recreate something of the household he had loved and been a part of before the balance had been knocked out of his life.

As he watched Charlotte's profile scanning the view under the grainy sky, David realized that contrary to her apparent concern, she had indeed won the match. Checkmate. She need not worry about Kate's allegiance, as Kate had made it plain that her coming back to Broughty Ferry was temporary. However, he would take it for whatever it was. All he wanted was the chance to restore some order, some familiarity and symmetry to this mess that was now his life.

"Thank you, Charlotte." The words were heavy in his mouth, but they needed to be said.

CHAPTER 51

———— ✦ ————

The house was cold. December was on the doorstep, and everything outside of the window wore the purple tinge of winter. Kate tried not to tremble as she sat down in her mother's chair. Shivering hurt her ribs, and the wound across her middle tugged as she maneuvered herself into the seat. Her arm was heavy in the cast, and her head was itchy where the skin was healing. All these irritations were like tiny stabs at her hard-sought sense of peace but the most overwhelming aftereffect of the accident, apart from the bone-deep sadness, was her exhaustion.

Getting out of the car and into the house, then walking down the long hallway and into the living room had zapped her of energy. Charlotte had helped her with a light hand under her elbow, and David had fussed around with bags and coats, turning on lights and flicking up the thermostat when Kate had commented that she could see her breath inside the hall. Charlotte was now upstairs putting Kate's clothes away in her childhood wardrobe, and David was in the kitchen making tea.

Elizabeth's chair sat close to the fireplace, but David had yet to light the fire, so the dark emptiness of the grate yawned wide and cold. Outside, the river was moving swiftly from right to left, the afternoon tide taking it out to sea, the choppy waves topped with foam. A solitary white sail jerked across Kate's view as a stalwart sailor made his way back to the local yacht club.

She adjusted the cushion behind her and pulled the pashmina that Charlotte had wrapped around her shoulders closer across her chest. She could hear the radiator ticking behind her as the metal began to expand, the sound taking her back to the many childhood winters spent in this house.

Her room upstairs had a long radiator that sat under the double -width window overlooking the garden. When she was seven or eight, she would lie on the floor to read her book and put her feet up against the hot metal struts, wrapping her toes around their edges until she could bear the heat no longer. She would look out at the sky and imagine herself inside the fictitious worlds she was reading about.

At the memory, she wiggled her cold toes inside her sheepskin boots. Those had been the days before she'd truly begun to cross swords with her mother. They'd been friends then, Elizabeth often tapping on her bedroom door with a slice of toast and jam or some biscuits and a glass of milk.

Kate smiled as she remembered some of her favorite times spent in this very room. Most of them had taken place during the winter, when she would walk home from school and get caught in the rain. Elizabeth would greet her with a towel, rubbing her dripping hair and taking her sodden shoes and coat to the pantry to dry. Kate would run upstairs and change into her jeans and a sweater, then come down to sit at the fireside.

Her mum would bring her a steaming cup of soup or a toasted sandwich and an apple. She would eat as she splayed her cold toes out in front of the flames and tell her mum about her day at school. Time had seemed to stand still on those afternoons. Everything was in its place, and the world inside their house was safe from the cold, inhospitable one outside its walls.

In those days, David's arrival back from work had felt like an intrusion on that perfect mother-daughter time. They'd hear his keys in the lock and Elizabeth would jump up, shattering the magic that held them together. She would take the empty dishes out into the hall, as if David shouldn't catch them languishing at the fireside when there were things to be done.

Sitting in her mother's chair now, Kate felt a new wave of loss. If only they had known to cherish those moments, stretch them out beyond themselves and keep each one locked in their minds and memories. If they had, perhaps there wouldn't have been so many years of tension, disappointment, and distance between them. She knew that looking back with regret was pointless, but it was part of the human condition, and she was nothing if not human.

David padded into the room in his socks. His hair was unruly, his face pinched and pale, and he still wore his coat. Kate accepted the cup he offered her and wrapped her fingers around its warmth.

"I'll get the fire going in a minute. We'll get some heat up soon." He smiled at her and slid the heavy coat off. "Charlotte upstairs?" he asked as he folded the garment over his arm like a waiter with a dishcloth.

"Yep. She's unpacking for me." Kate nodded and sipped the hot liquid.

David paced across the room and stood at the window with his back to her.

"Your mum sat here for hours, just staring at the water." His voice was rough. "Used to amaze me how long she'd do that."

Kate watched his weighted shoulders as he spoke. His frame was sharper, bonier than it used to be, and she wondered if he was eating enough. It had been the right decision to come here. It was difficult enough for her to be back in the house, in this room, sitting in this chair. She couldn't conceive of how it was affecting her father.

Davis turned and smoothed the coat over his arm.

"Is Charlotte staying tonight?" He looked at Kate, his face showing lightly shrouded dread.

"Dad." Kate met his eyes and frowned. "We talked about this." She leaned over and placed the cup on the low table at the side of the chair.

"I know, I was just asking." He pouted as he spoke, his lower lip protruding. Had it not been an irritating flash of his underlying objection to her relationship with Charlotte, Kate thought that it might have been comical.

"Don't start, please. You promised." She gave him a warning glare. "If she wants to stay, she can, and you'll make her welcome. OK?" She leaned back in the chair and winced as her damaged ribs reminded her that they were still not healed.

David dragged a socked toe across the carpet in a childlike manner, a dark shadow forming where he forced the woolen weave against the grain.

"I will." He looked over at Kate. "I will."

The stairs creaked as Charlotte started down them, providing

David and Kate with the warning they needed to change the subject. As she walked into the living room, she smiled broadly at Kate.

"What a lovely room you had. The garden looks fabulous from up there." The first comment was directed at Kate, the second at David, who still stood awkwardly holding his coat.

"That was all Elizabeth." He nodded towards the window. "Hours of work."

"Well, it paid off. It's gorgeous." Charlotte walked behind the chair and put her hands on Kate's shoulders. "Do you need anything, sweetheart?"

Kate shook her head.

"Nope. Got tea here. Dad's going to light the fire to melt the icicles off the chandelier." She smiled and rolled her eyes, sending David into action.

"Right. I'll get on with it." He trotted across the room and then stopped at the door. The two women watched as he hesitated, then turned back towards them.

"Our neighbor had left us a beef casserole in the fridge. In fact, we've got several dishes that people have left. You'll be staying tonight, won't you?" He looked directly at Charlotte.

"Em, yes. I'll stay. I have an early start, but I can sneak out before you two even wake up." She squeezed Kate's shoulders and smiled over at David. Kate reached up and clasped her hand over Charlotte's while looking over at her dad. That invitation had taken a herculean effort on his part, which needed to be recognized.

"Thanks, Dad. You're a gem." The edges of David's face became blurry to Kate as she watched him nod his acknowledgement and leave the room.

CHAPTER 52

———◈———

Charlotte burrowed farther down under the duvet. The bedroom was warming up, but the old house was taking its time to shake off the stone-deep cold that seemed to be hanging over it. Kate was reading, lying propped up on several pillows next to her, and Charlotte was anxious not to wriggle too much in case she inadvertently caused her any pain.

David had gone to bed before them, bidding them a hasty goodnight. She had watched him climb the stairs, his small overnight bag in hand, and had felt overwhelmingly sorry for him. He'd been polite at dinner, offering her wine, removing her plate for her, insisting that she sit with Kate while he cleared away the casserole and filled the dishwasher, and yet she had still sensed his discomfort. Kate had seemed to feel it too, watching her father as if something was bubbling under the veneer of propriety he was displaying.

Kate had been quiet since they'd arrived that afternoon, and while Charlotte was sensitive to her obvious struggle, being back in her parents' house, she felt an anxious knot in her stomach. Charlotte knew that she had a tendency to assume responsibility for other people's happiness, so by default, if they were unhappy she often fell into the trap of thinking that she was the cause.

"You comfortable enough?" she whispered.

Kate nodded and turned the page of her book. Charlotte, somewhat hurt by the wordless response, turned on her side and faced the door.

"Sorry. I'm fine. It just feels a bit weird, that's all." Kate laid a hand on Charlotte's hip.

Charlotte flipped over onto her back.

"What feels weird? Me being here?" Charlotte held her breath.

"No. Just being in the house. Knowing Mum isn't going to walk through the door. I won't see her cooking or hear her humming in the kitchen."

Charlotte nodded and, shifting over, curled up and laid her head on Kate's thigh.

"I know, sweetheart. It was bound to be difficult."

Kate put her book facedown on top of the duvet and stroked Charlotte's hair, spreading it out across her leg in a dark fan. Charlotte closed her eyes and let herself sink into the rhythmic sweeps of Kate's fingers. She'd often fall asleep while Kate did this, but tired as she was, she wanted to stay awake and be present for Kate tonight.

"It's Dad, too. He's so – I don't know – lost, desperate." Kate continued. "It's like he's afraid."

"Of what?"

"Life, this place, his future, us." Charlotte pulled herself back up and rested against her own pillows.

"What do you mean, us?"

"Us – as in you and me. What we are to each other. I wonder if he thinks he's alone now, that we'll shut him out of our lives." Kate looked anxious as she scanned Charlotte's face.

"Why would he think that? We're here, aren't we?" Charlotte could hear the irritation in her own voice. She struggled to disguise her annoyance so Kate would keep talking to her. In a moderated tone, she continued. "If we were going to shut him out, we wouldn't have agreed to this." She swept a hand around the room.

Kate nodded.

"While you were unconscious, he and I found a way to get on. I mean, we at least talked. We were able to agree on some things, we even went out and had a meal together. He didn't make it easy, Kate, and we're not exactly bosom buddies, but we got over the bad feeling and were adults because you needed us to be." Charlotte watched as Kate chewed her bottom lip.

"I know. He told me that, too. I know he gave you a hellish hard time, love. I just can't be angry with him anymore, he's so damaged by losing Mum." Kate swallowed. The bruise on her temple was fading, becoming a violet shadow, and her freshly washed fair hair fell to her jaw. She was so beautiful. Even injured and distressed, she was able to make Charlotte catch her breath.

"I'm not angry with him, either. We need to move on, and I think we all see that." Charlotte reached out and took Kate's hand. "What's really worrying you?"

Kate looked over at Charlotte. "That he might not get over it, that I might get trapped here. That he might come between us."

Kate's eyes were wide.

Charlotte was flooded with relief. She was not the pea under the princess's mattresses after all. Kate wanted to come home to Edinburgh, and that was all she needed to hear. She placed her arm around Kate's shoulder and pulled her gently towards her. Kate slid down in the bed and put her head on Charlotte's collarbone.

"It'll be good for both of you to be together for a few days. He lost his wife, but you lost your mum, Kate. You need to share the grief, grieve together. I'll be here as much as I can, and as soon as you feel like you've had enough, you can call me and I'll come and get you. You won't get trapped here, sweetheart. I won't let that happen."

Charlotte felt Kate relax into her neck. Kate's hair smelled of coconut, and as she exhaled, Charlotte felt her cool breaths across her chest. David needed help, there was no denying that, but Kate needed it, too. She hoped David was up to task of comforting as well as mourning, because right now, Kate needed her father.

CHAPTER 53

———◆———

Davidwalked briskly along the river path towards the town. He had a list in his pocket and carried two shopping bags. One of them contained an umbrella, as Kate had insisted that it looked like rain. He didn't like to leave her for long, but he had his mobile phone in his pocket so she could call if she needed him, and he would be no more than an hour.

The wind was cutting across the water, making his eyes water as he scanned for boats. It was the first day of December, and Elizabeth had been gone for two weeks. The weight of that reality hit him afresh each time he was reminded of it, and as he watched two small boats lurching on the incoming tide, he was caught again by the sharp edge of the truth. She would never walk this path with him again.

Kate had been emotional the previous evening. He knew she found it hard being in the house, and as he thought of the look on her face as she deliberately avoided Elizabeth's chair at the dining table, he felt a stab under his abdomen. He could stand almost anything at the moment, as had been proven, but he wasn't sure if he could bear seeing his daughter so obviously hurting. With all his own pain twisting inside him, he knew that he must remember that Kate had lost her mother. While her presence was a comfort to him, he must not start to lean on her or add to her burden. After all, she would be leaving him soon to return to Edinburgh, to return to her own life with Charlotte.

Charlotte had left that morning and, true to her word, had been gone before he had padded down to the kitchen to make coffee at 7:00 a.m. He had been tentative, tiptoeing past Kate's door, anxious not to wake her but more anxious that he not see Charlotte emerging from the room.

Despite being exhausted, he had not slept well, knowing that she was across the hall with his daughter. While he and Charlotte had declared a truce, even forged a friendship of sorts, he still struggled to let his walls down completely. There was work that needed to be done between them, and he recognized that the bulk of it was on his side.

The town was bustling with morning shoppers and "the coffee shop crowd," as Elizabeth had called them. She had been referring to the groups of elderly local ladies who met several times a week and drank cappuccinos or lattes, discussing their latest bridge game or what they'd seen on TV the night before. There were also the young mothers who bought a coffee and then let their children patter around the café tables. The women would nod in acknowledgement of each other while enjoying the freedom from the constant demands of their offspring, who were amusing themselves in the safe environment.

When Elizabeth characterized the various groups this way, David had laughed and asked where he fit in, as he often walked into town to meet Mike for a coffee and a chat. Elizabeth had said that she had christened his lot the golf groupies. They chose the only Italian coffee shop in town and sat in the four prime window tables, their Argyle sweaters and crossword puzzles making them stand out.

He had loved the way she observed life, and knew that he would miss the game they always played when people-watching, guessing people's life stories.

David passed the fish shop and headed for the baker's. Kate said she wanted a Scottish roll with her soup at lunch, and Kinsey's made the best rolls in town. As he pushed his way through the door, David saw that there was already a queue. Frustrated, he considered leaving, but then thought better of it. He joined the end of the line and stared down at his shoes as the people in front of him inched towards the counter.

"Dave. Is that you?" Someone tapped him on the shoulder. David turned to see Mike standing behind him.

"Oh, Mike." He smiled at his friend. "Clare sent you out to do the shopping today?"

Mike nodded. "She's got a cold. Damn nasty one, actually. I'm the man Friday, out with the list and a set of airtight instructions." Mike rolled his eyes. "Because I'm not capable of choosing the right mayonnaise or toilet paper myself." He laughed.

Memories of Elizabeth doing the same thing brought a smile to David's face.

"Liz was the same. She'd even write down the number of apples, and things like "Be sure to check for bruises." David shrugged. "I accepted my inadequacies as a shopper years ago."

The line moved again, and David stepped forward.

"Do you have time for a coffee before you head back?" Mike spoke to David's shoulder.

"Not really. Kate's at home, and she's still a bit wobbly, so I don't want to leave her too long." David shook his head as he spoke.

"Oh, right. I didn't realize she was here." Mike sounded surprised. "Is she staying long?"

"A couple of weeks. Just until she gets her strength back."

It was David's turn, so he asked for six rolls and a loaf of granary bread. As the lady behind the counter put them in a paper bag, he turned back to Mike. "She's pretty cut up about Elizabeth. It seemed a good idea to have her here for a while. Probably good for both of us."

Mike's face took on a pained expression.

"I totally understand that, Dave. Makes sense."

David paid for his goods and made to pass his friend.

"I'll give you a ring, Mike. Maybe next week we can have a coffee, once she's a bit stronger."

Mike watched David's face and, as he passed, reached out a hand and patted him on the shoulder.

"Don't be a stranger. I'll pop round in a few days and check on the pair of you."

David remained silent, and when he got no response, Mike continued. "Clare is worried about you. The gents at the golf club were asking after you yesterday, too."

David was overtaken with a sense of panic. What if Mike turned up unannounced and Charlotte was at the house? How would he explain her presence to his friend? How would he introduce her? David felt his insides lurch.

"No, it's best to call first. Kate's napping a lot, and I don't like to disturb her." David's response was abrupt, and he instantly regretted his tone. He looked at his friend and shrugged his apology. He hoped Mike knew him well enough not to take offense, as he hadn't deserved that.

"Of course. No problem. I'll ring first, then." Mike frowned and released David's shoulder. "Just call if you need anything, though."

David's heart was beating fast as he walked back out into the street. Scanning the shopping list, he planned the fastest possible route to cover all the stops he needed to make and set off, head down into the wind and hoping that he wouldn't meet anyone else he would have to talk to.

CHAPTER 54

———◆———

Kate stood in the kitchen. The kettle was boiling, and a mug with a teabag inside it sat on the counter. Elizabeth had always insisted they use the teapot to get a proper brew, but Kate and David had defaulted to the bag-in-the-cup method. The garden was retreating into its winter state, and Kate looked out at the bare shrubbery, the stark tree limbs, and the brackish lawn.

Being in the house by herself was disturbing. She had never been afraid to be here alone as a teenager. Her parents rarely left her, but when they had, she'd been quite confident that she was safe. Now, as she walked from room to room, she felt oddly displaced where she should have felt familiar. She tried to define the sensation, but all she could come up with was discomfort. It felt as if Elizabeth were watching her, could walk in and sit down any second, or come up behind her and touch her shoulder. Kate found that she was leaving the lights on when she left a room and closing the doors behind her as she came and went through the house. It made no sense, and yet she felt observed.

When her dad had put her dinner plate at Elizabeth's place in the dining room the previous evening, Kate had recoiled. She had silently picked up the plate and moved to a chair at the side, leaving Elizabeth's spot at the foot of the table empty. David had seemed alarmed, but had said nothing.

The fire popped in the living room, making her jump. Kate shook her head at her own nonsense. Even if Elizabeth *was* here, watching her, there was no reason to be uncomfortable.

David had gone to the post office and she had sat at the fire reading for an hour until the phone rang.

Charlotte was calling a couple of times a day to check on how things were going. It had been three days since she'd returned to Edinburgh, and Kate was missing her terribly. Charlotte had reported on how The Bakery was doing and filled her in on the blossoming romance between Chloe and Mungo. She had also said that she'd seen her own dad and told Kate that he had been out on a date with a woman from the lawn bowling club. Charlotte had sounded somewhat shocked and even wounded when she had told Kate about it. Kate couldn't imagine how it would feel if and when David took up with someone new. She couldn't picture it at the moment, his wounds gaping, so wide and fresh.

"Lottie, your dad's got a lot of years ahead of him. It's probably a good thing, love." She had tried to reassure her.

"Yeah. It just seems disrespectful to Mum, somehow. It feels like he's moved on, when I can't." Charlotte's voice had been tight and strained.

"Try to stand in his shoes. He's a loving, clever, and interesting man. He needs stimulation and company, and perhaps this woman is good for him? It's been almost eighteen months since your mum died." Kate had tried to play devil's advocate, but had understood Charlotte's reaction.

"I know I'm being childish and probably selfish, too. I don't want him to be lonely. I have my own life, and he needs his, too. I'm just struggling with it, that's all." Charlotte had sniffed down the phone. "It seems too soon."

Kate had talked to her for twenty minutes, and when Charlotte had hung up, she had agreed to meet the mystery woman and had even promised to try to be kind to her.

The button on the kettle popped, and Kate filled her cup with boiling water. She squeezed the teabag with a spoon, offering up a silent apology to her mum, and then walked back into the living room. The fire was getting low, so she reached into the copper cauldron and threw another log onto the flames. The TV was warbling with a daytime talk show, and her book lay facedown on the coffee table. Outside, the winter was closing in and the river looked angry and grey.

She picked up her laptop and opened it to check her email. She had been keeping in touch with the university frequently, and several of her students and friends on the faculty were asking if they could come and see her. While the idea of visitors was not in the least appealing, she appreciated their concern. She had fielded their requests, saying that she'd be back in Edinburgh soon and would love to see them then. Charlotte had offered to do triage on their calls, but Kate wanted to start taking responsibility for herself again. Charlotte had enough on her plate with The Bakery and coming back and forth to Broughty Ferry. She was due back the following afternoon and had said she could stay the weekend and return to Edinburgh late on Sunday night. Kate was looking forward to having two whole days with her.

As Kate sipped her tea, the warmth from the fire seeped back into her legs and feet. The wind was picking up outside, and as she thought about David walking back from town, she hoped he would make it before the rain that threatened to split the sky.

A white streak caught her eye, and as she focused on the window, two large seagulls glided past. They flew into the wind, their wide wingspans buffeted as they battled against the gusts that lifted them up and then dropped them down again, like two aircraft in turbulent skies.

She had always loved lying upstairs in bed hearing the gulls. The sound reminded her of childhood holidays spent on the south coast of England. The three of them had stayed in seaside bed-and-breakfasts, exploring various towns, walking the length of many a pier in search of warm doughnuts or paper cones full of piping hot chips soaked in vinegar. Elizabeth would tut at their unhealthy food choices while Kate and David giggled and ran ahead, leaving her mother to walk alone until they slowed down and let her catch up with them.

Kate closed her eyes. They had been cruel to Elizabeth in many ways. She had been excluded from much of their fun, and later, when Kate was grown, Elizabeth had been ridiculed, teased, and mimicked. As she let the memories come, Kate felt awash with regret. If she could have that time over again, she would be kinder.

The sound of David's keys in the lock startled her, and her eyes shot open. The door slammed, and she could hear his heavy footfalls as he made his way down the long spine of the house. He popped his head through the door, and she thought she could smell the brine of the river on him.

"Hi. You doing all right?" His hair was tousled and his cheeks pink from the wind.

"Fine. I made some tea. I've just been reading." She indicated the book on the coffee table.

"Anything good?" He ran a hand over his hair, smoothing it back into place above each ear.

"Michael J. Fox's biography. Pretty good, actually. I'll leave it for you when I go home."

David blanched. She hadn't meant to be insensitive, but he seemed stung by her words.

"Right, well, I'll go and get started on the dinner." He walked briskly away towards the kitchen as she clenched her fists in frustration.

She heard him clattering pots and the fridge door opening and slamming several times. Kate pushed herself up from the chair and walked in to talk to him.

"Dad, I didn't mean to upset you. I was just saying that…"

"It's fine, Kate. I understand." He cut her off, not turning to look at her as he filled a pan with water. His coat lay in a heap on a chair, and a pile of fresh green beans sat on the counter next to a small chicken and two large potatoes.

"Dad?" She waited for him to turn around. "Dad, come on."

David put the pan on the stove top and turned to face her. Whatever he had been feeling had been erased from his face, and he smiled at her.

"So, chicken, baked potato, and beans, OK?"

"Yes, perfect. Listen, we need to talk about what you're going to do."

David stood still and frowned, uncomprehending.

"Do?"

"Yes. Do you think you'll keep the house? I mean, do you want to stay here?" Kate watched as what she was saying permeated and his face sagged.

"I've not given it much thought. It is too big for just me, though." He dropped his eyes to the floor and ran a toe along the grout line between two of the terracotta tiles. "It feels odd being here now, but then, this is where your mum and I lived most of our lives together. Giving it up would be like letting all that go." He raised his head, and Kate saw his eyes glittering, and she felt bad for pushing him.

"Well, there's no rush for you to decide. I was just curious if you'd thought about it." Kate slid onto the long wooden bench at the table and put her cup onto one of the tartan coasters. "I don't like to think of you rattling around here on your own." Kate searched his face, feeling her throat tighten.

David walked over and sat opposite her at the table.

"I know, and when everything has sunk in and things have settled a bit, I'll probably think about moving." David reached out and turned the salt and pepper shakers around each other in a dance.

"Where would you move to? Would you leave Broughty Ferry, or maybe get a smaller place here, so you'd still be close to your friends?" Kate wanted to know what he was thinking, and she couldn't help but ask.

"I think I'd stay here. Maybe look at a nice flat along the water-front or something." David nodded to himself as he repositioned the salt and pepper and then ran a hand over the table, gathering up some stray grains of salt that, through force of habit, he then tossed over his left shoulder.

"I could see you in a nice flat. Maybe a ground floor, with a bit of garden?" Kate leaned in towards her father and took his hand.

"No garden. What would I want with a garden?" David's voice was shrill. He withdrew his hand and looked annoyed by her suggestion.

Kate wanted to kick herself as she remembered that the garden had always been Elizabeth's domain.

"Right, well, no garden then. Less to take care of." She smiled at her dad and held his gaze until she saw his momentary flash of anger dissipate.

"There's plenty of time to decide, anyway. I'll let you know as soon as I've got a plan." David reached out and placed a hand over Kate's.

She nodded and turned her palm upward so she could grab his fingers.

"Take your time. I just want you to be comfortable, whatever you decide." Her voice caught in her throat.

"I'll be fine, love. Don't you worry about me." David pushed himself up from the bench and walked back to the sink. "When is Charlotte coming back?" He spoke over his shoulder.

"Tomorrow afternoon. She's staying for the weekend. Is that all right?" Kate swirled the dregs of the now cold tea around in the mug in front of her.

David nodded silently as he pulled the chicken out of the wrapping and washed it under the tap. Kate watched his reflection in the window as he worked, and she wondered what he was thinking. She hoped he was coming to terms with Lottie's presence in the house and her position as a permanent fixture in both their lives.

CHAPTER 55

———◆———

Charlotte paced across the bedroom in the flat above The Bakery. She had packed herself a bag for the weekend and had put some things that Kate had requested into a backpack. Mungo was all set for the next two days, and she had been impressed with his organization and planning when they'd spoken downstairs in the kitchen.

She glanced at her watch. It was nearly 3:00, and she wanted to be on the road before 3:30 in order to beat the rush hour. As she lifted the backpack from the bed, Charlotte scanned the room for anything she might have forgotten. Satisfied that she had all she needed, she flipped off the light and walked into the living room.

Her phone vibrated inside her pocket, and she sighed, irritated at whomever might be distracting her from her scheduled departure. When she saw the number displayed on the screen, she smiled.

"Hi, love. How are you?" Kate's voice was bright.

"Good, just getting everything nailed down so that I can leave around half past three. What's up?" Charlotte tucked the phone under her jaw and picked up her coat.

"Nothing. I was just checking to see if you were on the road yet."

Charlotte knew that tone. Kate was holding something back.

"I will be leaving shortly. I just wanted to drop off an order for Monday with Chloe and then I'll set off. Is everything OK?" Charlotte walked out the front door, dumped the bags in the hallway, and locked the front door to the flat.

"Everything's fine, but I need a favor." Kate sounded apologetic.

"What kind of favor?" Charlotte slid the door keys into her handbag and lifted the two bags.

"I want to get Dad a nice bottle of whisky, just to thank him for taking care of me."

"Good idea." Charlotte started down the stairs.

"I don't think the shop here in town has his favorite so, if it's not too much of a pain, could you possibly grab a bottle from that little place on Rose Street before you leave?"

Charlotte's stomach clenched. Did she have time to run down the street to do this and still beat the Friday night traffic exodus?

"I'll see if I can, once I've talked to Chloe." She tried to keep her voice even, not to hint at it being a bother to have been asked.

"Sorry to spring it on you. If I could get out, I'd do it myself." Kate's voice was low, as if she was being overheard.

"Well, I plan on getting you out this weekend before you go completely stir crazy. If it's dry, why don't we drive down to the beach and then walk along to that little gallery? We can get a coffee at Visocchi's and sit on the bench at the front and smell the seaweed while we read the papers." Charlotte made her way down the stairs, watching her feet so as not to trip.

"God, that sounds great. " Kate's tone lifted. "It's fine being here, but it would be fabulous to get outside. Dad watches me like a hawk, and I think he's afraid that if I cross the threshold to the outdoors, I might be spirited away and he'll never see me again." She forced a laugh, but Kate's words caused Charlotte to stop her progress into the bakery kitchen.

"Well, we'll just have to sort that out when I'm there. Don't worry. If I go now, I can grab the whisky and still be there for around five."

Charlotte walked into the kitchen, where Mungo was sitting at her desk shuffling some papers. She nodded at him and mouthed, "Where's Chloe?"

Mungo pointed to the café and mouthed back, "Setting up tables."

"Right. Sorry. I didn't mean to delay you. You go and, oh, the whisky he likes is…"

Charlotte cut Kate off. "The Macallan. Yes, I know. Twelve-year-old, right?"

Kate was silent for a few moments as Charlotte made her way into the café at the front of the shop.

"Yes, the twelve-year-old is the one he likes. How did you know that?" Kate sounded puzzled, and Charlotte realized that she hadn't told her about the meal she and David had shared at the vampire-themed pub. The whole episode seemed bizarre now, and she didn't have time to go into it.

"Oh, I'll tell you all about it when I see you. Got to go." She blew a kiss down the phone and hung up.

Chloe was wiping down the glass-topped tables and rearranging the condiments into tidy clusters. She looked up as Charlotte approached.

"Hi, *patron*. You ready to go?"

"Soon. I just wanted to give you this order for Monday morning. Foresters, the insurance group on Princes Street, have a catered breakfast meeting at nine. Can you manage that for me?" She handed Chloe a crumpled sheet of paper that she had pulled from her handbag.

"*Oui*, sure. No problem." Chloe scanned the paper and then folded it before sliding it into her apron pocket.

"I'll be back around ten on Monday, so I can help with the lunch rush." Charlotte swiped at a stray spiral of hair that had fallen across her face. Despite the chill in the air, she could feel a trickle of sweat make its way down her back. She always got clammy when she was hurrying or stressed.

"Go. Relax. *C'est bon*. Say hi to Kate. Tell her we miss her." Chloe leaned over and pecked each of Charlotte's cheeks, then, holding her shoulders, turned her around towards the door and gave her a gentle push. "Go now."

Charlotte laughed and juggled the two bags she was carrying.

"OK, I'm going. Call me if you need anything."

Chloe wafted a tea towel at Charlotte as if she were swatting a fly.

"Shoo."

As she looked at the café behind her, Charlotte felt a pang of homesickness for the warm space she had created inside this old stone building. The caramel-colored walls in contrast to the terracotta of the exposed brick, the old-fashioned glass display case that she had bought at an auction, the two bay windows hanging like heavy eyelids over the cobbled street outside, and the green glass-paneled door that stuck in the frame each time you opened it … all made her heart lift. She missed being here every day.

By 3:50, she was heading out of Edinburgh towards the Forth Road Bridge. The view from the iconic suspension bridge along the Firth of Forth was classic Scotland. The water was silvery, and today it was deeply kinked as the tide turned back towards the sea. Once across the bridge, she always looked forward to seeing the ensuing sweep of green hills that welcomed travelers into Perthshire. It was a beautiful drive to Broughty Ferry, and even the stark winter scenery was stunning.

Charlotte tuned the radio to her favorite classical station and sipped some of the coffee she'd bought herself at the petrol station in South Queensferry. As the road curved left, taking her down a steep incline, she let her mind wander.

Elsie had often driven her over the bridge as a child to visit the aquarium. They would sing all the way across and then buy ice cream at Deep Sea World, no matter the weather. Charlotte's favorite thing to see at the aquarium was the seahorses. They struck her as magical, the way their tails curled and uncurled, forcing water away as they levitated above the bottom of the tanks. Elsie loved the coral, and they'd spend ages staring at the rainbow colors of the Martian-like animals.

There were so many memories of Elsie that made her smile, and yet they hurt her to replay. She missed her mother intensely, and the uncomfortable thought of her father taking some new woman out came back to her. She had promised Kate that she'd be open-minded, even meet the woman if Duncan wanted her to. She just hoped it wasn't going to happen anytime soon.

Kate had said that David was finding it hard to talk about Elizabeth. A picture of his face came back to her, standing in the doorway of Kate's room with the bag of Elizabeth's belongings in his hand. It was a visual she would likely never forget, and as she steered the car down the hillside, Charlotte resolved to remember it whenever she began to feel frustrated with David. It would be a good leveler, keeping her compassionate and fair in this gentle tug-of-war that was developing between them, with Kate as the rope.

When she arrived at the house, Kate was standing in the open front door, waving. It gave Charlotte a lift to see her there, and she jumped out of the car and trotted across the gravel driveway to throw her arms around Kate's waist.

"I missed you." Charlotte spoke into Kate's shoulder.

"Me too. So much." Kate squeezed her hard with her right arm and bent down to kiss the side of Charlotte's face. "Dad's in the kitchen. I was hoping he'd let you cook tonight. I'm about done with roast chicken." Kate laughed and linked arms with Charlotte, guiding her inside the house.

"Hang on, I need to get the bags." Charlotte disentangled herself and walked over to collect the bags from the boot of her car.

"So you're over chicken, are you?" Charlotte winked as they walked inside.

"Kind of, yes. I think it's the only thing he can cook."

"I'll cook tomorrow then. I'll make that Moroccan lamb you like, or beef stroganoff?" Charlotte smiled over at Kate.

"Thank you." Kate mouthed, rolling her eyes.

They inclined their heads towards each other and laughed softly as they walked down the hallway to check on the progress David was making, with yet another chicken.

CHAPTER 56

———◆———

David watched as Charlotte helped Kate into the car. He hadn't been keen on them going off to the town, but had done his best to swallow his objection and wave them on their way. It had been five days since they had brought Kate back to the house, and having her here had made being home bearable.

He raised a hand as the car pulled away, and then he stepped inside and closed the door. As she'd slept the entire way back from the hospital, David wondered if Kate would be nervous to get back into a car, now that she was compos mentis again. It would be perfectly understandable if she was anxious, as he'd noticed that, since the accident, he himself was paying closer attention to the other vehicles around him and taking longer to make decisions at junctions. An experience like the one Kate had lived through could shatter your confidence, there was no doubt about that.

The floorboard near the phone table creaked as he stepped

on it. He had been meaning to fix it for over three years, and Elizabeth had nagged him about it regularly. He would make an empty promise to repair it and then ignore it until another two weeks would pass and she would ask if he was intending on doing anything about it.

David was not handy around the house. Basic things like changing light bulbs and un-blocking sinks were within his capabilities, but anything requiring more than the most rudimentary skills made him nervous.

He stomped on the creaky board a few times, as if establishing whether it still needed attention. Now was the perfect time to fix it, with Kate and Charlotte out. He would find his toolbox, brush the inevitable cobwebs from the old hammer that his father had given him, and have this done by the time they got back.

David paced through the kitchen, went out the back door, and crossed the narrow path to the garage. The side door was stuck in the frame as he pushed on it. He seldom used this entrance, and the handle had rusted, being exposed to the elements. He tried again until eventually it opened under the pressure of his shoulder and he stepped into the darkness.

He flipped on the light, and the sight of Elizabeth's car stole his breath. The little blue Citroen glowed under the stark light bulb that hung above its bonnet.

The car had sat in the driveway for several days before David, unable to look at it, had put it into the garage. Now the smooth paintwork of the roof was spattered with bird muck. Elizabeth would have been mortified to see her car in this state; she had always been meticulous about keeping it clean.

As he walked around to the front of the vehicle, he saw that the windshield was dotted with smudges of sap, and a few slivers of brown leaves stuck to the tacky marks. He reached over and peeled a leaf from the glass. In an instant, David decided that the floorboard could wait.

Having gone inside to fetch a jacket and the car keys, he opened the driver's door and slid into the seat. Elizabeth's smell assaulted him and he felt his stomach fall away. The scent was so distinctive, a mixture of her floral perfume and the peppermints she always ate when driving.

He looked down at the central console and saw half a packet of Strong Mints, the silver paper wrapped back around the open end of the roll. He reached down and picked it up. Putting the roll to his nose, he inhaled, then tore away a strip of paper and put a mint on his tongue. It was powdery and began to burn immediately.

David sat still, moving the mint around his mouth, feeling the cold sensation of its heat as he inhaled against it. The taste was so familiar, and yet the grabbing that it caused deep in his stomach was not. Would everything Elizabeth had touched, used, or worn cause him to collapse in on himself this way when he came across it?

David sighed. He knew that at some point he would have to address the wardrobe, which was full of her clothes and shoes, the bathroom cabinet that contained her cosmetics, the hall coat cupboard, the drawer in the kitchen that she used like a sewing basket, and the magazine rack at the side of her chair. As the list grew exponentially in his head, he felt the weight of it settle on his heart.

Perhaps Kate could help him with the task before she left for Edinburgh, or was it too soon to ask her to go through her mother's things? He wished he knew the right thing to do in this instance. Elizabeth would have known, but of course she could be of no help to him now. Sighing again, he folded the paper back around the mints and tucked them into his pocket.

David slid the key into the ignition and started the car. Opening the door behind him with the remote that was clipped to the visor, he backed out of the garage and parked the car on the widest part of the driveway. He considered continuing on to the automatic car wash in town, but then thought better of it, afraid that the big brushes and long cloth tentacles that hung down from the arched contraption would smudge the mess rather than remove it properly. No, he would wash it himself.

He glanced out at the river. It was calm today, the wind being low. As he watched a batch of yachts go by in a white cluster, he was glad the weather was being kind to Kate and Charlotte. He knew that Kate needed to get out of the house, and while he had enjoyed having her to himself, he had to admit that he'd seen a certain light come back into her eyes as soon as Charlotte had arrived.

Charlotte was going to cook for them that evening, and had said that she would shop for whatever they needed after taking Kate to a gallery she loved. There was no denying the extent of Charlotte's baking skills. He had tasted several of the things that she had brought back from Edinburgh and it had all been exquisite. There was no reason, therefore, to doubt her abilities in other areas of the kitchen.

The kitchen had been Elizabeth's domain. David knew how to make a few basic meals, but he had enjoyed her pleasure in cooking, and for years had looked forward to trying new recipes that she'd been experimenting with, glad to be a guinea pig for a new soufflé or spicy meat marinade.

David closed his eyes at the thought of Charlotte moving around Elizabeth's kitchen, wearing her apron, opening cupboards, using the utensils and the copper-bottomed pots, touching the French linen tea-towels that Elizabeth had loved. If, as he suspected was the case, Charlotte was going to be around a lot more in the future, he would need to get over this feeling of her presence as an intrusion. As he pressed his eyelids down tighter and watched the tiny specks of white light that sparkled against the otherwise dark void he was seeing, David swallowed.

Charlotte's face floated before him, smiling, asking him if he was all right. He saw her kneeling down next to him when he lay on the floor in the hospital, his willpower spent, as he cried into her lap and she smoothed his hair. She'd asked for nothing from him that day, or any subsequent day, except for something that he was struggling to give her. The only thing that Charlotte Macfie wanted from him was acceptance.

CHAPTER 57

Kate flipped the page of the *Herald*. Her coffee was almost finished, and as Charlotte leaned over to steal a piece of the remains of the muffin that sat on her plate, Kate reached out and slapped her hand away.

"Get off." She grinned over the paper and pulled the plate closer to herself. "You ate yours already."

"It's market research." Charlotte leaned back in her seat and folded her arms across her chest. "Just checking the competition."

Kate watched as a slow smile crept across Charlotte's face, and she felt the usual grip of love that followed whenever she saw the mischievous expression.

"Well, check someone else's, please." Kate folded the paper and laid it on the table. The coffee shop was busy with weekend customers, and as she picked up the last of the muffin and popped it into her mouth, Kate noticed that there were people standing inside the doorway, waiting.

"We should go. They're waiting for tables." She nodded towards the door and Charlotte turned to look.

"Oh, right. Well, I'm ready if you are." Charlotte slipped her coat from the back of her chair and put it on.

Kate rose and pulled her own coat around her back with her right arm. Her left arm was still in the cast, and while she could use the fingers well enough, the casing was cumbersome. She longed to get the hard shell removed so that she could soak her arm in a warm bath and feel the water against her skin.

Charlotte stepped over and helped Kate drape the coat around her shoulders, then pushed a chair aside to let her pass.

As they emerged into the street, Kate felt the cold air seep into her lungs. She could see her breath. It was only a short walk back to the car, and she was glad that they'd parked close, as she was tired from the brief outing.

"Are you all right?" Charlotte was looking over at her, so Kate made an effort not to shiver.

"Yes, just a bit tired."

"I can drop you at home first, then go to the shops by myself." Charlotte hooked her arm through Kate's and pulled her closer.

"No. I'm fine. Let's go and attack the shopping. I haven't been into Tesco in weeks." Kate widened her eyes. "What if it's nothing like I remember it?" She grinned.

"Believe me, nothing has changed on that front." Charlotte laughed and steered her towards the car park.

Kate looked at the variety of faces that they passed. Some of them felt familiar, although she couldn't tell whether it was the individual she was recognizing or just the sense of home that they represented. The voices, the smells, the light, all filled her with a calm warmth that she forgot about until the next time she was here to experience it. She suspected that most people felt the same about the town or city that they had grown up in. A significant number of formative years spent in a place that was subsequently revisited in adulthood was bound to elicit this response. She was on the point of mentioning the feeling to Charlotte when she thought better of it. The last thing she wanted was for Charlotte to think that she was happier here than in Edinburgh. Besides, she loved Edinburgh, their unique home above The Bakery, and their life together in the city.

The supermarket had been so busy that Charlotte had insisted Kate wait in the car. Kate had mildly protested, but felt secretly relieved when Charlotte gave her the keys and wouldn't take no for an answer. Now, sitting inside the car, she turned on the ignition and then cranked up the heater. It was turning bitterly cold and she didn't want to start trembling, as it still hurt her ribs to do so.

The dashboard of Charlotte's car was dusty, and Kate ran her hand over it, cleaning a dark swathe through the film. She wiped her palm on her jeans and glanced over at the passenger seat. That was the side of her car where her mother had been. If she had been sitting there and Elizabeth driving, rather than the other way around, David would be mourning his daughter now and not his wife.

Kate pressed her eyes closed. She knew that she shouldn't be thinking like this, but she couldn't help herself. What if she had turned her head just a few seconds earlier, seen the lorry, reacted faster, or maybe reacted smarter? Would it have made a difference? Could she have done enough to buy them an escape?

She felt her diaphragm tensing and her jaw clenching, so she tried to focus on her breath. She needed to just breathe through this moment.

It didn't matter how many times David said that it was just an horrific accident and that there was nothing she could have done; Kate was afraid that there were some questions that would never be answered for her. She could ask herself the same thing a million times a day, but she was here and Elizabeth was gone, and that was everyone's new reality.

Charlotte tapped on the window, startling her. Kate snapped her eyes open and smiled as Charlotte lugged the heavy bags to the back of the car and lifted them into the boot. When Charlotte jumped into the driver's seat, Kate was wiping her eyes on her coat sleeve.

"What's the matter?" Charlotte twisted in her seat and took Kate's face between her palms. "Talk to me, Kate."

Kate gulped and pulled her face away, wiped at her cheeks, and tucked her hair behind her ears. When she felt she could speak, she turned back to see Charlotte's concerned expression.

"I'm just going over and over that day, those moments, in my mind. It's like a slow-motion film and I am wading through syrup, trying to steer, think straight, reassure Mum, and avoid the lorry." She swallowed. "It's just that it isn't always clear."

Charlotte nodded.

"Sometimes I can see Mum's face, hear her voice, then the next time I re-live it she is totally silent, like someone's muted the volume. Her mouth is open, but nothing comes out. Those times, all I can hear is my own heartbeat and then the crunch, those weird splintering sounds, and then her scream." Kate gave in to a sob as she leaned her head against Charlotte's shoulder.

Charlotte sat still, giving her exactly what she needed in order to cry, then fished a tissue out of her pocket and pressed it into Kate's hand. She reached over and lay her fingers on Kate's thigh; the contact was enough for Kate to know that she understood.

After what seemed like an age, Charlotte lifted Kate's head from her shoulder and wiped her eyes.

"You need to let it out, Kate, but you can't keep asking yourself the same things over and over, or you'll drive yourself mad."

Kate nodded.

"There was nothing you could have changed or affected. You did everything humanly possible, and the sad thing is that life just delivers us large amounts of shit sometimes, irrespective of what we deserve." Charlotte sniffed.

Kate realized that Charlotte was crying too, and hearing the pain in her voice made Kate sit up straighter. Enough of this feeling sorry for herself, she had Charlotte to consider, too.

"I know. You're right. I will get there, Lottie. It's just every time I see Dad, remember something she said to him, find something of Mum's in a drawer, or see her picture on the sideboard, my heart feels like it's going to be sucked out through my mouth." She spoke quietly and stared out of the side window. "I'll get through this, though, I promise."

Charlotte wiped her eyes and turned towards Kate.

"You don't need to explain it to me. I get it. I can't even imagine your dad's pain at the moment, but what I do know is that he still has *you*. In fact, he has both of us, if he wants us." Charlotte scanned Kate's face.

"He does." Kate nodded.

"What would I do without you, Lottie?"

"Well, I hope it's going to be a long time before you find out."
Charlotte wiped at her cheeks again and then dragged her hands
through the mass of dark curls that hung at either side of her
face. "Now, let's go home and cook something delicious, drink
expensive wine, and watch some mindless TV." She smiled at
Kate and started the car.

CHAPTER 58

It had been ten days since Kate had returned to Edinburgh, and David was adjusting to the solitude. She and Charlotte had been to Broughty Ferry twice to have dinner with him and spend the night, and each time he had found himself warming towards Charlotte.

They had arrived the previous evening, on Christmas Eve, with a car full of presents, and despite their assurances that they were desperate to get out of Edinburgh for a few days to escape the Christmas madness, David was under no illusion as to why they'd really come.

Charlotte had insisted that she would cook Christmas dinner for everyone at the house. Her father was coming with his new girlfriend, Helen, and David was looking forward to meeting Duncan Macfie, having heard much about him from both the girls. David had also invited Mike and Clare to join them. They had arrived about an hour ago and he was anxious, and a little nervous, to have them spend time with Charlotte.

David stood looking at the Christmas tree.

The circles of small white lights that his wife had preferred surrounded the slender fir, glittering against the darkening window behind. Putting the tree up had been a painful reminder of Elizabeth's favorite time of year, but it had also been yet another hurdle conquered.

He, Kate, and Charlotte had exchanged gifts that morning, and then he had made them pancakes for breakfast, which they'd eaten around the fire, wearing their pajamas. Several presents still sat underneath the lower branches of the tree, artfully wrapped in silver and black paper, and all with professional-looking bows that Charlotte had tied. She had spent Christmas Eve sitting on the floor and laughing while trying to teach him how to perfect them. David had given up, his thick fingers unable to master the intricate folding and twisting required.

As he glanced out at the violet sky, he could smell the turkey cooking, and the glass in his hand held an inch of his favorite Macallan. Kate was in the kitchen, making gravy while Charlotte issued orders. A pipe band CD turned in the player, *Silent Night* wailing across the room as the fire crackled in the grate.

Two of the remaining presents under the tree were from him to Kate and Charlotte. In identical small boxes, he had wrapped them as best he could and then tucked them away behind the rest. Out in the garage, in a tall vase, were two long-stemmed roses that he had driven into town for the previous morning. He was excited about giving the women their final gifts, but had decided to wait until their guests had gone. These presents were personal, and while he didn't want to be melodramatic about it, he felt that it would be more appropriate if they opened them in private.

Kate walked into the room, surprising him.

"What're you up to? You're shirking your duties." She nudged him with her elbow. "It's all hands on deck, according to the chef." She smiled. Her face was fuller again, now that she was recovering, and she was flushed from the heat in the kitchen.

"Right-o. I was just taking a moment to enjoy the tree." He nodded towards the window.

"It's lovely. We did an OK job, didn't we?" Kate hooked her arm through his and leaned her head on his shoulder.

"I think she'd have been happy." David nodded and then planted a kiss on the top of Kate's head.

The fire popped, and a twist of piney smoke spiraled up the chimney. They stood still and let the music, the light, and several years' worth of memories surround them.

David had felt Elizabeth's presence strongly over the past few days, and standing here with Kate, he could almost smell his wife's perfume and feel her breath on his cheek.

After a few minutes, Kate lifted her head.

"We'd better get back in there or we'll get fired." She giggled, planted a kiss on David's cheek, and headed out the door.

David swallowed some whisky, lifted the glass to the tree in a salute, then just as he was about to follow his daughter into the kitchen, Mike came into the room and sat down in Elizabeth's chair.

"Merry Christmas, Dave." He raised his glass in the air.

"Same to you, Mike. It's certainly a different one, that's for sure." David echoed Mike's gesture and sat back down.

"Well, yes. It was bound to be." Mike nodded slowly, then sipped his whisky. "The place looks great, though." He glanced towards the tree.

"We decided to push the boat out and decorate, just as Elizabeth would have. It seemed the right thing to do."

Mike nodded again and stretched his legs out in front of himself. "Charlotte is quite the chef."

"Yes. She's impressive." David sat back and lifted his feet up onto the coffee table. "She has a wonderful little business. A bakery in Edinburgh."

Saying it out loud felt good. Hearing himself, David realized that he sounded like a father would when bragging about a daughter. The past few weeks had seen his relationship with Charlotte slowly but surely gather strength. They had taken tentative steps towards a friendship, and he was proud, and hoped that Elizabeth would have been too, of the way that he was learning to share Kate with the new woman in both their lives.

Mike was watching him and David coughed, embarrassed that he had been staring into the space over his friend's head.

"What is it?" Mike asked as he leaned forward, the crystal glass held low between his knees.

"I was just thinking that it took me a while to see it, but it turns out that Charlotte's quite a remarkable young lady." David watched Mike's expression, trying to gauge whether now would be a good time to tell him about Kate's relationship.

Mike nodded and swirled the amber-colored liquid around the glass. He looked over at David and locked eyes with him.

"Are she and Kate together?" Mike's face was open, receptive.

David felt the question like a jolt to his middle. Mike was

taking the plunge, and this move was brave, if not a little fool-hardy on his friend's part. David let go of the breath he was hold-ing and drained his glass.

"Yes, they are a couple."

There, he had said it. The house was still standing, the sky had not fallen, the fire still glowed, and his friend still sat comfortably opposite him in this new accepting space he'd created.

"Well, that's good. Clare and I thought it might be someone from the university, a professor type, but when I saw Charlotte at the hospital…" Mike shrugged, raised his glass, and then drained the contents. "So, shall we go and see if we are needed?" He thrust his chin towards the door and stood up.

David nodded. Enough had been said, and whatever reaction he had expected, he supposed he should not have been surprised by his good friend being unfazed by this new development. He patted Mike on the back as they walked back towards the kitchen.

CHAPTER 59

———◆———

Their guests having left, Kate and Charlotte had gone for a walk to work off their Christmas dinner. David had finished clearing up the last of the dishes in the kitchen and now sat in his chair with his back to the river. The fire was glowing warmly, his eyelids felt heavy, and the book he'd been reading lay in his lap. He was trying to stay awake until Kate and Charlotte got home. He wanted to be alert and welcoming, rather than drooling like an old man at the fireside.

David had to admit that they had done a magnificent job of a Christmas that a large part of him had been dreading. The house felt warm and festive, and although he still saw Elizabeth in every corner of every room, he acknowledged that he was allowing himself to feel a pale shade of happiness.

David lifted the book from his lap, closed it, and placed it on the coffee table. Across from him, Elizabeth's chair stared at him, the cream fabric sagging slightly in the middle of the seat. Her rust-colored rug was draped over the back as if she had just left it there while she went to the kitchen for more wine.

David sucked in his breath and pushed himself out of his chair. He walked behind the tree, picked up the two small boxes he had hidden, and then headed for the kitchen.

On the counter a bottle of good Burgundy stood on the wine coaster with the opener beside it, and three crystal glasses sparkled as the overhead light bounced off them onto the granite surface underneath. He placed the two small boxes next to the wine bottle and then went out to the garage to retrieve the roses.

He had been relieved to find both yellow and pink roses at the flower shop, having researched which colors would be appropriate for his purpose. Elizabeth had a book on what different flowers symbolized, and he'd chosen pink for Kate, for grace and appreciation, and yellow for Charlotte, denoting friendship.

Back in the kitchen, he nervously adjusted the boxes and roses for the umpteenth time and then twisted the wine bottle around to inspect the label. It was a 2007, a good bottle that he and Elizabeth had been saving for a special occasion. As he turned the bottle back to face the table, he heard keys in the lock of the front door. David ran a hand over his hair, pulled his sweater down at the back, and headed out into the hall.

"Hi, ladies. Did you have a good walk?" His voice sounded bright, perhaps a little too loud.

"Yep. It was good to get out and walk off some of that plum pudding." Kate looked pale, and Charlotte's arm was under her elbow. His heart tilted at the thought that she had perhaps pushed herself too far.

"Did you do too much?" He tried to keep the concern from his voice as he walked towards her and took her arm from Charlotte.

"No. It was just right." Kate smiled at him and accepted his hand. "I'll just have a little sit down and I'll be fine." Kate headed towards the living room.

David pulled gently against her arm.

"Shall we sit in the kitchen for a while?"

She looked over at him and blinked. She seemed so tired.

"OK, if you want." She shrugged and let him steer her farther along the hall.

Charlotte followed behind, letting them dictate the pace. David looked over his shoulder at her and winked, and she seemed surprised by the intimate gesture, a slight flush blooming on her face.

David led Kate into the kitchen and helped her settle into a chair at the table. He looked over at Charlotte and pointed at another chair.

"Please sit down. I have something to say to you both." He felt tension gathering in the back of his throat, so he swallowed to release it.

The women sat looking at each other, appearing somewhat alarmed but attentive. Kate's eyes traveled to the counter, and then she raised her questioning gaze to his.

David picked up the gifts.

"These are from your mum." He looked at Kate as he handed them each a box.

Charlotte took the offering and smiled nervously. Kate snapped her eyes to his, and he saw a moment of anxiety cloud her face.

"It's OK. Just open it. You too, Charlotte."

David turned and lifted the wine from the coaster. "I thought we'd open this, if you both felt like a glass?" He swung the bottle out across the table for them to see. "It's a lovely Burgundy your mum and I... Elizabeth and I were saving for a rainy day."

The two women looked at their respective gifts, both nodding yes to some wine. David busied himself with the bottle opener and, having pulled the cork out, sniffed it before pouring an inch of wine into one of the glasses.

Kate flipped the lid up on the small box, and he heard her gasp. For a split second, he wondered if this had been the right move, but when she raised her head and her mouth was slightly open and her eyes were shining, he knew it was right.

"Mum's engagement ring. Dad. Are you sure?"

"Yes. I'm sure. She'd want you to have it, darling." David felt his voice crack.

Kate pushed herself up out of the chair and walked towards him. "I don't know what to say."

As he opened his arms to her, she folded herself into his embrace, burying her face in his neck just as she had done as a child, on the many occasions that she would climb onto his knee. David felt himself choking up and cleared his throat.

"You just say, 'I forgive you, Dad,' and then we can move on." He pushed her gently away from him so that he could see her face. She was flushed, and silent tears slid down her cheeks and hung under her jaw. She leaned back from him, and he saw that her hands were shaking as she showed the beautiful solitaire to Charlotte.

Charlotte sat with her unopened box balanced on her thigh. She was watching them and smiling.

"Come on, Charlotte. Your turn." David sniffed and gently

disengaged himself from Kate's grip.

Charlotte looked over at Kate as if for approval, then, seeing her nod, opened the lid on the box. Inside were two perfect, brilliant diamond earrings. Charlotte, still silent, looked up at Kate, who was now standing over her to see what was inside the box.

"Oh, they were Mum's. The ones you got her for your twenty-fifth anniversary, right, Dad?" Kate crouched down next to Charlotte and put an arm around the back of her chair.

"Yes. She loved them. I know she'd be happy that you have them now, Charlotte."

Charlotte seemed to be struggling with something. She was frowning and biting on the inside of her cheek. After a few moments, she closed the box and set it on the table.

"I can't take them, David. It's too much." Her voice was rough.

"You can and you must." David stood, his arms still open where Kate had just vacated them. "Elizabeth wanted them to stay in the family, so…"

He was aware that he was shaking. He swallowed again and widened his arms. Charlotte, reading the signal, stood up and took a tentative step towards him, then stopped. He locked eyes with her, then nodded, inviting her in. She looked over at Kate, who was smiling and then, taking small steps, she moved forward and let him put his arms around her.

David noticed how tiny she felt compared to Kate, almost brittle in his embrace. He said nothing, listening to her light breathing against his collarbone.

"Can you forgive me, too?" He spoke to the top of her head. For a number of seconds, there was nothing, no movement or sound, then Charlotte nodded her head and he felt her thin arms go around his back, returning his hug.

"Of course I can." She spoke against his sweater, and the simple words she rewarded him with made David feel lighter than he had since before his world had imploded.

"Thank you, both of you." His voice was full.

Charlotte stepped to the side as Kate moved forward to put her arms around them both.

"I mean it. I'm a silly old fool and I don't deserve you." He addressed them both.

"Dad, we're all going to be fine, as long as we stick together." Kate nodded as she spoke. "We can handle anything as long as we're on the same side."

David stepped away from their huddle, lifted the bottle of wine, and poured out three glasses. Handing one to each of the women, he turned and picked up his own.

"To us, and to Elizabeth, who had the wisdom to know that we could do this, together."

Kate and Charlotte raised their glasses, the three crystal goblets singing out as they met.

"Here's to us." Charlotte put the glass to her lips. "And to Elizabeth."

"To Mum." Kate said as she took a sip of wine. "To Mum."

EPILOGUE

———————◆———————

On New Year's Eve, Kate and Charlotte sat on the sofa reading books. David nursed a mug, and his slippered feet were once again on the coffee table while he leafed through the first issue of the *Architectural Digest* subscription Charlotte had bought him for Christmas. A Debussy prelude was floating around the room, and the combined light from the fire and the tree flickered against the walls.

David sat up and laid the magazine on the table.

"Who's for a nightcap?"

He padded over to the sideboard to deposit his cup and fetch three brandy glasses and the box of dark chocolate mints that Helen had brought on Christmas Day. As he filled the three wafer-thin balloons with Armagnac, Charlotte and Kate sat head to head as Kate pointed to something in her book. The room smelled of wood smoke, the roast beef that they had had for dinner, and the sharp pine resin from the tree. The lights from across the river decorated the water, and all felt almost right with the world.

As David watched the two women on the sofa, he was struck by the realization that this was all that he had ever wanted for Kate. She was happy, loved, and in love, and thank god he had woken up in time to be a part of it.

Here, in his and Elizabeth's house, where all they had ever wished for was to be a loving family, was a loving family. It might not be made up of the components that he had first imagined, but far from being unbalanced, there was a wonderful symmetry to this new father-daughter club.

ACKNOWLEDGEMENTS

Heartfelt thanks to everyone who supported me in this undertaking especially my editors Amanda Sumner and Carol Agnew.

Special thanks go to Lesley Shearer, Rasheeda Syed, Annie Augenstein White and Sharon Erksa for all their support advice and encouragement.

As ever, last but not least, to Bob Ragsdale, for his constant encouragement, endless moral and technical support and most of all for his unshakable belief in me.

ABOUT THE AUTHOR

Originally from Edinburgh, Alison now lives in Virginia with her husband and two beloved dogs. A former professional dancer, marketing executive turned author, Alison was educated in England and holds an MBA from Leicester University.

The Father-Daughter Club is Alison's second novel. For more information on upcoming books, and a selection of short stories, go to www.alisonragsdale.com.